The Ka Mystery Series

In chronological order

Hushabye
Requiem
Imago
Snarl
Chimera
Joy (a short story)
Echo
Creed
Sanctuary
Valentine (a novella)
Siren
Pulse
Descent (a novella)
Fury
Tasteful (a novella)

Table of Contents

Joy 1
Valentine 37
Descent 129
Tasteful 229

Joy

A Kate Redman Novella

Joy

KATE REDMAN PAUSED BY THE bottom of the escalators and frantically tried to locate the payment tills. She was still wearing her thick winter coat and woolly hat and a scarf was wrapped snugly around her neck. All of this, plus the department store's formidable central heating, meant she was currently bathed in sweat, despite the temperatures outside in the street dropping to minus figures. Her arms were piled high with goods in imminent danger of crashing to the glossy tiled floor.

Ah, there *they were*. Kate spotted the tills and, simultaneously, the long queue snaking back from the desks. She groaned. Determined to just get this over with, once and for all, she panted over to join the back of the queue and shifted the pile about a bit in her arms to settle it more comfortably. Of course, Kate pondered, there was something to be said for doing your Christmas shopping early and beating the queues. But then, she'd learned the hard way that one could sometimes be a bit *too* efficient. For at least two years on the trot, Kate had dutifully made lists and bought Christmas presents throughout the year, when she saw something suitable or when various shops were running a sale. She would then stash the presents somewhere secure, like the back of her wardrobe or under the spare-room bed, promptly forget she'd bought them and then, in

December, she would panic-buy a whole load of *new* presents for people she'd already bought gifts for. The worst case was when she'd snapped up an expensive Thomas the Tank Engine toy for her godchild, Harry, stashed it, forgot about it, rediscovered it sometime the next Spring and thought philosophically, 'Oh well, I'll give it to him *this* Christmas,' only to find, the ungrateful child had switched his allegiance to Spiderman by the time the holiday season rolled round.

No, this year Kate was doing things by the book. Once she'd paid for this little lot, that was the bulk of the present buying out of the way. She could then think about getting the Christmas food and decorations. Kate's brother, Jay, and his wife, Laura, were coming over for Christmas Day, with Kate's fellow officer Mark Olbeck and his husband, Jeff, joining them in the evening. Hot and tired as she was, Kate couldn't help the warm anticipation that spread through her when she thought about Christmas Day. It would be the first time she'd 'hosted' and she was looking forward to it. Even the knowledge that her own boyfriend, Tin, couldn't make it down on the day itself didn't dampen her spirits. They had their own plans for Boxing Day – a wintry countryside walk in the day and a visit to the theatre in the evening – and Kate had to be content with that.

Kate's mind was so taken up with these seasonal musings that she scarcely noticed that she'd reached the front of the queue for payment. Thankfully, she unloaded all her gifts onto the desk in front of the cashier and reached for her purse.

Packages safely stowed away in her massive cotton

shopping bag, Kate made her way towards the exit. As she passed the ground floor displays of ten foot tall Christmas trees, hung so thickly with baubles and ornaments their foliage could scarcely be seen, the base of each tree heaped with gifts and goods and neatly folded piles of Christmas jumpers and soft leather gloves and cashmere scarves, she became aware of an altercation taking place just up ahead, by the exit. With a police officer's fine-tuned sensitivity to trouble, Kate realised that the security guard for the store had apprehended a shoplifter – or so it seemed.

She paused; a small selfish part of her didn't want to get involved. It was late, nearly eight thirty at night, and she had a whole heap of household chores to do at home, her cat Merlin to feed and dinner to make. She was back at work tomorrow, so tonight was the only chance she had to get on top of everything. Kate looked at the guard, a heavy, middle-aged man, remonstrating with the person he'd apprehended. She looked at the miscreant more closely and sighed.

"Can I be of assistance?" she asked as she walked up to the pair of them. A small crowd of late night shoppers was beginning to gather, silent but observant.

For a moment she thought the security guard was going to tell her to sod off, and before he could think of it, she pulled out her warrant card and thrust it under his nose. He blinked and then said reluctantly, "Oh, right, officer. Yes, we've got a problem here."

"I should say so," Kate said. She looked at the man standing in front of her, noting his old tweed coat was in an even worse state than usual. He'd wound a dirty scarf around his head and wisps of greasy grey hair stuck out from beneath it. Kate shook her head. "Charlie, Charlie, I thought we'd seen the last of you in here. Didn't the last time teach you anything?" She was amazed that he'd even got through the door without being apprehended, looking as he did.

Charlie Petworth hung his head. "I wasn't doing any harm. I was only looking. Come in here for a bit of a warm and—"

"He blatantly took three ornaments off that tree," the security guard said hotly. "I was watching him. They're in his pocket."

Kate sighed. "Come on, Charlie. Turn 'em out."

Charlie, his head hanging down, dutifully did so. His fluff-filled pockets disgorged three golden glass baubles.

"Oh, Charlie," Kate said, shaking her head. "What are we going to do with you?"

"I d'nt mean any harm," mumbled Charlie.

Kate shook back her hair, wishing she looked a bit cooler than she actually felt. "Look, Charlie, you know this isn't right, don't you?"

"—es..." Charlie whispered. He was in his fifties, but at that moment he sounded like a small boy.

Kate turned to the security guard. "You can leave him with me. I'll take him to the station."

"But—"

Kate put a hand on his arm and turned him around a little. "Are you new here?"

The guard looked confused. "I started last month—"

"Ah, well, you probably haven't run up against

Charlie before." Kate spoke low enough so the subject of her conversation couldn't hear. "He's a habitual thief. Always steals something small, something cheap. You'll probably see him in here again next month."

The guard looked truculent. "Why does he do it?"

Kate shrugged. "I would imagine he did it tonight so he can get a bed for the night. He's homeless, you see." She turned back to Charlie. "Am I going to have any trouble, Charlie?"

"No, ma'am." Charlie stood blinking and confused in the bright department store lights.

"Is Baxter outside?"

"Yes, ma'am."

Kate patted the security guard on the arm. "I'll take it from here, thank you."

Outside the shop, Kate stopped to let Charlie gather up the lead of his dog, Baxter. "Come on, then. Down to the station with you."

Once they were all in Kate's car, she turned the heater up to full. Charlie was shivering.

"When was the last time you ate, Charlie?" she asked. She could smell the booze on him now they were both shut into an enclosed space.

"Dunno."

"Okay, well – I'll get the duty sergeant to get you something when we get to the station." There were many things Kate would have liked to say to the man, but she knew it was hopeless. *Why do you drink so much, why don't you go to the refuge, what made you end up on the streets?* Instead, she shook her head and drove to Abbeyford Police Station.

"Evening, Charlie," said Constable Boulton, who was manning the front desk. "Usual, is it, Kate?"

"Yep. I'm not here, officially. Just dropping Charlie off. Can you make sure he gets something to eat, please?"

"Of course."

Kate watched as Charlie was led away to the cells. Baxter, veteran of the police station, watched as his master was led away, his tail drooping.

"Here you go, boy." PC Boulton indicated a spot over by the radiator and Baxter, after a moment, sloped over and lay down with an almost human sigh.

"See you tomorrow, then," Kate said, waving. She hugged her coat tighter to herself as she walked back out into the cold.

Driving home, she spared a thought for Charlie Petworth. She'd lost count of the times he'd been arrested for theft. It was almost always something small, something inconsequential. Occasionally he got sent to prison and was then released back into the community – which meant he went straight back to the streets. He'd got Baxter about a year ago and – now she came to think of it – this was the first bit of trouble they'd had with him for a while. Kate wondered whether Charlie had been 'good' so that he wouldn't have to lose the dog if he ended up in prison again. Her thoughts flew from Charlie's dog to her own cat, Merlin. He'd be yowling

JOY

for food by now... She drove home, her mind full of Christmas lists and tasks and things to do.

***

THE NEXT MORNING WAS COLD and bright, everything glittering with frost. Kate shivered as she scraped ice from the windscreen of her car before she could drive off. At least the central heating at work was efficient – almost too efficient. As Kate got to the office, she divested herself of scarf, gloves, hat, coat and cardigan, dumping them all in a pile by her desk.

There was a garish, badly wrapped parcel sitting prominently in the middle of her desk.

"What's this?" Kate said suspiciously.

Theo bounded up to her desk, grinning. "Secret Santa, innit? Didn't you bring yours?"

Kate had forgotten. "Oh. No." she said lamely.

"Well, aren't you going to open it?"

"Is this from you?" Kate asked.

"It's secret!" Theo cried in mock horror. "Go on. Open it."

Sighing, Kate did so, revealing a large cardboard box containing chocolates. On looking more closely, she realised the chocolates were shaped like tiny penises.

"Theo," she said, sharply. "This is definitely from you."

"Why do you say that?" Theo asked innocently.

Kate sighed again. "No one could ever accuse you of subtlety."

"Aren't you going to try one?"

Kate gave him a look. "No. I am not."

Shoving the box of chocolate willies underneath a pile of paperwork, she turned to her computer, ignoring Theo's giggles as he went back to his own desk. Shaking her head, Kate looked at the long list of emails awaiting her attention. There was one from PC Boulton, telling her that Charlie Petworth had been released that morning. The department store had declined to press charges. Kate sent a quick message of thanks back and then deleted the email.

It was a quiet day, for once. Perhaps criminals like to take the holidays off as well, thought Kate, as she got to grips with paperwork that had been lying fallow for three weeks. She even had time to do her expense claims, something that almost never happened. At about three o'clock, she caved and ate a chocolate penis with her afternoon coffee, trying not to let Theo see her do it.

It was five o'clock and Kate was thinking about heading home when the phone rang. It was the desk sergeant. "Kate? It's Steve. I've got a couple here, reporting a missing baby."

"What?" Kate said sharply, although she'd heard perfectly well.

"A missing baby."

"I'll be right down."

The reception area of the police station was unusually empty, except for the two people standing by the front desk. Even if the area had been full of people, Kate would have been able to pick them out. They were so different to the people who usually frequented this area.

"How can I help?" Kate asked, stepping up and introducing herself.

The woman, tall and blonde and thin, swung around. "Oh, thank God. This is such a nightmare." Tears glistened in her eyes. "I just turned around and Sophia was gone, just gone—"

"I realise this must be very distressing for you, Mrs...?"

"Walker. Amelia Walker. This is my husband, Paul." Kate shook hands with the husband, a tall, handsome man in his forties.

"If you could both just come through here with me..." Kate led them through to one of the more pleasant interview rooms. She sat them both down in chairs facing the desk, asked one of the PCs in the reception area to bring in coffee and returned to the room, shutting the door.

"Now, how can I help you?"

The woman, Amelia, spoke with a sob in her voice. "Our baby, Sophia – she's been taken. I put her in the car and I went back to the house to get my bag and when I came out – she was gone."

Kate nodded. "Did you see anyone near the car?"

Amelia was crying freely now. "No – no, nobody. I – I screamed and I ran down the road but there was nobody there. It was as if she'd just vanished into thin air."

Kate turned to the husband. "Mr Walker, were you there when this happened?"

Paul Walker nodded. He was older than Kate had first assumed; fine lines radiated from the corners of his eyes and grey threaded through his dark hair. "Yes, I was working from home today – I'm a financial advisor – but I didn't see anything. I was shut up in the study and the first I heard of it was Amelia screaming."

"And you came straight here?"

Amelia shook her head. "Yes. I couldn't wait for the police. I just had to come here straight away."

"Right." Kate knew the machinery had to be set in motion. "Can you give me a description of Sophia? We'll put out a call and get a search in motion. How old is she?"

"She's eighteen months." Amelia fumbled in her handbag and withdrew her mobile phone. "Here she is."

Kate contemplated the photograph of the child; cherubic, blonde, blue-eyed. For a moment, she saw the photograph reproduced on the front pages of the broadsheets and the tabloids and she saw the newspaper headlines of the future. Her gut twisted.

"Please wait here, I'll be back as soon as I can," she said and virtually ran out of the room.

By sheer luck, Anderton was in his office. He looked up, startled, as Kate skidded into the room.

"Missing child? My God. Right before Christmas," was all he said, but he was already reaching for the phone before Kate had even finished speaking. She waited, jigging from foot to foot, as he spoke to various people, making sure that every box was ticked. Abbeyford didn't often deal with child abduction but there was still a standard procedure to be followed. Waiting impatiently, Kate remembered the Charlie Fullman case, her first case upon joining the team here. She prayed for another happy ending in this instance.

Kate ran back upstairs and back to the incident room, where the Walkers were waiting. Olbeck was already there, obviously alerted by Theo. Kate stood by the door, watching as he spoke to the Walkers with his usual gentle courtesy, glad that he was able to take over. He was so much better at this sort of thing than she was. She eyed Amelia Walker uneasily. The woman was clearly on the verge of breaking down – well, understandably. She was very thin. It was only now that Kate realised how thin she was. Fashionably dressed, wearing expensive labels that couldn't disguise the too-big joints of her elbows, the jutting collar bones, the hollows beneath her cheekbones. Perhaps she was ill? Kate wondered but said nothing.

After a moment, Olbeck paused and Kate was able to interject. "I've just informed the Chief Inspector, Mr and Mrs Walker. You can rest assured that we'll be doing everything we can to find your daughter."

Amelia Walker said nothing. Her thin cheeks were glazed with tears. Paul Walker muttered a distracted "Thank you."

Kate hesitated but knew there was nothing more to add. She exchanged an eloquent glance with Olbeck – they'd worked together for so long now they could communicate without words – and muttered a goodbye, backing out of the room and shutting the door behind her.

She was walking back through the reception area when she spotted the filthy back of Charlie Petworth's tweed coat. Baxter was standing quietly and obediently by Charlie's legs.

"Now, Charlie, what's the problem—" she began to say, and then Charlie turned and Kate stopped speaking abruptly.

He had a baby in his arms. A toddler; a blonde child, sleeping peacefully.

"*What the hell?*"

Charlie's bloodshot, watery blue eyes met her gaze. "I found her."

Kate's arms were already reaching out to take the child. "What do you mean, you found her?"

Charlie sounded defiant. "I found her on the step. Where I sit sometimes. Just turned up and there she was."

Kate recalled the photograph she'd seen of Sophia Walker. This was the same face. Relief made her legs weak. "What do you mean?" She reached out for the baby but Charlie pulled the child closer to him. "Charlie, don't be ridiculous. Give her to me."

Charlie shook his head. "No. She's safe with me."

Kate could feel the backwash of adrenaline, spiking within her. "Charlie, for f—" She recalled herself. "For God's sake. Give her here. You know I won't hurt her."

People were gathering, drawn by the intimation of drama and by Kate's rising voice. Charlie looked down at the sleeping child and then looked at Kate.

"Her name is Joy," he said, very distinctly.

Kate had got her arms underneath the child now. In this close proximity to Charlie, she tried not to breathe too deeply. "Just give her here, Charlie. She'll be safe with me."

"She will be?" Charlie said, doubt in his voice but he allowed Kate to take the child. Feeling the weight of the sleeping child, the warmth and life of her, Kate felt almost sick with the relief of it.

"Now, what's all this then?" Sergeant Bill Osbourne was looming. Kate, her throat thickened, found it hard to speak for a second.

"Bill, take Charlie into one of the interview rooms. I need to – this is the missing child, Sophia Walker. Her parents are right over there. Oh Christ, we need to let them know we've got her, right now."

Even as Kate spoke, there was a scream behind her. A second later, Amelia Walker had snatched the baby from Kate's arms and was holding her close. Sophia jolted awake and immediately began to cry.

"Sophia, oh, Sophia..." The rest of Amelia's words were lost in a torrent of sobs. Paul Walker had come up behind her and laid a hand on her shoulder, tears standing in his eyes.

Unnoticed in all the commotion, Charlie Petworth was being led away by Bill Osbourne. He stopped still and shouted loud enough to be heard over the tumult. "Her name is Joy!"

For a brief moment, silence fell. Kate, her gaze on Amelia Walker's face, saw for a moment the look of shock that occurred. Paul Walker was frowning.

"Come on, Charlie. Let's not have any trouble." Bill Osbourne placed a hand on Charlie's arm.

For a moment, it looked as though Charlie wouldn't

concur. Then, his head drooping, he allowed himself to be led away.

***

SEVERAL HOURS LATER, KATE FACED Anderton across his desk.

"Christ," was his eloquent remark.

Kate was not religious but she didn't like to hear the Lord's name taken in vain. "Don't."

Anderton pushed one of the pens on his desk. It rolled to the edge and dropped to the floor. "What made him do it?"

Kate was silent. She and Anderton both knew the usual reason a middle-aged man would abduct a young female child.

"There's nothing in his history, nothing to indicate he is – is that way inclined." Anderton spoke reluctantly.

Kate looked over at Olbeck, sitting next to her. He'd so far remained silent. "What do you think, Mark?"

Olbeck lifted his shoulders in a shrug. "Maybe – well, you know Charlie's always nicking things so he can get a bed for the night, isn't he? Is it beyond the realms of possibility that he decided to commit a much more serious crime so he'd get a prison sentence? Somewhere relatively warm and safe to stay over the whole of the winter?"

They all contemplated that thought. "It's possible," said Anderton.

Kate was shaking her head. "I don't think he would have done. He wouldn't have wanted to leave Baxter."

"Baxter?" questioned Anderton.

"His dog. He loves that dog. That's why he won't go to the refuge, because he wouldn't be able take his dog with him."

Anderton bent down and picked up the pen that had dropped to the floor. "Well, I'm not sure that we have any other choice than to charge him with child abduction." He looked at them both. "Anything you want to add?"

Kate and Olbeck both shook their heads.

"Okay." Anderton pushed his chair back from the desk and sighed. "Well, it's hardly filling me with Christmas cheer but there we go."

Kate got up, quickly followed by Olbeck. "I'd better talk to the Walkers, check that everything's okay."

"Good. Do that." Anderton rubbed a finger along his chin. "There's something... Did you say Walker?"

Kate nodded. "Yes. Why?"

"That name is ringing a faint bell. There was something... Hold on a minute..." Anderton sat back down, grabbed his keyboard and began typing something. "Hold on. Yes, I thought so. My God, I thought so. What relief the child came back—"

Kate was thoroughly lost and, from the look on his face, so was Olbeck. "What's the problem?"

"There's no problem. It's just that the Walkers lost a child about five years ago. A tragedy – the little girl fell down the stairs." Anderton swung his computer screen around so that Kate and Olbeck could see it. There was a local newspaper account of the accident. Biting her lip, Kate read it quickly. What immediately jumped out at her was the name of the baby who'd died.

"'Joy'" she said, softly.

"Yes, little Joy Walker. Dreadful accident. She was only about eighteen months."

"Joy," repeated Kate. She looked at the two men. "Don't you remember that's what Charlie said when he brought Sophia into the station?"

"What's that?"

"He called her Joy. Charlie did." Kate pointed to the screen and the flaring black capitals of the headline. "That's the name of the Walkers' first child, the one that died."

Both men looked at where Kate was pointing. "He's confused," said Anderton. "Not surprising, really, the amount he drinks."

For a moment they all continued to stare at the screen. Then Kate turned away. "Maybe," she said.

***

WHEN KATE GOT BACK TO her desk, she sat for a moment, thinking about what to do. Then, slowly, because she wasn't exactly sure what she was looking for, she brought up Charlie Petworth's records. She looked at all the things he'd been accused of stealing. A hand trowel. A flowerpot. Some gardening gloves. Kate scrolled back down the page. What a lot of things he'd taken and yet all of them so inconsequential. Why would Charlie go from stealing a packet of flower seeds to taking a baby girl from her car seat?

Remembering the Walkers, she jumped up and hurried back to the interview room, where they were still waiting. Sophia had calmed down by now and was lying quietly in Amelia Walker's arms, her big blue eyes fixed on her mother's face.

"Well, Mr and Mrs Walker, we won't keep you much longer." Kate sat herself down in the chair opposite the two of them. "Would you like our on-call doctor to have a look at Sophia?"

Amelia Walker blanched. "Why would you say that? Did he – oh, God, did that man do something to her?"

"No, no." Kate hastened to reassure her. "There's nothing suggesting any kind of abuse took place. I know it's hard to believe but the man who took Sophia, Charlie Petworth, is really completely harmless. He's never done anything like this before, it's totally out of character."

"He must be a goddamn lunatic." Paul Walker was angry, and Kate couldn't blame him.

"Well, he'll certainly be charged and remanded. You won't have to worry about him any longer." Kate leant forward a little. "Could you say that you recognised him, Charlie Petworth, I mean? Had you ever seen him outside the house before?"

Paul Walker was already shaking his head. Amelia cuddled her daughter closer to her, her head down. Then she looked up. "No, I don't think so. I can't remember seeing him."

It was odd, but even as she was saying it, Kate got the impression that Amelia was saying something quite other than what she wanted to. She frowned, and was going to probe a little further, when Amelia's gaze met her own and there was something in her eyes that silenced Kate.

"I've never seen him before in my life," Paul Walker said emphatically. "And now, Sergeant, might we be permitted to take our daughter home? I think I can speak for my wife when I say we're all quite exhausted."

"Yes, I understand," said Kate. "Now we've got your statements and so forth, I don't see why you can't head home. You'll be contacted in due course about the case, obviously, and you can also expect a visit from Victim Support."

"That's kind but I don't expect we'll need them," Paul Walker said in a tone that was polite but firm. Kate looked over at Amelia, but she was looking down at Sophia, who was drifting into sleep again.

Kate ushered them through the reception area, shook hands with them both, and watched them walk out the door. Was that *snow* she could see in the light from the doorway? She squinted harder, almost convinced she could see tiny white whirling flakes. Then she realised that Amelia Walker had come back into the station, almost hurrying.

"I forgot my gloves, I won't be a sec – you settle her," she was saying over her shoulder, clearly to her husband. Then she caught sight of Kate and hurried over.

"I just wanted to say – it's just that I think my husband's – well, I'm not sure, it might be that he doesn't remember because it's quite a long time ago, but I've realised I did recognise him. The man who took Sophia, I mean. I think it was him."

Kate was alert now. "You think you recognised him? From where?"

Amelia looked worried. She cast a glance over

her shoulder. "I can't say for certain, but he did look familiar."

"You mean you've seen him recently?"

Amelia shook her head. "No – not recently. Sometime in the past, but I can't exactly remember when or where." She paused and said, "It's probably not very helpful."

"Well, it's something we can look into," Kate said. "Could you please let me know if you remember anything more? Feel free to call me at any time."

"Yes, yes of course. Oh, I must go—" Amelia said a hurried goodbye, pivoted on her heel, and scurried back out of the main entrance. A little flurry of snow blew in after her. So it *was* snowing – perhaps they would have a white Christmas after all.

Kate was about to call after her – what about the woman's gloves? – but then she realised that had been the pretext for Amelia to come back into the station. Shrugging a little, she made her way back to the office, thinking about Sophia and Charlie and whether this case was as straightforward as it first appeared. She switched off her computer, wondering whether the snow would be too deep as yet to drive home. Surely not? Still, there was no point hanging about here any longer, waiting to find out.

She was about to leave the office – she was the last one there, as usual – but after a moment, she dug out the box of chocolate willies that Theo had given her and proceeded to decorate his desk profusely with them, until scarcely a pen pot, folder, keyboard or square inch of desk space was clear. There. That would take him a while to clear up the next morning – if the cleaners didn't move them first. Giggling, Kate left the office, gleefully anticipating the look on Theo's face the next morning.

***

By eight o'clock the next morning, the snow had settled in earnest. Kate abandoned her intentions to drive in, swapped her office shoes for her walking boots, packed her things into a rucksack and set off for the station on foot. She'd forgotten all about her little redecoration of Theo's desk in the chaos of the morning and was pleased to find he hadn't yet made it into the station. Rav and Anne were already there and laughing.

"Don't touch them," Kate warned as Rav went to eat one of the chocolates.

"Come on, there's tons here."

"I know but I want him to experience the full effect—" Kate realised Theo was walking in through the door of the office and immediately swung her chair back to face her computer, pretending nothing was wrong. Rav and Anne did the same, although Kate could see Rav's shoulders shaking with suppressed laughter. She held her breath for Theo's reaction.

"Oh, ha ha. And ho bloody ho."

Kate started laughing. "Serves you right." She ducked as Theo threw a fusillade of tiny chocolate phalluses at her. "Don't be so childish."

"*You* can talk—" Theo was laughing himself now. They all got up to help him clear his desk and eventually settled back to work, each fortified with their own stash of chocolates.

Still grinning, Kate turned to her emails. There was one from the duty sergeant from the cells downstairs, informing her that Charlie Petworth would be moved to a remand prison later that day. Kate frowned, her good mood dipping. Of course, for an offence as serious as the one he'd committed, the chance of bail was unlikely... Who on Earth would bail him out anyway? No, being on remand was probably the best thing for him. Was that why he had done it?

Kate tapped her fingers on the edge of her desk, chewing her bottom lip, thinking. Then she got up and headed for the stairs, collecting a cup of tea from the machine along the way.

When the door to cell three was opened for Kate, she could see Charlie sitting quite peacefully on the edge of the narrow bed – well, hardly a bed; more a ledge with a thin foam mattress upon it. He looked up as Kate came into the room.

"Here you go, Charlie. I thought you might like a cup of tea."

"Ta, love." Kate handed it to him and then leant back against the wall of the cell, seeing him sip it with shaky hands.

"I just wanted to let you know that Baxter's been picked up by the RSPCA, okay? They'll keep him until we get everything sorted out." Charlie looked anxious. "He'll be fine, Charlie. Don't worry about him. They might even be able to get him into foster care so he won't have to stay in kennels."

"He don't like kennels, does Baxter. He doesn't like being locked up."

"I know." Kate, watching Charlie's shaky hands, made a mental note to be sure that the doctor should come and see him if she hadn't already. Kate wasn't sure exactly how much Charlie drank on a regular basis, but she didn't want him having a fit or something similarly awful because of having to go cold turkey.

It was warm in the cells, and Charlie had divested himself on his awful old tweed coat and the scarf he'd wrapped around his head. He was wearing a big black fleece with an old faded logo across the front of it. *Greenfingers Gardening*. Kate recalled all the little petty thefts that Charlie had committed and thought of something. She pointed at his top. "Do you like gardening, Charlie?"

He looked at her as though she were stupid. "I *am* a gardener. This is my company."

"Your company?" Kate asked, confused.

"Aye. This." He pointed to the faded logo. "Been a bit quiet recently but once I get myself together, it'll be fine."

Kate smiled sadly. "Of course it will, Charlie."

She left him then and made her way back to her desk. Absentmindedly removing a chocolate penis that Theo had sneakily placed on the seat of her chair, obviously hoping she'd sit on it, Kate brought up a browser on her computer screen. Idly, she typed in the URL for Companies House, found the appropriate search box and typed in *Greenfingers Gardening*.

There were at least twenty companies with that

name or variants thereof. Kate cast her eyes down the list, wondering why she was doing this, why she was bothering. Well, well. Right at the bottom, a gardening company was listed to a Charles Petworth. Kate clicked on it to bring up any further information. She sighed. Written under the company name was the date of its insolvency, some four years ago now.

Kate shook her head and shut down the browser. Poor old Charlie. Had he lost track of time so badly that he genuinely thought his company was still flourishing? Why had he gone bankrupt? Did he drink because of his failure as a businessman, or had the collapse of his company come about because of his drinking?

Kate got up to make herself a hot drink. While she was waiting for the kettle to boil, she wandered over to the window. Snow was still falling, the air a mass of fluttering white flakes. Lucky she didn't live too far away... She remembered the forerunner of all this bad weather last night, the tiny flurry of snow that had blown in as Amelia Walker left the police station...

Kate stopped dead, her hand holding a heaped spoonful of instant coffee. She let it fall, scattering brown grains everywhere, and ran back to her desk. There was something, just a glimmer; if she thought too hard about it, it would disappear. Frantically, she grabbed her phone and stabbed at the buttons. How difficult would it be to get hold of the thing she wanted? Was it likely that the information she was seeking had already been archived?

She made the call, spoke to someone, got a number from them and then she spoke to someone else. There was a frustrating wait for yet another person to get back from their lunch break. An hour and half later, a cardboard folder was deposited on Kate's desk and she thanked the young officer who had brought it up.

"What are you up to?" Olbeck paused by the desk on his way back through the office.

Kate, who had her nose practically buried in the contents of the folder, merely grunted.

"Can I help?"

Kate waved him away. "Can't talk. Concentrating. I'll come over in a minute." She heard Olbeck sigh but he obediently went away.

Kate continued reading slowly and thoroughly. Her search was hampered by the fact that she wasn't exactly sure what she was looking for. It was on the second sweep of the report that she spotted it and drew her breath in with a hiss.

It wasn't much but it was something. Pondering her next move, she thought for a moment and reached for her phone.

Amelia Walker answered the call in a polite but rather hesitant manner. Her nervousness increased when she realised it was Abbeyford CID on the end of the line.

"Please don't worry, Mrs Walker, it's nothing to fret about," Kate hastened to reassure her. "I just had a very few quick questions."

"Yes?"

"You said to me last night that you thought you might have recognised Charlie Petworth. Is it possible that he might have once worked for you? As a gardener?"

There was silence on the other end of the line and then Amelia spoke with comprehension dawning in her voice. "Oh, yes. Why, yes, of course, that's how I know him. Yes, he used to come and do the lawns, the hedge-clipping, things like that. How stupid of me not to remember."

"Did he work for you for long?"

"A few years, I think. This was some time ago."

Kate pushed her for the exact dates, as closely as Amelia could remember them. As she jotted down the numbers, she looked at the date of the report she was reading. *So, that tallies...*

"Thank you, Mrs Walker, that's very helpful. One more thing; can I ask if your husband has always worked from home?"

Amelia Walker sounded confused at the question but answered it anyway. "Yes, he has done for the past few years. Actually, longer than that. At least five or six years, I think."

"Right, thanks very much. Have Victim Support been in touch yet? Oh good. Well, please don't hesitate to let me know if you need anything else or remember anything else. I'll be in touch."

***

AFTER KATE RANG OFF, SHE sat silently, staring blindly across the office. Then, slowly, she got up and went over to Olbeck's office. "I know you're probably busy but would you mind sitting in on an interview with me?"

Olbeck looked surprised but smiled in acquiescence. "It's pretty quiet at the moment, actually. Hope it keeps up until Christmas." He got up from his desk. "Who are we interviewing?"

"Charlie Petworth."

***

As LUCK WOULD HAVE IT, one of the duty solicitors, Nathan Anstey, was just walking out of the cell block area as Kate and Olbeck entered it. Kate grabbed him by the arm. "Nathan! Just the person I wanted to see. Would you be an angel and just sit in on a quick interview with us?"

Nathan groaned. "Oh, Kate, I was just leaving..."

"I'll be quick, promise. And Mark and I will take you for a festive pint afterwards."

Nathan rolled his eyes. "That's bribery and corruption."

Kate grinned. "Come on. I promise I won't be long."

She found a free interview room and collected Charlie from his cell. He stood a little uncertainly, waiting for Kate to lead him to where they were going.

"In here, Charlie. I just want to ask you a few questions. It'll be all right."

They all seated themselves. Kate leant forward. "Charlie, what was the name of the little girl you – you brought into the station yesterday?"

Charlie looked down at his trembling hands. "Her name is Joy," he almost whispered. Then he blinked. "Or is that the other one?"

Kate said gently "Do you know the Walkers, Charlie? Did you used to work for them as a gardener?"

Charlie was blinking. He looked at Kate and nodded.

"You used to work for them?"

"Yes." Charlie folded his hands back together. "Used to work for them, years ago. Did their lawns, did their flowers. Used to see the little girl in the garden. She used to give me daisies, pick 'em off the lawn. Couldn't talk much, she was too little, but she had a lovely smile. Little Joy."

"You knew Joy Walker?"

Charlie nodded. A tear fell from his rheumy eye. "She died," he said hoarsely.

Kate sat forward a little in her chair. This was the biggest leap of faith she'd ever taken in an interview. She swallowed hard before she asked her question. "Charlie, were you working at the Walkers' house on the day little Joy Walker died?"

The silence hung in the room. Nathan Anstey was frowning. Kate could feel Olbeck tense beside her.

After a moment, Charlie nodded. "I was there. I looked up and I could see through the window. See the landing at the top, it were a big window, round like a porthole."

He stopped speaking, his voice trembling. *Don't interrupt*, Kate prayed silently to Nathan and Olbeck. *Let him speak*. She wondered how many years Charlie had choked this down, this memory, had tried to drown it with whisky and lager and cheap cider.

"What happened, Charlie?" she asked, as softly as she could.

Charlie gulped. "They all said she fell but she didn't fall. He was angry. He picked her up and threw her down the stairs."

And there it was. Kate clenched her fist under the table. "Who threw her, Charlie? Who threw Joy?" She could see Nathan opening his mouth to speak and shot him such a glare that he shut it again with a snap.

"He did," whispered Charlie. "Mr Walker. He was angry, always angry. Used to hit his wife, too. Saw that too once, through the kitchen window." His voice cracked. "Never said anything about that either." He began to cry, softly.

Kate took a deep breath. "Charlie, why didn't you say anything at the time?"

Charlie's head hung. Kate saw a tear fall into his lap. "I was confused. I was drunk at the time, I was drinking even then. I thought I'd made a mistake, I thought I'd imagined it. Everyone was so sure it was an accident I – I didn't know..." He trailed off and then his head came up and he looked Kate straight in the eye. "Who was going to believe me over him?"

There was another moment of silence. Then Kate asked, gently, "What happened yesterday, Charlie? Did you go to the Walkers' house?"

Charlie nodded jerkily. "I go there sometimes. Never inside or anything. I just – sometimes I have to remember." He took a deep, ragged breath. "I hid in the bushes by the driveway. It's a long driveway, you can't see the house from the road. No one could see anything but I heard them. I heard him. He was shouting again, shouting at his wife. Calling her a stupid bitch, saying he was going to kill her. And I looked over at the car and the little girl was there, in the car seat. And I was so frightened..." He took another gulp of air. "I just walked over and got her out and walked down the drive with her. I had to keep her safe, you see."

There was a silence in which Kate fancied she could almost hear the soft flurry of snowflakes falling from the darkening sky.

Charlie cleared his throat and spoke again. "I had to keep her safe."

***

Outside the interview room, Kate and Olbeck looked at one another. Olbeck was looking a trifle pale.

"Anderton?" was all that he said, and Kate nodded.

"Are you completely determined to ruin Christmas?" Anderton demanded, after listening to Kate's five minute summation of what had just happened. "Opening an investigation this late in the day? Are you mad?"

Knowing him for as long as she had, Kate knew when her boss was merely venting steam. "Come on, sir. You've got a witness to the crime. At the very least, that's enough to re-open the investigation."

"A chronically unreliable witness, a homeless alcoholic to boot. The defence will make mincemeat of him."

"It's not just that." Kate pushed the folder she'd been carrying under her arm across the desk. She indicated the part of the report that she'd highlighted in fluorescent yellow. "What about that?"

Muttering, Anderton did so. Kate watched his lips purse as he read. "That's not much either."

Olbeck spoke up. "Actually, I think Kate's right. The post mortem on Joy Walker revealed that she'd already had her arm and her collarbone broken once before. Two broken bones in eighteen months? There could be some quite serious questions raised about why that wasn't flagged up."

"Hmm," said Anderton.

"I'm sure if we pulled all the medical records of the family, we'd have something else to go on. Even the hospital attendance of Amelia Walker. You know the kind of thing to look for." Anderton still looked unconvinced "Come on, sir. We don't want yet another case of abuse where it all gets swept under the carpet just because the parents are wealthy, middle-class and professional," Kate said with an edge of impatience in her tone,

"True." Anderton looked up. "God, this is going to cause a fuss, though."

"Well, we should be used to it by now," said Kate.

Anderton barked laughter. "True! Okay, leave it with me—"

"There's something else too," Kate added. "Paul Walker lied. Blatantly lied about not knowing Charlie Petworth. He would have recognised him – his wife certainly did."

"Okay." Anderton scribbled something down on a notepad. "All right. You've convinced me. You have my word that I'll be recommending another investigation into the death of Joy Walker, given the new information that's come to light. Okay?"

Kate and Olbeck looked at one another and then back at Anderton and nodded.

"Fine. Right. Let me get on with it then." Anderton waved a hand, dismissing them. Then he looked up. "Oh, Kate. Have a word with Social Services as well, will you? This is not just a new investigation, we have the issue of child safeguarding to take up with regards to Sophia Walker."

Kate had already made a mental note to do just that. "Of course. Leave it with me."

"Good stuff. Well, see you later. And Happy Christmas," Anderton added.

***

KATE AND OLBECK HEADED BACK to the office. Kate stood by her desk for a moment, irresolute.

"Don't you have a phone call to make?" Olbeck asked on his way past.

"Yes. It's just – hang on a minute. I'll be back in a flash." Quickly, she grabbed her coat and her bag and hurried out of the door.

The pavements had finally been gritted and Kate was able to make good progress to the city centre. It had stopped snowing but it was bitterly cold, the wind like a knife-blade against her face. Kate hurried thankfully into one of the department stores, loosening the scarf around her throat. It didn't take her long to find what she was looking for.

"Shall I wrap it?" asked the jolly-looking lady behind the till. Kate nodded and thanked her. Then she took up her purchase and hurried back to the station.

Down on the cell floor, Kate approached Cell Three and peered through the viewing pane in the door. She saw, with compassion, that Charlie was fast asleep on the narrow bed.

Kate turned to the duty sergeant at the desk in the corner of the room. "George, could you give this to Charlie Petworth when he wakes up?"

George Smithfield took the paper-wrapped parcel from Kate suspiciously. "What is it?"

"Nothing dangerous. It's just a calendar."

"A calendar?"

Kate nodded. "A gardening calendar. With lots of pictures of flowers." George was still looking at her suspiciously. "Don't worry, it's fine. Have you got a pen?" She took the one he proffered and wrote on the front of the package. *Happy Christmas, Charlie. A fresh start? Kate Redman.* Then she handed back the pen and the package.

"I'll give it to him," George said, still frowning.

Kate tipped him a wink. "Thanks," she said. "And happy Christmas."

"Humph."

Kate smiled to herself as she climbed back up the stairs. Halfway up, a window showed her the snow-covered streets of Abbeyford, the twinkle of the Christmas streetlights, the hurrying shoppers slipping and sliding through the snow. Kate paused, hugging her elbows. She thought about Charlie, peacefully asleep downstairs, and hoped he was dreaming of gardens; not snow-covered and dead, but glorious, green, verdant gardens, abundant with flowers.

She stayed there a long time, looking out at the snow, thinking about what had happened and what would happen in the future. Would justice be served? "All we can do is try," she muttered to herself under her breath. Then, tearing her gaze from the snowy vista before her, she turned and began climbing the stairs again, back to the office.

THE END

Valentine

A Kate Redman Novella

This book is for my niece Georgia Lucas-Going, with my love.

Chapter One

Terminal Five at London Heathrow Airport was never less than busy, even first thing in the morning or last thing at night. Now, at nearly one o'clock in the afternoon, it was chaotic; people rushed from one gate to another pulling luggage trolleys loaded with baggage behind them, argued with staff at the check-in desks, and raced wailing children to the baby-changing areas.

Kate Redman had hoped for some sort of romantic farewell with her boyfriend, Tin, before he got on his plane to New York that afternoon. As they stood by the departure gates, she realised she'd been a bit naive. She could scarcely hear herself think in all the tumult, let alone exchange meaningful and heartfelt last words before they had to say goodbye.

"God, this is hell," Tin said, yanking his carry-on bag out of the way as a large woman pushed past him, giving him a glare and a tut for his trouble.

"I know. You'll be happy to get on the plane, just to get a bit of peace."

"Look, let's move. How about we have a drink at the champagne bar? One last treat before I have to go?"

Kate agreed; not because she had much of a liking for champagne but more so she could sit somewhere without being buffeted on all sides by stressed humanity. They waded their way through the crowds to the relative peace of the champagne bar and seized the first seats they could find. Kate took one look at the prices of the drinks and nearly fainted.

"It's all right," Tin said, noticing her bog-eyed look. "My treat. It's the least I can do, seeing as I'm flying out just before Valentine's Day."

Kate tried to smile. She'd bought Tin a gift and a card and tucked it away in the inner pocket of his suitcase. Should she mention it now or leave it to be a surprise? But then he might not discover it until much later and he'd think she hadn't got him anything...

The glasses of champagne were placed before them, on top of black paper napkins. Kate watched the bubbles as if hypnotised.

"So – cheers, then," Tin said, clinking his glass gently against hers.

"Cheers." All of a sudden, Kate's throat was aching. *Don't cry*. She stared at her champagne glass, watching the bubbles rise in the golden liquid, blinking hard.

"Hey," Tin said gently. "It's okay. It's not for ever."

"I know." She didn't say any more because she didn't trust her voice.

"I fully expect to see you out there with me in a few months' time."

"I know." She managed to smile and look him in the eye. That was the biggie, the pachyderm in the room. Would she join Tin in New York permanently? She swerved from thinking it would be a great opportunity and she should really just go for it, to thinking that it would be the death of her career and the worst decision she'd ever made. She could often hold these two opposing viewpoints in a matter of minutes.

They finished their champagne and then Tin looked at his watch. "God, I'm really going to have to go."

Kate tried to smile encouragingly. She could tell that they were reaching the stage of goodbyes where everything had been said and the traveller was wanting to just *go*, just get the journey started. "Go on, then. You don't want to miss your plane."

"I'll call you as soon as I land," said Tin. He pulled her into an embrace and hugged her very tightly. "I won't say goodbye, I hate goodbyes. I'll say *au revoir* instead."

"*Au revoir*, then. Have a good flight." Kate's voice betrayed her.

"Hey, now." Tin kissed her and then let her go. "I'll see you soon."

Kate blinked back tears and forced a smile. She waved him off, watching him disappear through the departure gates. She couldn't wait to get back to her car so she could have a proper cry. Head on the steering wheel, tissue in hand, let it all out for a few minutes and then it would be back on with the stiff-upper-lip and giving herself a stern talking to as she drove back to her home in the West Country. *Pull yourself together, woman. It's not as if you'll never see him again.* But first – one good hard sob, Kate told herself, and as she reached the escalator that led up to the short stay car park, she could feel her eyes beginning to brim.

***

Back in Abbeyford, the pretty market town that stood on the banks of the River Avon, Police Constable Paul Boulton was taking his shift in manning the front desk at the police station. He'd already dealt with a teenage runaway, two elderly gentlemen who had almost come to blows over a parking infraction, and the now almost-weekly arrest of local drug dealer Jason North. Paul was beginning to suspect that Jason was allowing himself to get caught because of some as yet unascertained reason. Although every time Jason was collared, he requested the same duty solicitor, a very pretty, glamorous young lawyer, so Paul was pretty certain that Jason was getting careless because he'd fallen for his brief and this was the only way he had of spending time with her. The idiot.

Shaking his head at the stupidity of youth, Paul straightened the paperwork littering the desk, returned an errant pencil to a pot and looked up into a blast of wintry air as the main station door opened. He suppressed a sigh, bracing himself for more trouble. But the woman who walked through the door didn't, he had to admit, look like she'd be here to report anything more startling than a lost dog. She was in her early forties, with a carefully shaped mane of glossy brown hair, discreet make-up, diamond earrings sparkling under the harsh strip lights above. She was carrying a cardboard box displaying the logo of a very expensive and exclusive patisserie shop in Abbeyford's town centre in her hands. Paul Boulton brightened up. She was clearly just delivering a cake. Was it for him? It's not my birthday, he thought, before he switched on a smile and asked if he could help her.

"I'm so sorry, I wasn't sure whether to call someone out or not. I mean, you hear all the time about the immense pressures the police are under. I didn't want to, well, be a *nuisance caller,* or something like that. So I thought perhaps I'd better just come here myself." Her voice matched her appearance – a well-bred accent, softly spoken. "I'm Mrs Houghton – Valerie Houghton."

"You have something to report, Mrs Houghton?" Paul Boulton was conscious of a little stab of disappointment at not getting any cake and inwardly chastised himself. How old did he think he was, five?

"Yes, I'm afraid I have," said the woman, almost apologetically. She placed the cake box directly on the desk before him. "I found this on my doorstep this morning."

She raised the brown and blue lid of the cake box. Paul Boulton leant forward a little to see what was inside it and recoiled sharply, just about managing to stifle a cry of shock.

"I'm sorry," said the woman. "But you can see why I thought you might want to know about it."

The cake box contained two objects, both incongruous against the luxurious packaging. The first was a lump of viscera, a bloody object of about four inches in diameter that Paul's disbelieving gaze identified after a moment as a heart. An actual heart. It was pierced through the centre by the other object, a thin, metal-tipped arrow.

"Good God," he said, on his feet now to look at it more closely. Was it *human*? Dear God, if it was, this was a damn sight more serious than he'd first thought. He looked up at the woman. "You found it on your doorstep like this? In the box?"

"Oh *no!* No, I thought I'd better put it in something, and this was the only box I had. It was just lying there on the doorstep in a puddle of blood. Disgusting."

The sound of a set of footsteps preceded an exclamation from Detective Inspector Mark Olbeck, who had just walked through the door. "What the hell have you got there, Paul?"

The woman turned and gave a cry of recognition. "Why, Mark – it is Mark, isn't it?"

Olbeck smiled in response to her greeting. "Hello, Valerie. What on Earth brings you here?"

This was an added complication that Paul Boulton could have done without. "Do you two know each other?"

"Her husband works with my husband," explained Olbeck. "How *is* John, Valerie? Haven't seen you both for ages."

"Oh, he's fine. Very busy, you know. Well I'm sure you do, it must be the same for Jeff—"

They were carrying on as if they'd both forgotten there was a bloody body part lying on the desk in front of them. "Excuse me?" demanded Paul Boulton. "DI Olbeck? What am I to do with this? Should I have forensics check it out?" He drew Olbeck to one side, out of earshot of Valerie, and murmured, "What if it's human?"

Sergeant Bill Osbourne had come up to both of them unnoticed. "It's not," he announced, peering over at what was in the cake box.

They both turned to face him. "How do you know?" asked Olbeck.

"My dad was a butcher. This is a pig's heart or a cow's heart, maybe. It's definitely not human."

"You sure, Bill?"

"Aye. As sure as I can be. Our dad used to bring them home sometimes, for the dog."

Paul and Olbeck exchanged looks of relief. "Well, that's something," said Olbeck. "Tell you what, Paul, shall I do Valerie's statement? It shouldn't take long. It's probably just some malicious prank, youngsters making trouble. That sort of thing."

Paul felt a little troubled by this. Detective Inspectors didn't normally do the routine statements but if Olbeck was happy to do so, then that was one less thing he had to worry about... "That would be great, thanks," he said and returned to his station at the desk, watching with relief as Olbeck ushered Valerie Houghton into one of the interview rooms and bore the cake box away with him.

Chapter Two

IF KATE HAD PLANNED THINGS better, she would have booked the whole day off work to drop Tin at the airport. As it was, she'd promised to go into the office that afternoon and so had to take a few moments to repair her eye make-up in the rear view mirror of her car when she parked in the station car park. She regarded herself suspiciously. Not too bad – not *too* red-eyed. She practised a bright, uncaring smile in the mirror. Perhaps coming in was a better idea anyway – she would be able to keep busy, and not sit at home brooding over whether she'd make the biggest mistake of her life by not going to New York with Tin as soon as he'd asked.

The office was quiet when she got there. Only Detective Sergeant Theo Marsh bent industriously over his keyboard, two desks down from Kate's. He looked up as she sat down. "Tin get off okay?"

"Fine," Kate said shortly.

"Never mind, Kate. He's only thousands of miles away, surrounded by gorgeous young American beauties. Dunno what you're upset about." He caught sight of the expression on her face and dropped his usual facetious tone. "Oh, mate, sorry. I was only teasing."

"Yes, well," said Kate, hating the wobble in her voice. "Don't."

"Sorry."

They worked in silence for a few minutes. Kate opened her emails and stared, unseeing, at the long list of unanswered ones. She was startled a moment later by Theo's hand appearing in front of her bearing a mug of coffee.

"Blimey," she said, taking it. "You really must feel sorry. I think the last time you made me coffee was when I came back from compassionate leave."

"Yeah, well, then you really appreciate it when I do it, yeah?"

They bickered amiably for a few minutes, interrupted by the phone ringing. Kate picked it up.

"Kate?" It was Olbeck. "How are you doing? Tin get off okay?"

"Fine," said Kate, wishing she'd kept her mouth shut about her boyfriend's departure date. She still had three or four colleagues' commiserations to suffer. "What's up?"

"It's nothing serious but it's a bit odd. We've had three reports from women who've had a dead pig's heart with an arrow through it left on their doorstep."

"*What*?"

"I know. Like I said, odd. It's probably nothing more than a malicious Valentine's Day prank, but do you think you could do some preliminary digging into the victims, just see if there's any obvious link between them?"

Kate nodded and then realised he couldn't see her doing it down the phone. "Sure, no problem."

"It's not top priority, anyway. I know that, but if you could when you get a moment, that would be great."

"I will." A thought struck Kate. "Where are you?"

"Downstairs. Just finishing up a statement. I'll be up shortly." He gave her the details of the three women he wanted her to investigate.

"Okay, got it. See you soon." Kate hung up and looked up to see Theo looking over with raised eyebrows.

"What's up?" he asked.

Kate explained. It sounded even more bizarre in the recounting. "Pretty weird, isn't it?" she said. "A dead pig's heart?"

Theo snorted. "Well, it would hardly be a *live* pig's heart, would it? Jesus, woman. It's like those old anti-smoking adverts. 'This is the lung of a healthy person'. He's hardly healthy if he's bleeding *dead*, is he?"

Kate laughed and turned back to her computer with renewed interest. Coming into work had been a good idea after all. Even so, she looked at the clock, wondering whether Tin would have landed by now...

As luck would have it, she wasn't as absolutely snowed under with work as was usual. She started with a simple Google search on the three names of the women who'd reported the hearts. Valerie Houghton, Caroline Spendler, Kiki Dee. *Kiki*? What kind of name was that? The search on Kiki's name brought up a multitude of Google links. Miss Dee was a drama student at the Abbeyford School of Art and Drama – Kate knew it well, after a particularly nasty spate of suicides had occurred there a couple of years previously. According to the website of Decadence, a nightclub in Arbuthon Green, Kiki Dee was also a part-time burlesque dancer, performing under the name of Miss Dee-Licious. Kate's eyebrows rose. The accompanying photograph on the website showed a very pretty girl, with a sharp dark bob and well-marked dark eyebrows, like a young twenties starlet.

Kate checked on the other two names. Valerie Houghton barely appeared on Google, only mentioned by name in a newspaper report when her husband had been awarded some sort of academic science award. Kate opened up the link and regarded the accompanying photograph. Valerie Houghton appeared somewhat younger than her white-haired husband, although the grainy newsprint wasn't very clear. They apparently had two teenage children and she was described in the article as a 'full-time home-maker'. Kate stopped the curl of her lip with difficulty. *Now Kate, feminism is about choice. If it's some women's choice to stay at home full time, you should support that choice...*

Political thoughts were distracting her. She searched for the last name, Caroline Spendler. A LinkedIn profile was the first link to appear. Caroline Spendler was a solicitor, specialising in family law, apparently working in nearby Salterton. She had what seemed to be a much underused Facebook account and the remaining links were mostly to do with academic and professional sites where her name was mentioned in various contexts, all apparently work-related.

Kate fired up various police databases and ran checks on all three names. Nothing came up for any of them. She searched the National DNA Database, where again she drew a blank. She looked at their addresses on a map of Abbeyford – all three lived in different suburbs. She sat back, tapping a pencil against her jaw, as was her habit when stumped. On the face of it, there was nothing connecting these women – nothing except someone had left each of them an animal's bleeding heart on their doorstep, pierced with an arrow.

Kate looked at the clock. Time was ticking on, and whilst she might not be as busy as usual, she *did* have other things to do, things that were slightly more pressing than this odd but surely harmless case. Taking one last punt, she checked the arrest database to see if anything like this had ever occurred before in Abbeyford. There was nothing that she could find, despite searching under various parameters. Sighing, she closed the slender cardboard file she'd created and decided to concentrate on something else.

Chapter Three

KATE WAS BACK AT WORK the next morning, bright and early, and feeling better about things, generally. Tin had texted her on his arrival at JFK and, even better, Kate had woken that morning to a ring on the doorbell and opened it to find a delivery driver with an enormous bundle of red roses in his arms. Exclaiming in delight, Kate had signed for them and taken them in to discover a note attached to the bundle. Inside the bundle was a note from Tin professing his love and including a flight reference number, a flight to New York that he'd already booked and paid for in two months' time. Kate, half aghast, half delighted, was already feverishly plotting her leave requirements and thinking about packing and who would look after her cat, Merlin, while she was away...

As she seated herself at her desk, she had a moment's regret that Tin hadn't thought to have the enormous bundle of roses delivered to her desk at work. That would have given her bragging rights for at least a week... But no, on second thoughts, Theo would never have let her live it down. Even by the time Halloween rolled around, he would still have been teasing her about the flowers. She hugged the memory of Tin's words, and the flight he'd booked, to herself as a delightful secret.

The macabre Valentine's gifts that had been left for the three women she'd investigated the day before had completely left her mind. It wasn't until Olbeck beckoned her over and asked her whether she'd found any connection that Kate remembered.

"Sorry," she said, feeling a little guilty. "But I couldn't find any link between them, spurious or otherwise."

"That's okay. Thanks for looking." Olbeck sounded a trifle absent-minded. Kate watched as he opened his desk drawer, looked inside for a moment, unseeing, and then shut it again.

"Anything wrong?" she asked.

Olbeck looked up and smiled briefly. "No, it's nothing. It's just – oh, you know how sometimes you get a bad feeling about something? A case, I mean."

"Yes," said Kate, cautiously.

"Well, I've got one about this one. The pig hearts, I mean."

Kate crossed the floor of his office and shut the glass door. Then she returned to his desk, seated herself opposite him and fixed him with a gaze. "Go on."

Olbeck leant back in his chair with a sigh. "This reminds me of something." He saw Kate sit up a little and said hastily, "Not the pig hearts themselves. I've never known of anything like *that* around here. No, it was a domestic incident case I was working on, years ago now. Long before you joined. Started out quite innocuously, if you can say that about a domestic violence case, and ended up with a whole family being killed."

"What?" Kate said, shocked.

"I know. You'd probably remember it, it made the

national press." He named a name that Kate did indeed recall, from a variety of newspaper headlines. Olbeck went on. "Maybe I'm wrong about this. God, I hope I am. But it's just..." He trailed off, pushing a pen around on his desk top. "I've just got a bad feeling about it, that's all."

"A feeling is not evidence," Kate said, mock-sternly, trying to cheer him out of his mood. It worked, sort of. Olbeck laughed and then sighed.

"Well, anyway," he said. "Keep me posted on any developments."

Kate threw him a salute, which he acknowledged with a grin, and then took her leave. Her desk phone was ringing as she left Olbeck's office and she ran quickly to answer it.

"Kate? It's Paul Boulton. I've just had a call from Miss Dee, Kiki Dee. Isn't she one of the ones who—"

Kate interrupted him, feeling a jump of something – unease? Excitement? "What did she want?"

"She called to report someone's killed her pet cat. Left it on the doorstep for her to find. I know it's not normally something you'd be interested in but I thought—"

Kate spoke over him again. "You thought exactly right, Paul. Thank you. Can you give me the details and I'll take it from here?" She scribbled down what he told her, said goodbye and then ran back to Olbeck's office.

***

Kiki Dee lived in a large, three-storey Victorian house. Kate, pausing outside to look up at the exterior of the house, thought it an enormous place for one young woman to live in. A moment later, she chastised herself for her stupidity. Of course Kiki didn't live there on her own – she shared the property with other girls, probably all students at the Abbeyford School of Art and Drama. The house was a monument to femininity – or perhaps the dramatic arts. Piles of clothes were draped here and there, the air was perfumed with a multitude of different scents, and a feather boa was draped artistically around the banisters of the stairs, shedding pink feathers that had dropped to the dirty hallway carpet below.

Kiki Dee was composed but red-eyed when they introduced themselves. She was a tiny girl, no more than five foot two, and as dainty as a china doll. Unlike the publicity photograph on the Decadence club's website, she wore no make-up and her skin was as smooth and unlined as a baby's.

Kate and Olbeck were ushered into a sitting room, stuffed with worn armchairs and an old leather sofa covered in knitted throws and furry rugs. There was a light fitting over the mantelpiece in the shape of a huge, red mouth, pursed in a smiling pout. A pair of gold, sparkly stilettos stood by the empty fireplace, one shoe fallen over on its side. Kiki obviously saw Kate's gaze drawn to the shoes and explained "Those are mine, I use them for the show. I'm a dancer. Only part-time, of course."

"Yes, so I understand, Miss Dee." Olbeck seated himself on the edge of the sofa amidst a pile of soft furnishings.

"They must be terribly hard to walk in," said Kate.

Kiki Dee gurgled a laugh. "I don't have to do much walking, actually. Just gyrate around a chair, twirling my nipple tassels." Kate caught the quick sideways glimpse Kiki gave her as she said this. The girl seemed extremely confident for one so young – she couldn't have been more than twenty – but perhaps that was the attitude one needed as a burlesque dancer.

When they were all seated, Olbeck leant forward. "So, Miss Dee, I understand you found your cat this morning, dead on the doorstep?"

Kiki's blue eyes filled with tears. "Yes. I opened the door this morning – I thought I'd go to college early for once – and poor Frosty was lying there on the doorstep. Just like the other day, when I found the – the heart."

"What did you do?"

Kiki wiped a hand under her eyes. "I moved him. I had to. The others would have had to step over him otherwise and – and I didn't want to leave him there."

"No, that's understandable." Olbeck looked down at his notebook. "You think that somebody may have deliberately killed him? He couldn't have died from natural causes."

Kiki's face hardened. "His neck was broken. I could feel it, once I picked him up. It was horrible."

"Yes, I'm sure it must have been." Olbeck scribbled something down and looked across at Kate, who took up the cue.

"Do you have any idea who might have done this, Miss Dee?" she asked.

"You can call me Kiki. It feels strange being called

Miss Dee." Kiki gave her a watery smile. "And no, I can't think of anyone. I can't think of anyone who would do anything so awful."

"You haven't received any threats, strange messages on social media, anything like that?"

Kiki shook her head. "No. No I don't remember getting anything that I thought was weird."

Kate persisted. "Have you recently broken up with a boyfriend, a partner? Anything like that?"

Kiki's blue gaze dropped. "Well – I kind of did break up with someone recently. Fairly recently."

"When was this?"

"About a month ago. But she wouldn't do something like this, I'm sure of it." Again, that quick sideways glance at Kate, checking whether she was shocked. Kate smiled blandly back.

"Who was this, Miss – Kiki?"

"Laura Ellis. She's on my course at college. But she wouldn't – we didn't really have a serious thing going on, you know? It was a bit of fun, quite casual, you know."

"We might have to talk to her anyway, Kiki. Could you give me her phone number and address details, if you have them?"

Kate scribbled in her own notebook and then looked across at Olbeck, wondering whether she should continue along this line of questioning. It was some time since they'd interviewed together – Olbeck was a bit too senior now for the routine enquiries – and while it had been a while, Kate was pleased to find that they both still worked well together, batting the questions back and forth, working as a team. It was still a partnership, despite the difference in rank. A bit like a marriage, she thought, with an inner grin.

"Had any arguments with anyone, lately?" asked Olbeck. "Any rivalries at college, things like that? Anything you can think of that might have sparked this?"

Kiki shook her head at all his questions. She looked tearful again. "I'm getting quite frightened," she whispered, as Olbeck finished speaking. "What if there's someone out there who really wants to hurt me?"

"I'm quite sure there's not," Olbeck said in his most fatherly and reassuring tone. "But if anything else happens – anything at all – don't hesitate to call us. If you're actually threatened, then dial nine nine nine at once. You might also want to think about getting a personal alarm of some sort. Now, do your friends – your housemates – know about this?"

Kiki nodded. "They do about the heart. I couldn't keep *that* from them. Jenna almost stepped in it."

"Well," said Olbeck. "I'd also keep them abreast of developments, if I were you. The more people looking out for anything suspicious the better."

Kiki looked at him gratefully. "Thank you, DI Olbeck. You've made me feel better already." There was something almost flirtatious in her gaze and Kate smiled quietly to herself. *Wasting your time there, Kiki...*

"What do you think?" she asked Olbeck as they drove away from the house.

Olbeck made an indeterminate noise. "Not sure. I still don't like it much. Of course, there's a good possibility that that cat died of a road accident or something and the person who hit it thought they'd leave it there on the nearest doorstep. Not very kind, but it does happen."

"Really?" Kate said dubiously. She thought for a moment of getting home herself one night and finding Merlin's dead body on her doorstep. She had to physically stop herself from shuddering.

"Look, if something else happens, we'll get someone to take a quick look at the cat." The body of poor Frosty was, at that moment, in the boot of Olbeck's car, wrapped in a large evidence bag. "If it's a case we're building, we'll need all the evidence we can get. But – and I say this with some trepidation – at the moment, it's just conjecture. The only real evidence we've got is those hearts, and that could quite easily just be a malicious prank."

Kate smoothed an errant wisp of hair back from her face. "That's not what you said earlier."

"I know. I'm just saying now that there's nothing more to go on. Like *you* said earlier, feelings are not evidence."

Kate made a noise of agreement. "Shall I check up on the other two women, Valerie Houghton and Caroline what's-her-name, Spendler, and see if they've got anything else to report?"

"Yes, good idea." Olbeck drove in silence for a few moments and then said, "You know, I think that's partly what's making me uneasy about this case."

"What is?"

"The fact that Valerie Houghton is involved. It's just not the kind of thing that happens to people like her. Finding a dead heart on the doorstep, I mean. That's why I can't help but think it's just some random nutter."

"Why isn't it the kind of thing that happens to her?"

Olbeck shrugged and flicked the indicator to turn into the station carpark.

"Oh, you know. She's not the type that has things like that happen to her. She's so, you know—"

"Boring?" Kate said, unclipping her seatbelt as the car came to a halt.

Olbeck gave her a look. "Respectable, I was going to say."

"Oh, *respectable*," Kate said, heaving herself from the car. "Well, you know what they say – the quiet ones are always the worst. Come on, let's get back to the office."

Chapter Four

THE INTERIOR OF VALERIE HOUGHTON'S house couldn't have come as more of a contrast to that of Kiki Dee's. Instead of startling lighting statements and feminine fripperies lying here, there and everywhere, the Houghton residence was furnished in all that was in safe good taste. *Boring*, thought Kate and hid a grin as she was shown into the living room.

"No, there's been absolutely nothing else untoward," Valerie Houghton said, bringing in a tray on which reposed a white china milk jug and two matching cups and saucers. A silver and glass cafetiere steamed beside a plate of biscuits. "Absolutely nothing. Which is a relief, I have to say."

"I'm sure it must be," Kate said, pleasurably anticipating the biscuits. It was only eleven o'clock in the morning but breakfast seemed like a long time ago.

Valerie handed her a cup of fragrant coffee and sat down on the cream-coloured sofa on the far side of the room. "It's a shame Mark – I mean, Detective Inspector Olbeck – couldn't come today."

"He's very busy, I'm afraid, Mrs Houghton," Kate said with a neutral smile. It got like this sometimes, when you knew people outside of work. They got to the point where they thought you were their own personal police officer. She brought herself back to the point.

"This is just a routine follow-up, Mrs Houghton. One of the other women who reported the – the same sort of incident as you did – has had something else happen to her which might be suspicious, so we're just following up to see if anything else strange might have happened to you."

"The other women?" Valerie said blankly.

"Yes, were you not informed?" Kate asked, a little puzzled. "Two other women reported having a pig's heart with an arrow through it on their doorstep, the day before Valentine's Day. You weren't aware of this?"

Valerie Houghton had gone a trifle pale. "No. No, I had no idea. I thought – I thought it was just me."

Kate watched her keenly. "Of course, the fact that it happened to two other people means it is more likely to be just a random individual playing a malicious trick. We've not been able to ascertain any kind of link between the three of you, so far."

"Yes," said Valerie. "Yes, I can see that. Who are these other women?"

"I'm afraid I can't divulge that information at present, Mrs Houghton. But if anything develops, we will, of course, let you know." Kate paused, aware of the tension emanating from the other woman's body. "Is there anything else you'd like to tell me, Mrs Houghton?"

"What do you mean?" Valerie asked sharply.

"Oh, nothing serious. I just meant, have you anything else to tell me that you think might be pertinent to this inquiry?"

Valerie frowned. "I'm sorry. I don't know what you mean." She clearly then recollected how defensive she sounded and smiled placatingly. "I'm sorry, Detective Sergeant, but all of this is quite new to me. I have no idea as to who could have done this, if that's what you want to hear."

"You haven't had any strange phone calls? Any strange emails or letters?"

"No. Nothing like that."

"There's nobody you know who might harbour a grudge against you?"

Valerie blinked several times in quick succession. "Nobody. I'm – I'm not the sort of person who has enemies."

"Quite," said Kate, bending her head to her notes to hide an incipient grin. *Boring*. "Well, if there's nothing else, I'll be on my way. But—" She looked up again and fixed Valerie Houghton with a steady gaze. "If anything comes to mind, anything at all – you will let me know, won't you? Mrs Houghton?"

Valerie's gaze met hers, equally steadily. "Of course I will. Thank you."

ONCE SHE WAS OUT OF the house, Kate hesitated for a moment by her car. Then, acting on impulse, she crept back towards the house and around the side, making for the kitchen window. Keeping herself flattened against the wall, she watched as Valerie Houghton entered the kitchen and moved with quick, decisive steps towards the kitchen dresser at the back of the room. Kate watched as Valerie took down a bottle of brandy from the top shelf of the dresser, poured herself a generous measure and downed it in one gulp. Kate saw her put the empty glass on the lower shelf of the dresser with a shaking hand. Then Valerie just stood there, gripping the edge of the dresser with both hands, her head bowed.

Kate watched for a moment. Then, frowning, she crept away again.

"I THINK SHE'S HIDING SOMETHING," SAID Kate. She swung the swivel chair in Olbeck's office back and forth, kicking her legs to keep the momentum going.

"Would you stop that? You're not six." Olbeck was trying to answer emails, listen to Kate and book a table for dinner that night at an Abbeyford restaurant, all at the same time. "Yes, I'll hold. Thanks. Now, look, Kate—" He grabbed the receiver from between his shoulder and ear. "Oh, hello. Yes. Eight thirty would be great. Thanks. Bye."

He put the receiver back in its holder with obvious relief. "Now, what were you saying?"

"Valerie Houghton," said Kate. "She's hiding something. She was nervous as hell when I interviewed her this morning."

"Well, she's not really had a lot of dealing with the police before," Olbeck said reasonably "And it probably shook her up a good deal to find a dead body part on the doorstep."

Kate gave him a look. "Oh, come on. You know if I think she's hiding something, it's going to be more than that."

"True." Olbeck gave up on his emails and turned to face her fully. "So, what is it?"

Kate told him what she'd seen when she left the Houghton house that morning. "She's obviously worried about something. Either that or she's got a drinking problem."

Olbeck looked troubled. "I don't think that's the case. I can't say I'd ever noticed any of the signs whenever I've seen her."

Kate raised one shoulder in a half-shrug. "Well, all I'm saying is that she's definitely hiding something." She gave the chair one last wild swing and then got up. "*But,* as she's the victim in this scenario, it's probably not something that important – or that criminal."

"Okay." Olbeck turned back to his computer. "Anything else before I get on?"

"Theo's gone to interview Laura Ellis – you know, Kiki Dee's former girlfriend. Just to see if she might be the culprit behind this."

"But how can she be?" Olbeck demanded. "Why send dead hearts to two complete strangers as well as Kiki?"

Kate raised her eyebrows. "I don't know. Camouflage?" She thought for a moment and then added, slowly, "Or there's a link between them we haven't found yet."

She and Olbeck stared at one another for a moment. Then Olbeck blew out his cheeks and slumped back in his seat. "I'm starting to think this is all a waste of time," he said. "It's not as if we haven't got some more serious cases to worry about."

"Well, you were the one who thought this might... escalate."

"I didn't say that," Olbeck said with a frown. "I said I had a bad feeling about it. I don't know. Maybe I'm wrong."

"'Maybe'?" Kate said, and gave him a wink. He grinned and waved a hand, dismissing her.

WHEN KATE GOT BACK TO her desk, Theo was standing by his own desk divesting himself of his coat and scarf, shivering theatrically.

"Still cold out?" asked Kate, somewhat unnecessarily.

"You could stay that."

"How did it go with Laura Ellis?"

Theo grinned and sauntered over to her, rubbing his hands in a manner that could have been interpreted as lascivious. "Lesbians have got a lot hotter since I was at college, I'll tell you that."

"Theo!" Kate shook her head at him. "Stop being so homophobic."

"Am I being?" asked Theo, in honest confusion.

"Well, you're being bloody sexist then," Kate said. "As usual," she added.

"Well, whatever. She denied all knowledge anyway, totally indignant that we should suspect her. Said that she only had a short-term thing with Kiki and it wasn't serious. In fact, she said she thought Kiki—" He stopped talking for a moment, looking thoughtful.

"What?" prompted Kate.

Theo perched himself on the corner of Kate's desk.

"Well, that was the one thing that made me pause, actually. I got the impression that Laura thinks Kiki went out with her, well, not because she fancied her or anything like that, but because of some other reason."

Kate was nonplussed. "I don't understand."

Theo rubbed his jaw. "Laura said that Kiki sort of went after her, hell for leather, and Laura was flattered and, let's face it, attracted, 'cos that Kiki's seriously hot, right?" Kate fought the urge to roll her eyes. "Well, anyway, so they get it on and then almost immediately Kiki loses interest and they break up."

Kate frowned. "Well – maybe Kiki's one of those people who always want what they can't have – and then when they get it, they're not interested anymore."

"Maybe." Theo pushed himself upright. "Anyway, the crux of it is that Laura says she didn't send the heart or kill the cat."

"And you believe her?"

"I do, actually."

"Right." Kate barely noticed as Theo went back to his own desk. Her thoughts were echoing Olbeck's. This was a waste of time. She shook her head, dismissing the memories of the dripping hearts, the glint of the metal arrow, the stiff, white body of Frosty the cat, and reached for the top folder from the teetering pile in her in tray.

KATE GOT HOME REASONABLY EARLY that night. She decided to cook herself a proper meal for once, nothing fancy, but something fresh and tasty. Merlin twined around her ankles as she chopped the vegetables and crushed the garlic. Once the herb-smothered chicken breasts were in the oven, Kate poured herself an orange juice and wandered through to the living room. Tin's roses still looked beautiful up on the mantelpiece; the multitude of red, velvet buds reflected in the mirror. Kate leant over them and took a deep, grateful sniff. Delicious.

Thinking of Tin was not quite so uncomplicated. Kate paced back and forth in front of the fire, glass in hand. Should she go to New York? As in, *move* to New York? Tin was there, he wanted her to come. It would be a great opportunity. But an opportunity to do what, Kate asked herself. What was it that she would actually *do*? She wouldn't be able to work as a police officer, that was for sure, and what else was she going to do?

A small reckless part of her wanted to call Tin that instant and say 'yes'. Just for the hell of it. Just so she could stop thinking about it, stop going over the pros and cons, get over the 'should I or shouldn't I' once and for all. She didn't call him, though. She sat there on the sofa, staring at the flickering flames in the grate, waiting for the beep of the oven timer.

Chapter Five

"So, Kate," Detective Chief Inspector Anderton said pleasantly, the next morning. "How's young Tin getting along in the Big Apple?"

Kate made a solemn, silent vow never again to share any aspect of her personal life with her work colleagues. "He's getting on fine, as far as I know. And you do know he's over forty? Hardly young!"

"That's young to me," sighed Anderton. "Glad to hear it, though. You were looking very down in the mouth for a week or so."

Given Kate and Anderton's history of romantic and sexual entanglement, his comments were particularly unwelcome. Kate gritted her teeth, smiled and said, "I'll try to cheer up from now on, sir."

She managed to detach herself from his presence without appearing rude – she hoped – and made for her desk. She could see Olbeck in his office with the phone to his ear, talking to someone and looking serious, but his office door was shut so she couldn't hear what they were talking about. Kate sat down at her desk, waved to Rav and Anne, noted that Theo was absent, and then turned her attention to her work.

She was soon so immersed in answering her emails that she jumped when Olbeck came up behind her and laid a hand on her shoulder. "Got a minute?" was all that he said. Kate raised her eyebrows but followed him back to his office.

"What's up?" she asked.

"I just had another call from Kiki Dee. She says she's received a threatening message on her Facebook wall. A death threat, if you could call it that."

Kate eyebrows remained raised. "What did it say?"

Olbeck picked up his notebook and cleared his throat. "'You'll end up the same way as your cat, bitch.'"

"Blimey." Kate sat down in the swivel chair and put her chin in her hands. "So, what do we do now? I presume we're taking it seriously?"

"Of course we are. I'm asking IT to look into where the message came from, track down the IP address, find the server, that sort of thing. And I think we might go back and re-interview Kiki, see if she can shed any more light on whether there's someone out there who might mean her harm, for whatever reason."

"Now?"

"Yes, I think so. Let me just talk to Sam, to get the tech stuff rolling, and then we'll go."

KIKI DEE HAD LOST A little of the self-confidence she'd displayed on their first meeting. She was dressed in a shapeless grey dress and thick brown cardigan, and her dark hair was greasy and uncombed. She took some time to open the front door of the house and when she did, Kate noted the dark half-moons under the girl's eyes with concern.

"I can't think who'd be doing this," she almost

wailed, at Olbeck's question. "I can't see any of my friends being so – so *mean*. And as for—" She shot a quick glance at Kate before she addressed Olbeck. "I guess you've talked to Laura?"

"We have," said Olbeck. "And I have to say I don't think she's had anything to do with this."

"I *know*. That's what I told you before. I just – I can't think of anything else…"

She trailed off, biting her nails. Kate thought of something.

"Kiki, forgive me if this sounds rude, but in your work as a burlesque dancer, do you ever get, well, unwanted attention from people? Men watching the show, things like that?"

Kiki sniffed. "I'm not a *stripper*, you know."

Kate repressed a sigh. "I know you're not. But sometimes, when you're a public performer, some people – men especially – react rather strangely to that."

Kiki looked at her with red-rimmed eyes. "Right."

"Has there been anything, any sort of contact with someone at the club perhaps, that's – shall we say – given you pause? Made you concerned? Anything like that?"

Kiki sniffed again. "No. No I can't think of anyth—" She stopped abruptly, staring into space, her hand at her mouth. Kate held herself tense.

Kiki slowly dropped her hand. "There was one thing," she said eventually, slowly. "It was nothing, really, but…"

"Go on," Kate prompted.

Kiki sat up a little from her slumped position. "It

was just – a couple of months ago, this guy sent me over champagne after my dance. Real champagne, you know, expensive stuff. The whole bottle and two glasses. He'd put a note with it."

She stopped talking, clearly thinking over the memory. "What did the note say?" asked Kate.

"Nothing bad. Something like 'I'd like to drink this with you,' something like that."

"And did you?"

Kiki shot her a wary look. "Did I what?"

Kate smiled. "Did you drink it with him?"

Kiki looked a little sheepish. "I did, actually. We had it at the bar together. He seemed nice and it was a nice thing to do. It's not often people buy me real champagne. I guess I was a bit flattered."

"Can you tell us anything else about him?"

Kiki's hand went back up to her mouth, one finger slipping into the corner of it like a little girl. "His name was Joel. That's all I know, I didn't get his surname or anything like that – I mean, he did tell me but I've forgotten it. He was, um, older than me, maybe thirty-five, maybe?" A smile tugged at the corners of her mouth, dislodging her finger. "He was married – well, he was wearing a wedding ring."

Kate and Olbeck exchanged glances. "Anything else?" asked Kate. "What did he look like? Would you recognise him again?"

"Oh yes, of course. That night with the champagne, we sat together for over an hour, just chatting. He was nice, like I said. But not really good looking or anything like that. Just ordinary."

"Can you describe him?" asked Olbeck, pen poised over his notebook.

Kiki shrugged. "Just ordinary, like I said."

"You'll have to be a bit more specific than that," said Olbeck, smiling. "What colour hair, what colour eyes? What ethnicity?"

Kiki looked startled. "Oh, well, he was white. Um... brown hair, short-ish, you know, normal. Um, I don't know what colour eyes he had."

"Well, we can always bring you into the station to do a more formal identification," said Olbeck. "Did you see him again after that night?"

"No," Kiki said with a firmness that surprised Kate slightly. Then she corrected herself. "Oh, wait, sorry. Yes, he did come back into the club, about two weeks later but I didn't speak to him then." Kiki looked a little coy. "I was with Laura by then, and I didn't want to – well, encourage him, or anything like that."

"And you haven't seen him since?" checked Kate.

Kiki said nothing but shook her head. Her gaze dropped and the animation that had returned to her features suddenly waned.

"Please don't worry," said Olbeck, who must have also noticed the look of fear that had suddenly returned to Kiki's face. "We'll make sure you're okay. There's no need to panic."

"BUT IS THERE?" KATE ASKED, as they drove back to the office. It had started to rain heavily and the windscreen wipers of the car moved back and forth in a way that was almost hypnotic.

Olbeck was driving and didn't glance over but she could see him frown. "I'm not sure."

Kate tapped her fingers on her leg. "That message on Kiki's Facebook page seems to make it clear that the cat was killed deliberately. It takes a fairly dangerous person to do something like that, I would have thought."

Olbeck's frown remained. "I know. I'm thinking we might have to get Kiki a panic button, or something. Some kind of alarm."

"Well, that's a good start." Kate watched the raindrops roll down the passenger side window. "But it's odd, isn't it? How does this tie in with the other women, Valerie Houghton and Caroline Whatsit, you know, the lawyer?"

This time, Olbeck did look at her. "I have absolutely no idea."

"Hmm," said Kate, equally stumped. Then she cheered up a little. "Oh well, hopefully Sam or someone in IT will have tracked down the sender of that message by now."

"That would help." Olbeck slowed the car and indicated for the turn-off into the station carpark.

Unfortunately, when the two of them got back to the office, the results from IT were still outstanding. Kate could understand it – the department was snowed under at the moment, concentrating on gathering evidence for a big case involving a recently exposed paedophile ring – but it was still annoying. She fetched a tuna salad from the canteen and ate it hurriedly in front of her computer, trying to catch up on all the work she should have done that morning.

She'd just about got on top of it by four o'clock that afternoon when her telephone rang. She could see, by looking at the display, that it was a call that had been rerouted from Olbeck's phone. He often did that when he was going to be out of the office or stuck in meetings. Kate answered it.

"Oh – oh, I was hoping to speak to Detective Inspector Olbeck," said a woman's voice that Kate didn't recognise.

"I'm sorry, he's not available at the moment. Can I help?" Kate gave her rank and name and added "I'd be happy to help if I could? I work under DI Olbeck, if that helps."

The woman sounded a little diffident. "Well, it's – perhaps I should wait."

"Can I take a message?" asked Kate.

Suddenly the woman's tone changed. She sounded firmer, more decisive. "No, no it's fine. I'll tell you. I'm Caroline Spendler, by the way." Kate felt a small jolt of surprise. Surprise and something else. Anticipation?

Caroline Spendler was still speaking. "I think I might know who sent me that pig's heart."

Now Kate did sit up. "*Really?*"

The diffident tone was back in Caroline Spendler's voice. "Yes, I've got a pretty good idea. I wonder – this is quite hard over the phone... could you possibly come to see me and I can tell you face to face?"

Kate's eyebrows went up and she looked at the clock. Merlin wouldn't need feeding for some time yet, and she had no other plans for after work. She reassured Caroline Spendler that a home visit would be no problem. "I'm on my way, Ms Spendler." She got the address details, said goodbye and put the phone down, the anticipation climbing with every minute it took her to switch off her computer, gather her things and leave the office.

Chapter Six

Caroline Spendler lived in a modern apartment, part of a renovated warehouse that stood on the banks of the Abbeyford canal. Parking her car in the marked space for visitors to the building, Kate looked around her. What had once been a shabby wasteland of abandoned buildings and empty concrete spaces had been transformed into a smart, chic housing estate of new-build houses, trendy restaurants and a water-side promenade where hip young couples drank artisan beer in pop-up bars, and where an arts, crafts and vintage market was held every Sunday. Kate remembered investigating a serial killing case here, years ago now, before the area's transformation. It was hard to remember now what it had been like.

Caroline Spendler matched her shiny new apartment. She had short, geometrically cut blonde hair, subtle but expensive clothes, a single piece of striking statement jewellery worn on a short chain around her slender neck and a general air of confidence and self-sufficiency. Kate knew she was regarding her with favour, just as she had regarded Valerie Houghton with condescension. She made the effort to dial back her approval, to try to remain neutral.

Caroline Spendler shook hands firmly and offered Kate coffee. Kate accepted, knowing that the coffee would almost certainly be freshly ground and made from the highest quality beans. She took a seat on the grey modular sofa while Caroline moved about the galley kitchen with quick, efficient movements.

"Here you are," said Caroline, handing Kate a white china cup in a fashionably square saucer. Kate sniffed the fragrant steam rising from the cup appreciatively. Caroline sat down in a chair opposite the sofa and regarded Kate steadily. Kate had the impression Caroline was finding in favour of her, just as Kate had done so with the other woman.

"I have to admit, I was a bit embarrassed to call," Caroline said eventually. She prevaricated, taking a long sip of coffee. "Silly, really. There's not normally that much that embarrasses me. But – oh well, as you'll see—" She broke off and got up, walking over to the small dining table in the corner of the room and picking up the slim little laptop that stood on its surface. "I'm very busy, you see, I work such long hours and – well, it make it hard to meet people, normally. In the normal way. You know."

Kate tried to smile reassuringly but Caroline wasn't looking at her. She sat back down on the chair and opened the laptop, balancing on her knees.

"I've been using this – site," said Caroline, her gaze fixed on the laptop screen. "There's nothing wrong with it, it's all adults, it's just – well, it's a bit like Tinder, really. If you want to meet people, you can contact them through here."

Kate was beginning to understand. "A dating site?" she asked in the most neutral tone she could muster.

A tinge of pink became visible in Caroline's cheeks. "Well, look, to be honest, it's not quite a dating site. More of a – more of a hook-up site, if you know what I mean." She gave an embarrassed laugh. "I never thought I'd do something like that but, you know, being single and all that..."

Kate leapt in to try and diffuse the situation. "What you do in your private life is absolutely no concern of mine, Ms Spendler. You think the person who sent you the heart might have been someone you met on this site?"

Caroline nodded. "Yes. In fact, I'm almost sure of it. No, I *am* sure of it. He sent me this message yesterday. See?" She turned the laptop so that Kate could see the screen. The website currently showing was a mass of moody blues, black and gold. '4Adults' seemed to be the name of the site. Kate kept her face as blank as she could – she could almost feel the other woman's embarrassment radiating off her like heat. Caroline pointed to a message box in the upper corner of the screen. *How did you like your present, bitch?* was the one line of the most recent email.

Kate drew in her breath. The message sounded uncannily similar to the one Kiki Dee had received on her Facebook page. "May I?" she asked, reaching out for the laptop. Caroline handed it to her without protest.

Kate clicked on the link on screen that led to the message sender's profile on the site. It was disappointingly blank – no photo, no other information. "How do you know who sent you this?" she asked Caroline.

"Well, I don't know for sure. As you can see, he's set

up a new profile. But it made me recall something that happened about a week before I got the – the heart." Caroline was definitely blushing now.

"Go on," prompted Kate.

"Well, I'd arranged to meet up with this guy from the site. He was seriously gorgeous, I mean, model-material, and he sounded nice enough." Caroline stopped speaking for a moment. Kate raised her eyebrows, urging her to continue. "Well, we arranged to meet and when I got there, it wasn't the guy from the picture at all. I mean, nothing like him! He'd obviously used a fake photograph."

"Right," said Kate. "I understand that can happen. So what did you do?"

Caroline looked down. "Well – and I know it wasn't very kind – I said I was going to the toilets and I – I made a run for it."

Kate fought back a grin. "You didn't tell him you were going?"

Caroline smiled reluctantly. "Well, no. I thought, if he can't even be honest enough to use his own photograph, then why the hell should I be polite enough to let him know I was going?" Her gaze flickered. "I know it was rather rude. I didn't want to get into some sort of big argument, though, to be honest."

"So, what did he look like?" asked Kate. "The real life man, I mean?"

Caroline made a sort of half-grimace. "Nothing memorable about him at all. He looked totally ordinary. A bit overweight, not particularly tall."

"Was he white?"

Caroline looked slightly startled. "Yes."

"Can you give me any other description? Hair colour? Eyes?"

Kate watched the other woman turn inward a little, obviously thinking. "He had brown hair, receding a little. Um, I don't know what colour his eyes were."

Kate was thinking. "Forgive me, Ms Spendler, but have you met a lot of people through this site? I mean, what makes you think it could have been this man?"

Caroline's gaze met hers. "Well, I have met a *few* people through here but – but he's the only one I've ever stood up. I thought it must be him because he was obviously, well, pissed off."

"It seems likely," agreed Kate. "But nothing is definite. I'll need you to come down to the station, Ms Spendler, and give an official statement. We'll also need you to sit down with one of our visual composite artists and try and build up an accurate picture of this man." She hesitated and added, "You're aware that there were other women targeted as well as you?"

Caroline nodded. "Yes, the liaison officer told me that. Obviously she didn't go into details but I did know."

Kate leant forward. "If you can work with us to get an accurate picture of this man, we can show it to the other women and see if they recognise him too."

"Yes, I see that." Caroline hesitated and then asked "You'll presumably be able to trace him through the website?"

Kate smiled. "Yes, Ms Spendler, but don't you worry about that – you can leave that with us. Now, if I could just get a time from you when you'll be able to come in and make a statement?"

Driving away from the apartment building, Kate felt another piece of the puzzle click satisfyingly into place. If it were true that this man was present on the 4Adults website, and that was the missing connection between the women, then no wonder Valerie Houghton had looked so disturbed at the thought of any further investigation into the crime. Had she, Valerie, been meeting other men illicitly through the site? Kate thought that was probably exactly what had happened. It was strange that Kiki Dee hadn't mentioned it though, sexually aware and confident as she seemed to be. Something to ask her about, anyway. Kate drove home, her thoughts moving from the case to her boyfriend.

What was Tin doing right now, over in New York? Did he miss her? Was he thinking about her right this second? I'll try and call him when I get home, Kate promised herself and put her foot down just a little harder on the accelerator.

Chapter Seven

"Well, well," said Anderton, as Kate and Olbeck convened in his office the next morning. "He should be easy enough to find, anyway. I presume IT are already on it?"

Kate nodded. "Yes, Sam's got his team working on it right now. It won't take long anyway, I could probably do it myself. This guy, whoever he is, might have hidden his identity but you need a credit card to register at that site and we can get his address from that."

Olbeck was looking troubled. "I can't believe that *Valerie*..." He broke off and then resumed. "Well, she doesn't seem like the kind of person to be into that sort of thing."

"What did I tell you?" Kate said, grinning. "It's always the quiet ones."

Olbeck didn't look as though he got the joke. "I know, but..."

He trailed away just as there was a knock on the door and Sam Hollington, the head of the IT department, poked his head around the door. He waved a sheet of paper. "Got him," he said, with some satisfaction. "Ian Neely, thirty-six, of 15A, Rackham Avenue, Charlock."

"Brilliant," said Kate. She looked across at Anderton who inclined his head.

"Go on, then," was all that he said but with a grin of approval. "Go and bring him in."

Olbeck got to his feet. "We'll both go," he said.

"Come on, then," said Kate. "I'm driving."

SEVERAL HOURS LATER, KATE REGARDED Ian Neely from across the table of Interview Room Three. He was almost exactly as Caroline Spendler had described him: mid thirties, slightly overweight, beginning to bald. Short, brown hair, brown eyes. Nothing memorable about him whatsoever.

The duty solicitor, Katy Watson, sat next to him. Kate had seen her here before – to be frank, the young woman was quite hard to forget, being quite improbably gorgeous with long, auburn hair and equally long, shapely legs. Ian Neely seemed oblivious to her beauty. He was staring at the surface of the table, looking white and ill.

"So, Mister Neely," Olbeck said, leaning forward a little. "Do you want to tell us about the pig hearts?"

Silence from Neely. Kate, looking at him, wondered why he'd done something quite so stupid as to use a fake photograph on his dating profile. How could he have thought that he would get away with it, once he'd met up with women in real life? But perhaps that was why – he was so insecure, so full of self-loathing, that he engineered reality so as to have his paranoia confirmed. Kate had spoken to Valerie Houghton and had shown her the photo-fit that Caroline Spendler had assisted in putting together. For the second time, Valerie had gone white. "Yes, that's him," she said faintly and then burst into tears and pleaded with Kate not to tell her husband. "I didn't even wait to meet him," she'd cried. "I saw he wasn't – he wasn't who I thought he'd be – and then I'd just left, without even waiting to meet him. Oh, God, please don't tell John—"

Thinking back on that scene, Kate felt a vicarious embarrassment rushing through her. It wasn't often she felt so awkward, but there was so much pain and humiliation in the woman's voice that it was difficult not to feel a queasy pity. Her thoughts went from Valerie to Kiki Dee, who she hadn't yet been able to get hold of...

"Why did you give those three women the pigs' hearts?" Olbeck asked Ian Neely, who so far had remained silent or muttered 'no comment', clearly on the advice of Katy Watson. Kate observed him. He looked so unmemorable, so forgettable. But did that mean that he wasn't dangerous?

"What about the death threat, Ian?" Kate knew that when Olbeck dropped the 'Mister' in addressing a subject, he was losing patience. "What do you say about that?"

Something in Ian Neely's dull face sparked to life. "It wasn't a death threat," he said, surprising them all. His voice was rather soft and reedy. "I was just – just pissed off, that's all."

"Come on, now," said Olbeck. He read, rather theatrically, from his notebook. "You wrote on Kiki Dee's Facebook page, 'You'll end up the same way as your cat, bitch'. Do you deny that?"

Ian Neely didn't protest. He merely blinked. "What?"

Olbeck repeated the sentence. Kate saw his solicitor shoot Ian Neely an anxious glance but one look at his face, creased in confusion, told its own story.

Kate found herself interjecting, sharply. "Are you saying you *didn't* write that on Kiki Dee's Facebook page?"

Ian Neely was still blinking. "What cat? What are you talking about?"

The confusion in his voice was palpable. Kate thought, with a sudden rush of coldness through her, *he didn't write that. He didn't kill the cat*. Which meant...

She and Olbeck convened outside the interview room, Olbeck having hastily adjourned the interview and brought it to a temporary close.

Kate found she was hugging her arms across her body. "He's telling the truth, isn't he? He sent the hearts but he didn't do anything else. Nothing else except write that message to Caroline Spendler."

Olbeck squeezed his eyes shut temporarily, as if he had a headache. "So if Neely hasn't been stalking Kiki Dee, then who has?"

They both stared at each other. Kate said, slowly, "I've been trying to get in touch with her, to tell her we'd made an arrest. I've left messages on her mobile—"

Olbeck cut across her. "You'll need to go and try and find her. Try the college, try the house. If Neely isn't the one who's been threatening her, then she might still be in danger." Kate nodded and began to hurry away down the corridor, feeling the rush of blood in her ears as her heart began to thump.

JUST BEFORE SHE STARTED HER car, Kate tried Kiki's mobile again. It was fully dark by now, past six o'clock, and cold, with a sharp wind that laid a blade of ice against her cheek. The night sky above was ragged with rushing clouds that blotted out the thin crescent moon. Kate could see her breath steaming, even in the interior of the car, and reached to turn the heater up to full.

Kiki's phone was switched off and went straight to voicemail. Kate left another message, this time allowing some urgency to infuse her tone. Then she turned the key in the ignition and set off, making for Kiki Dee's house.

No one answered the door to Kate's knock, when she arrived. Frustrated, Kate peered up at the blank windows. The curtains weren't drawn but there definitely didn't seem to be anyone at home. Baulked for a moment, Kate stood on the windy pavement, tapping her foot. Should she try the college? But there were hundreds of students there, the chances of tracking Kiki down seemed increasingly unlikely. After a moment, she used her phone to search for the address of the Decadence bar and club and then keyed the postcode into the sat nav.

Decadence was situated in Arbuthon Green, just down the road from the pub where Kate had once listened to a band with her younger brother, Jay, and met the violinist, who was later to be found murdered. Kate found a parking space along the road from The Black Horse and walked past it quickly. The Decadence bar and club was situated in the basement of a four storey Georgian townhouse, a remnant of elegance now sadly decayed. Kate was surprised to see a short queue of people waiting to get in, even at this early hour. She walked to the front of the queue and flashed her warrant card in the doorman's face, causing a sudden tide of tautness and whispering in the waiting crowd.

Frowning, the doorman let Kate through. She walked through a small, dark reception area, showing her card to the woman taking the money at the entrance, and moved on through a pair of red velvet curtains which brought her out to the main area of the bar and stage.

Now, Kate could see why people were waiting to get in. There was a swing band playing and the dance floor in front of the stage was packed with couples, most of whom were dressed in vintage and retro styles. Other people sat around the edge of the dance floor at the delicate little gold-painted tables, drinking cocktails and laughing and talking loudly over the music. There were a lot of Victory rolls, plenty of red-painted lips, tea-dresses and frothy petticoats. Kate, blinking against the flash of the stage lights, thought for a moment she'd been transported back in time to the late nineteen forties.

It was less sordid than she'd imagined. A lot less. The stage backdrop was a glittering curtain of gold threads and there was a giant stiletto shoe over by the side of the stage, big enough for a person to climb into.

Kate recollected herself and made for the bar. She couldn't see Kiki anywhere but this was a long shot anyway, she could very well not be here...

Kate reached the bar, a long curving shape with a mirrored surface and located the most senior looking member of staff. "I'm looking for the manager," she shouted, over the noise from the band.

"That's me," said the man with a silver ring through his eyebrow and dark brown hair combed into a greased DA. "I'm Jack. How can I help?"

Kate showed him her credentials and watched the silver ring in his eyebrow move sharply upwards. "I'm looking for Kiki Dee," she added.

"Kiki? What's she done?" Jack the bar manager looked serious. "She's just finished up her set. I think I saw her go outside for a smoke."

"She's definitely here then?" checked Kate.

"Yes, she was on stage about half an hour ago. You can go backstage, the door's over there."

Kate walked towards where he had gestured. Stepping through to the backstage area was like entering another world, oddly reminiscent of Kiki Dee's house, with its plethora of female inhabitants. There were girls everywhere, in various states of undress, some with feathery wings strapped about them, some with glittery nipple tassels firmly in place. There was even a young man wearing the top half of a pinstripe suit and a leather G-string, stocking and suspenders on his lower half. Kate blinked and averted her eyes.

"Can I help you?" asked a girl with pink hair, who

was dressed in nothing but a bunch of pink balloons that bobbed around her.

"Erm—" said Kate, distracted by the balloons. "Sorry, I'm looking for Kiki Dee. I was told she's here?"

"Kiki? She went outside for a ciggie," the girl said. Then she frowned. "Actually, that was ages ago. She can't still be out there, she'll be freezing. She must have gone home." She turned to the girl next to her who was pulling on a skin-tight black cat suit. "Zoe, have you seen Kiki? Did she leave?"

Zoe shrugged. "I haven't seen her," she said without interest and turned to observe herself in the big mirror. Kate could see her own reflection over Zoe's shoulder. She looked worried.

"Where do you girls go for a smoke?" she asked.

The pink-haired girl showed her and then bustled away, balloons bobbing and bouncing in her wake. Giving her head a mental shake, Kate stepped outside and back into the freezing night air. She was beginning to think this was something of a wild goose chase. Kiki had obviously finished her set and decided to go home. Why hadn't she responded to Kate's numerous voicemails? As Kate thought this, the answer came to her – because Kiki had been on stage and unable to answer her calls.

The area Kate stepped out into was the neglected courtyard of the original building, a dank, dark hole of bare concrete and crumbling walls. A large flowerpot stood by the back door, choked to the brim with cigarette butts. Kate stood for a moment, uncertainly, looking about her. The unshaded light above the back door cast a harsh rectangle of light for about ten feet. Beyond that was darkness. There was nobody here, and Kate turned to go back inside before realising the door had swung shut behind her. She was locked out here.

Cursing, she drew out her keyring, on which she kept a little torch. It had come in handy on more than one occasion. Could she walk back to the main street by going around the back of the building? Only one way to find out... Kate stepped cautiously forward into the darkness, following the feeble line of light cast by her torch. Then she stopped dead.

There was a foot in front of her, pale in the torchlight. A foot attached to a leg, attached to a body that was crouched hunched and shivering on the dirty concrete. Kate gasped and ran forward. The girl on the ground was curled into a foetal position, her dress ripped open, dirt on her knees. Kate could see blood, black in the semi-darkness, spattered across the girl's neck. She trained the torch directly on the girl's face, wincing as the light made the girl recoil and throw one dirty hand up to shield her eyes. It was Kiki Dee.

Chapter Eight

"What *happened*?"

Kate stood back to let the doctor through into the room where Kiki Dee was lying on a bed, wrapped in a hospital blanket. Then she took Olbeck by the arm and propelled him away into the corridor.

"I think she was raped," Kate said, in a tone that made much of the grim news. Olbeck's face tightened.

"My God." He looked back at the door to the room, as if he could see through it. "Does she know who?"

Kate nodded. "I think so. She didn't want to tell me though, and she wasn't in any fit state for me to push her. We'll wait until the doctor gives us the go ahead, and then we can ask again."

Olbeck was looking very troubled. "It can't have been Ian Neely. He's been with us all day."

"I know that. It wasn't him who killed the cat and made that death threat anyway."

"So who is it?"

Kate raised her shoulders. "We can't do anything unless we get a name from Kiki." A though struck her. "Actually, hang on. Let me call Theo. He can see if he can pull anything from CCTV. There's bound to have been some on that street. Perhaps he can get a sighting or something."

"She didn't give you a name or anything?"

"*No*, Mark. She could barely speak when I brought her in here—" Kate broke off as the door to the room opened and a harassed looking doctor stepped out.

"DS Redman?" she asked, looking from Kate to Olbeck.

"That's me." Kate stepped forward.

"Kiki's asked to speak to you. I have to admit, I warned her that she didn't have to – it could wait until she was feeling stronger, but she was insistent." The doctor stepped back a little and indicated the open doorway. "So, if you want five minutes with her now..."

Trying not to appear too eager, Kate hurried forward. Olbeck went to follow her and the doctor held out a hand. "I'm sorry, officer, but I think one person is enough. Especially as – well—" She broke off, looking a little embarrassed. "A female officer would be better. In the circumstances."

Kate didn't wait to catch Olbeck's look of quickly suppressed outrage. She sympathised – Olbeck was about as likely to rape someone as she was – but this wasn't the time to debate the issue. She closed the door to the room behind her and walked quietly over to the high bed.

Kiki was curled on her side, her dark hair mussed around her bruised face. She looked very young – too young to be a college student, not least a burlesque dancer. Kate smiled tentatively at her and sat down, not too near and not too far.

"How are you feeling, Kiki?"

Kiki closed her eyes momentarily. "Sore," she said after a moment, in a whisper.

Kate made a sympathetic noise. "Do you want to tell me about what happened?"

Kiki blinked. She hadn't yet moved from her foetal position. "I – I know who it was," she said, with difficulty.

"You do?" Kate tried to unobtrusively reach for the notebook in her bag. "Don't mind me, Kiki. Go on and tell me what you can. No rush."

Tears trembled on the edges of Kiki's eyelashes. "It was him, the guy who bought me champagne." She blinked and the tears rolled down, making a tiny damp patch on the hospital sheet. "I never thought – I—"

She was becoming incoherent. Kate soothed her as best she could, trying not to push for more details.

After a moment, Kiki seemed to gain a little more control. She sat up a little, wincing as she pushed herself back against the high pillows. "I went outside for a ciggy. He – he appeared out of nowhere, he must have walked around from the front. I was – it sounds so stupid—" She drew in a breath that was almost a sob.

"It's okay," said Kate, gently. "Take your time."

Kiki rubbed her hand under her eyes. "I was even quite pleased to see him," she said after a moment, hoarsely. "I was *flattered*. I remembered how nice he'd been when we'd drunk that champagne at the bar that time. And he – he asked if I had a spare cigarette and when I went to get one from the box he – he grabbed me—"

She started crying in earnest then, holding the sheet up to her eyes in lieu of tissues. Kate, spotting a box over on the bedside table, held out a handful to Kiki.

"Oh – thank you." Kate watched as she mopped her face, sniffing.

"Can you give me his name, Kiki?" Kate asked, as casually as she could.

Kiki's gaze fell to the soggy tissues in her shaking hands. "I've been thinking about that," she said, her voice still ragged with tears. "I remembered." She looked up and fixed Kate with swimming eyes. "His name is Joel, Joel Hunter, I *think*. I think that's his surname. I can't be sure though, it was so long ago that we talked."

"'Joel Hunter,'" Kate repeated, scribbling busily. "Well, we can certainly look into that. Now—"

She was unable to say more as the doctor opened the door, popped her head into the room and gave her a sharp look. "That will have to be all for now, detective."

Kate sighed. For a moment, she felt like arguing, but it was pointless. At least now they had a name to go on. She smiled at Kiki as kindly as she could. "Try and get some rest, Kiki. We'll be in touch very soon, and you're in good hands here. Is there anyone you'd like us to contact, to come and be with you?" Kiki shook her head, closing her eyes and lying back down on her side again. "Okay," said Kate. "Take care now."

When Kate got back out in the corridor, she found someone else waiting with Olbeck – a tall, slim young woman with a mass of chestnut curls, a silver stud in her nostril and wearing what looked like an original nineteen sixties leopard-print coat. Kate was about to ask her if she could help when Olbeck forestalled her.

"This is Laura Ellis, Kiki's former partner," he said. "She's come to wait to see if Kiki needs her."

"Oh I see." Kate shook hands with Laura, who looked almost as upset as Kiki had done. "It's good of you to come and support your friend, Miss Ellis." She shot Olbeck a glance of warning before she said, "Unfortunately, given the seriousness of the incident, you may be waiting a long time. And—" She hesitated, wondering whether this was going too far. "I'm afraid you won't be able to see her without a police officer accompanying you."

Laura's eyes filled with tears. "I understand," she said in a soft voice. She looked down, the curtains of curls framing each side of her pretty face. "I just wanted – I thought I could just be here if she needed me, just in case. I don't mind waiting."

"How did you know Kiki was here?"

There was no hesitation in Laura's voice and no shade of guilt. "One of the girls from Decadence called me. I was so shocked... Of course, I had to come straight away."

"Well, that's fine." Kate could see a uniformed officer – someone she vaguely recognised from Abbeyford Station – walking towards them down the corridor. He'd be able to take on guard duty and then she and Olbeck could get on with tracking down this Joel Hunter. The irony of his surname hadn't occurred to Kate before, but now it did and she nearly shuddered.

"Well, we'll be off now, Ms Ellis," said Kate, shaking hands with Laura. Laura nodded silently.

"Goodbye," Olbeck said, turning to go. He stopped as Laura said suddenly and fiercely, "It's too cruel. Kiki's never had any luck with men. Her useless father walked out on her when she was eight and now *this* happens..."

She trailed off, blinking. Kate and Olbeck, nonplussed for a moment, both murmured something sympathetic and then left.

They greeted the uniformed PC as they passed, informed him of what they knew, and left him and Laura Ellis in the corridor. Once they were out of earshot, Kate asked Olbeck if he thought she'd gone a little bit too far in restricting access to Kiki.

"No-o. Not exactly." Olbeck hesitated. "I know that Laura Ellis was originally a suspect, when we were looking at a stalking case, but—"

"I know it's ridiculously unlikely," said Kate. "That the rape is incidental to the stalking. I mean, it's not possible that Kiki's actually got *three* separate stalkers, is it?"

"No," said Olbeck, more firmly this time. "But until we know more, we proceed along the lines of caution. Come on, we need to find this Joel Hunter before he does any more damage."

Chapter Nine

JOEL HUNTER LIVED IN A prosperous looking house in an up-market suburb of Abbeyford. The houses here were large and well-kept, the driveways sporting a gleaming range of BMWs, Audis and the latest in large, family four wheel drives. As they drew into the curb, Kate spotted the black Toyota in the driveway that had been spotted on CCTV in the vicinity of Decadence. The times on the tape had tallied with the times given by Kiki Dee as to when she was attacked.

There were three of them making the arrest this time – Kate, Olbeck and Theo. Olbeck, as the senior officer, took the lead.

A man who Kate assumed was Joel Hunter answered the door. The first surprise, to Kate, was how good-looking he was. Given Kiki's description of 'just ordinary', Kate had been expecting someone like Ian Neely: running to seed, pudgy-faced, dishwater-coloured hair. Joel Hunter was tall and broad-shouldered, with high cheekbones and – noticeable even in the dim light of a winter morning – very striking, dark brown eyes. He was dressed in a suit and had a briefcase in his hand.

"Yes?" asked Joel Hunter, looking puzzled at the three of them standing there in a grim-faced circle on his doorstep.

"Mr Joel Hunter?" asked Olbeck.

"Yes," Joel Hunter said, beginning to frown.

Olbeck showed his card, quickly followed by Kate and Theo. Hunter's gaze went from each of the cards to the officers' faces with increasing alarm.

"Oh God, what's happened?" Hunter asked. There was a call behind him, a woman's voice, low-pitched and feminine.

"Who is it, Joel?"

Hunter didn't answer her. Olbeck cleared his throat. "We'd like you to accompany us to Abbeyford Police Station, sir. We have some questions about a case of serious sexual assault that took place yesterday."

Kate was closely watching Hunter's face. When Olbeck mentioned the words 'sexual assault' she saw a look of shock flash across his features and narrowed her eyes.

"What?" said Hunter. He looked from one police officer to the other. "Is this some kind of joke?"

Olbeck didn't dignify that with a response. "Will you accompany us, sir? Or will I have to arrest you?"

Hunter was blinking very rapidly. "What – my God – I—"

A woman appeared in the doorway behind him, a small, pretty-faced woman with her hair tied up in a loose knot. She had a young baby settled asleep against her shoulder.

"What's happening?" she asked. Kate noticed the dark circles of exhaustion around her eyes.

Hunter had visibly paled. He turned to his wife with a dreadful attempt at a reassuring smile. "It's nothing, Sarah, nothing serious. I just have to go and answer a few questions at the station, that's all." His voice wavered a little. "It's – it's just that traffic accident I witnessed last month, that's all. Nothing to worry about."

Kate and Theo exchanged a glance, but nobody contradicted him. Sarah, protesting a little, was ushered back inside the house and then Hunter was led to the car that awaited them in the street.

JOEL HUNTER WAS COMPLETELY SILENT on the way back to the station. He only spoke once, when Olbeck asked him if there was anyone he wanted to contact to be his legal representative.

"Of course I don't have a bloody criminal defence lawyer," Hunter snapped. "I've never been arrested before in my life. That's why – oh, there must have been some kind of mistake. This is – it's all *wrong*."

Nobody said anything. Kate, glancing at him in the rear-view mirror, where he sat next to Theo, was struck by the note of panic in his voice. Was that guilt? Or was it the natural reaction of someone accused of a crime they hadn't committed? She remembered the CCTV footage of Hunter's car, there in the street by the Decadence club, the way it had driven off soon after the time of the attack on Kiki Dee. Hunter himself had been seen getting into the car, rather quickly. He'd been *there*. That was undisputable. Kate thought of all the swabs and samples, taken from Kiki Dee's body, even now being tested for DNA...

Once Joel Hunter had been cheek-swabbed and fingerprinted and photographed, they sat him down in an interview room with John Harbrook, one of the duty solicitors, and quickly reconvened outside.

"I'll take the lead on this," said Olbeck. "Kate, do you want to sit in or would you rather start chasing up some of the details, checking records, stuff like that?"

"I'll sit in to start with," said Kate. Theo looked a little disgruntled that he hadn't been asked, but he was too much of a professional to start bitching about it. They parted; Olbeck and Kate to begin the interview, Theo making for the stairs back to the office to start gathering what evidence he could to enable them to keep Joel Hunter in custody for longer than twenty four hours. After that, they would have to charge him or release him.

"WELL, MISTER HUNTER," OLBECK SAID, sitting back down opposite the man who sat hunched and anxious in his seat. "I suppose Mister Harbrook here has filled you in on a few details. You know we're investigating the rape of a young student, a Miss Kiki Dee. Do you have anything to tell us about that?"

Joel Hunter shifted on his seat. "No, no I—" he began, muttering and then at a swift glance from his solicitor. "I mean, no comment."

Kate sighed inwardly. They were off to a flying start.

Olbeck persisted. "Do you know Miss Dee?"

"No comment."

"Have you ever seen her before?"

"No comment."

"Could you confirm whether you've ever had any contact with her at all?"

"No comment."

Kate sat back a little, listening to Olbeck trying to probe for details, for guilt, for anything. Nothing was forthcoming. How stupid of her to think that they might have actually got a confession out of the man. He'd looked so shaky and panicky when they'd picked him up that Kate had actually wondered whether he might break down in a fit of remorse. How much easier that would have been rather than having to sit here listening to the same two words over and over again...

She regarded his handsome face closely. Why had Kiki Dee called him ordinary looking? But then, Kiki was gay, wasn't she? So perhaps she hadn't been attracted to him at all. Or had she? She'd sat with him a long time at Decadence, more than a few hours at the bar, drinking champagne. Would she have done that for anyone? Perhaps she would have done; perhaps she was a kind, polite type of girl who wouldn't have wanted to upset anyone. If so, that made what had happened to her even more terrible. Kate set her jaw. Suddenly, she knew she didn't want to be here, listening to this arrogant man repeating 'no comment' at every question from Olbeck. She wasn't adding anything to the interview. She tapped her foot against Olbeck's under the table and, when he looked over, jerked her head mutely towards the door.

He suspended the interview and went with her out into the corridor.

"Listen," said Kate. "I'd do more good helping Theo

track down his records, looking at his past history, stuff like that. If you're okay with me leaving you to get on with it?"

"Absolutely." Olbeck dismissed her with a wave of his hand. "I don't think I'll be hearing anything too earthshattering, anyway."

Kate gave him a grin as she turned away. "Good luck."

"Thanks."

Chapter Ten

THE FIRST THING KATE DID when she got back to her desk was check that the DNA swab from Joel Hunter's cheek had been biked over to the labs for their fast-track, twenty-four-hour turnaround. It had. Kate ticked off that item on her 'to do' list with satisfaction. If Joel Hunter's DNA matched the samples taken from Kiki Dee then they were a giant leap ahead. It might not be enough to charge him, but it would be a good step forward.

What else? Kate tapped the pencil against her jaw for a moment as she contemplated the long list of things to do. Previous records – although perhaps Theo had already done that? She looked over at his desk, realising he was out of the office. Oh well, she'd do it herself – it wouldn't take long.

An hour later, she sat back in her chair, blowing her cheeks out with frustration. Joel Hunter was clean – impeccably so. The only thing she'd managed to find was a speeding fine from three years ago, and that was only a matter of points given. She'd have to wait for the lab report before they could check the DNA database, but hopefully that would be coming back soon. Was there anything else? She looked at her list of scribbled notes. Eye witnesses, CCTV footage, Kiki's own statement...

Kate wondered whether Olbeck had got any further with Hunter yet. She doubted it.

She telephoned the hospital for a progress report on Kiki Dee and was reassured to hear that she was doing well and would be discharged that afternoon, apparently back to the care of her mother. Kate made a mental note that she would have to get Kiki's mother's address from someone. She thought of something and rang down to IT to talk to Sam.

"Still working on it, sorry, Kate," he said apologetically. "You know what it's like at the moment, we're snowed under and understaffed."

"You can't give me anything at all? Come on, Sam, throw me a bone here."

She heard the grin in his voice. "Well, we have established that Ian Neely definitely sent that message to Caroline Spendler on the 4Adults site."

Kate snorted. "I *know* that. What about the message to Kiki Dee?"

"Um, no, he didn't. Not unless he's got a secret computer we haven't found yet."

Given than Ian Neely's house had already been searched, Kate didn't think that was likely. "So do you know who *did* send it?"

Sam's voice became apologetic again. "Still working—"

"—On it. Right, I got it. Bye." Kate banged the phone down vindictively.

She looked at the clock. It was coming up to five o'clock. If she left for home now, she might miss the DNA report coming back in. But then Merlin was probably waiting for his food at home... Making up her mind, she grabbed her coat and handbag and called over to Rav who was pounding away at his keyboard. "Just heading home for half an hour to feed the cat. I'll be back soon."

Rav waved a distracted hand in answer, and Kate headed for the door.

When she got home, she felt the usual pull of her cosy little house begin to ensnare her. She thought of the office, the glaring strip lights and the pile of reports awaiting her attention, the frustration of not being able to elicit the confession they needed, and then looked at her comfortable sofa, with the soft furry throw that lay over one end. The fire that lay waiting to be lit in the grate. She could pour herself a glass of wine, stretch out her toes to the dancing flames and relax. Call Tin for a chat – oh no, wait, he'd still be in the middle of his working day. *Damn the time difference.* Kate thought then of Kiki Dee, curled like a child in her hospital bed, lost and alone and hurt, and sighed. She stroked Merlin goodbye, picked up her coat and bag again and left, locking the front door securely behind her.

When she got back to the office, she felt better. She'd stopped off for a box of doughnuts from the bakery just down the road from the station, which immediately made her the most popular person in the office – for five minutes, at least.

"Nice one," said Theo, grabbing two.

"That means you have to make the coffee," Kate said, grinning as he groaned.

There was a call from Rav's desk. "DNA report's in."

Kate whooped and jumped up. "So, what's the dice?"

"Match. Definite match with the samples taken from Kiki Dee."

Kate whooped again in triumph. "Give it here, then. I'll take it down to Mark."

She grabbed it from Rav's hand and pounded for the door. "Wait, there's more," she heard Rav call after her, but there wasn't time for hesitation. This could be just the thing Olbeck was waiting for, the piece of evidence that would force a confession.

As luck would have it, she found him outside the interview room. Joel Hunter was in the room with his solicitor, enjoying – or not – a meagre supper of cheese and pickle sandwiches and the dishwater tea from the canteen dispenser.

Olbeck smiled when Kate handed him the report. "Great stuff. Let's see him argue his way out of this one."

Kate's immediate elation was cooling rapidly. She had a nasty feeling that Joel Hunter would follow the most obvious path and give the excuse of nearly every sexual predator she'd ever encountered.

"What's up?" asked Olbeck, watching her frown.

"Oh, nothing. It's just – I just know what he's going to say."

Olbeck looked grim. "Yeah, so do I. It was consensual, right?"

"Right," said Kate, with a sigh.

Olbeck was silent for a moment and then patted her on the shoulder. "Well, we can but try. Leave him to me."

Kate nodded. She had been going to ask if she could sit in again on the interview but she realised then that she didn't want to. She didn't want to hear Joel Hunter tell them that Kiki Dee had willingly had sex with him. The arrogant bastard... Kate wondered how he'd explain the scratches on Kiki's face and thighs. But then, they also had witnesses who could confirm that Kiki had willingly sat and chatted to the man for several hours and drunk champagne with him. Not that *that* should matter but, sadly, Kate knew very well that an able defence lawyer would leap upon that evidence like a cat upon a feather and *bang* would go Kiki's credibility in one fell swoop.

She climbed up the stairs to the office, feeling depressed. In some ways, the rape cases were harder than the murder cases. Two people's words against each other, that's what it mostly came down to. And the conviction rate was pathetic. She'd moaned about that to Olbeck once, and he'd pointed out, in his usual calm and reasonable way, that it was because the British justice system was mostly extremely robust and effective. "But—" Kate had started and then stopped.

Olbeck had sighed and said, "Yeah, *but*. I know how you feel."

Setting her jaw, Kate sat down at her desk. Now that she was here at work, she might as well get on with things. She picked up another copy of the DNA report the laboratory had sent back and sat down to read it but try as she might, her attention wandered. There was a little knot of anxiety in her stomach that she'd felt before on a case. Were they missing something – something important? And if so, what? And how on Earth could you find it, if you didn't know what was missing? She found herself staring across the office, tapping her fingers on the edge of her desk in frustration.

Chapter Eleven

Kate was walking along the corridor at the station the next morning, lost in thought, when a roar from Anderton's office just up ahead made her jump. A second later, he appeared in the doorway, brandishing a newspaper and looking furious. Kate was immediately in his line of sight – there was no escape.

"What the *bloody hell* is this?"

"Sir?" asked Kate, startled and confused.

"Get in here, *now*."

Kate, by now seriously concerned, hurried forward. As she got to the office doorway, Anderton was already speaking angrily into the phone to someone who turned out to be Olbeck, who hurried into the office a minute later, looking worried.

Anderton said nothing but spread the paper out on his desk before them both. Kate read the headline and gasped.

"'Police missed chance to catch my rapist stalker'," Olbeck read aloud in a horrified tone. "Dear *God*."

Kate was frantically scanning the text. Illustrating it all was a large colour photograph of Kiki Dee and a woman who was obviously her mother, both doing the obligatory tabloid 'sad face'. Kiki was dressed in white, the bruising and scratches on her face in no way detracting from her beauty. Kate read on in disbelief, fragments of text jumping before her eyes. *Bungled investigation. My cat was killed and left on my doorstep.* There was a picture of Kiki's house, the one she shared with all the other girls, which incorporated the street name sign. Wow, her fellow housemates were going to love *that*... Kate imagined a load of tabloid reporters camped on the doorstep, waiting to pounce on anyone brave enough to leave the house.

"Why would she do this?" Kate asked, horrified and baffled. She read on. "'Kiki bravely waived her right to anonymity, as she believes this is a matter of public interest.' What the *hell*?"

Anderton was looking very grim. "The Chief Constable is going to have his boot up my arse over this one, mark my words. I'm expecting him to call any minute now."

Olbeck was shaking his head. "I don't know – surely she's making herself vulnerable to a libel case with this? We haven't even charged Hunter yet, and quite frankly, I think we're going to have to let him go, for now."

Anderton put his head in his hands. "Mark, Mark, tell me that's not true. Can't you charge him?"

Olbeck slumped down in one of the office chairs. "He says that it was purely consensual sex between them and sticks to that. Just as you thought, Kate." He looked over at Kate, who rolled her eyes. "I could apply for an extension to the questioning time."

"Do it. We can't go releasing someone who might be a danger to society – or a danger to a vulnerable young girl – especially after this total shit-storm." Anderton indicated the paper. "God knows what the IPCC would do if something else happens on our watch." He tapped the article. "She won't get sued for libel – she doesn't name any names. They wouldn't have printed it, if she had."

They all stared at the picture of Kiki. There didn't seem to be much else to say.

Once they were dismissed, Olbeck headed straight for his office to make the telephone call for the extension of custody. Kate trailed back to her desk. She was still shocked by the newspaper article, but the twist of anxiety that sat in her stomach was getting worse. The case was getting out of control, or so it felt. Or was it something else? She stared ahead, unable to put her finger on what it was that was making her so uneasy.

She worked in a desultory way for an hour or so, feeling as though she was making no progress. At lunchtime, she gave up and decided to go outside for a short breath of air and to grab a pasty for lunch from the bakery.

She was walking back into the station after her lunch break, crossing the reception area, when her attention was caught by a woman standing by the front desk, remonstrating with PC Boulton. Kate walked closer. The woman was thin, with straggling brown hair twisted up into a messy pony tail from which multiple wisps were escaping. She had the harassed look of a person with too much on their plate and not enough time to do it.

"I said I'm sorry, but I know it's not an *arrestable*

offence," she was saying irritably, to the superbly poker-faced Paul Boulton.

Kate stepped up smartly. "May I help?"

The woman turned. She looked both angry, embarrassed and defensive. "I was just saying that I know I should have left a note, but really, there wasn't time, and I'm sorry, but it was just a cat—"

Kate held up a placatory hand. "I'm sorry, Mrs—"

"It's Ms. Ms Greythorpe. Look, I don't want to get into trouble, it's just that I saw it in the paper this morning—"

Kate managed to steer her towards a chair over towards the far wall, where it was a little more private. "Now, Ms Greythorpe, what seems to be the problem?"

Ms Greythorpe took a deep breath. "Look. I saw that article in the paper this morning, about the girl who was raped." She took another breath. "Poor thing," she added, perfunctorily. "Anyway, I don't know about all the rest of it, but the cat wasn't killed by whoever was stalked her."

Kate blinked. "How would you know that, Ms Greythorpe?"

The woman sighed irritably. "Because I ran it over. I'm really sorry, but it was a total accident. The stupid thing just ran out in front of me, there was nothing I could do."

"I see," said Kate, trying to keep the disapproval from her voice.

"Look, I know I should have run the doorbell and not just left it on the step, but I was in a real hurry and to be honest, I'd had such a day I couldn't face having to deal with a tearful owner." Ms Greythorpe folded her arms across her narrow chest defensively. "It was only a cat, after all."

"Yes, indeed," said Kate unable now to keep the frost out of her voice. "Well, thank you for letting us know, that was public-spirited of you. How did you know where to leave the cat? Did it have a collar on?" She saw the woman nod, pursing up her mouth. "Well, thank you. We'll need to take a short statement from you – I'll just get one of my colleagues to help you. Please just wait here."

WALKING BACK DOWN TO HER office, Kate smiled rather grimly. All that fuss and it turned out that the cat had died naturally after all – just as Olbeck, come to think of it, had suggested when they'd first gone to Kiki Dee's house when she'd reported it. The poor girl must have been very wound up by the delivery of the pig's heart and just assumed the worst. Shaking her head, Kate sat back down and almost immediately jumped back up again. What was she thinking? The cat might have died accidentally but then what about the death threat? She could remember it word for word. *You'll end up like your cat, bitch*. But then if nobody had killed the cat, what the hell was that message all about?

Kate sat back down again, feeling her stomach knot. More than ever, she could sense that there was a big piece missing from this case, something that literally nobody had yet seen. What *was* it? She sat there for a few tense moments, chewing her lip. Then she reached for the DNA report on Kiki Dee, determined to read it through properly this time.

Olbeck walked past her desk and she reached out an arm to stop him.

"What's up?"

Kate told him about her conversation with Ms Greythorpe. She saw her own confusion mirrored in Olbeck's face.

"So if nobody killed the cat, who sent that death threat?" he asked.

"Exactly," said Kate. "Something's not adding up here."

Olbeck frowned. "Look, I've got the extension to continue questioning Joel Hunter. I'm going down there now." He rubbed his forehead as if he had a headache. "Do you get the feeling—" he began and then stopped abruptly.

"What?" asked Kate.

"Nothing," he said shortly. He patted her on the shoulder and walked off.

Kate watched him go. Then, frowning herself, she turned back to the report and began to read.

Chapter Twelve

"Kate. *Kate*. Hello? Anyone home?"

Kate looked up with a start, suddenly realising that she was being addressed. "Oh, sorry, Sam. I was miles away. What's the problem?"

Sam Hollington sat down on the edge of her desk. "There's no problem. I just wanted to let you know that we've traced that other message, you know, the one you've been asking about."

By now, Kate was fully awake. She felt a little ashamed of how she'd last spoken to Sam on that very subject. "Look Sam, I'm really sorry I was a bit snappy with you about that—"

"No worries," Sam said cheerfully, interrupting her. "Anyway, we've caught up on a few things now. That message, the threat to Kiki Dee, we traced it to a computer at the Abbeyford College."

Kate stared at him, her heart beginning to thud. "Seriously?"

"Yep. Got the IP address and everything. It was sent from one of the computers in the library there." Sam paused. "Are you all right?"

Kate snapped out of the trance that she'd momentarily slipped into. "Fine. I'm fine. Thanks, Sam, that's really helpful."

Sam stood up. "I'll send the full report up shortly."

"Great," said Kate, on autopilot. She stared blankly ahead as Sam left the office. Was what she thinking correct? Could she possibly be right?

After five minutes, she got up and walked carefully to the door. Her heart was still thumping. Was it *possible*? She remembered that sense of uneasiness that had grown stronger by the minute. She remembered Joel Hunter saying in the back of the police car *this is all wrong*. Was it? Was she?

By now, Kate had reached the floor where the interview rooms were located. She hesitated outside the one in which Olbeck was continuing to interview Joel Hunter. Then she took a deep breath and knocked.

"Detective Sergeant Kate Redman has entered the room," said Olbeck, looking at her quizzically. For a brief moment, Kate thought better of what she was going to say. Then she set her jaw and sat down next to her fellow officer.

"I've got a couple of questions for Mister Hunter," she said and then decided that rushing headlong into Olbeck's interview was just too rude. "Actually, DI Olbeck, I'd like to have a quick word with you, outside? If I may?"

Out in the corridor, Olbeck was still looking curiously at her. "Something's happened," he said. "What is it, Kate?"

Kate took a deep breath. "I think Kiki Dee might be lying. I think—" She broke off for a moment, aghast at what she was saying but knowing that she had to say it. "In fact, I'm pretty sure she is lying."

Olbeck's eyes bulged. "Lying about the *rape*?"

Kate nodded, biting her lip. "Yes. About all of it. The cat, the death threat, the rape."

Olbeck put a hand up to his forehead, ruffling his hair. "Care to tell me why?"

"Of course." Kate tugged on his arm, leading him towards the stairs. "But I think we need to tell Anderton at the same time."

"What the hell is this?" Anderton demanded, five minutes later.

Kate sat up straight. Now that she came to say it out loud, her evidence had started to feel rather thin. But surely she was right? "I'm saying it's a set-up. The whole thing. Not the pig's heart, that was genuine – Ian Neely sent it to her like he did to the two other women, because he's a weirdo and Kiki probably stood him up just like the other two women did, and that was his bizarre way of getting back at her. But that's all that *really* happened. All the rest of it; the cat being killed, the death threat, the rape—" Her voice faltered for a moment and she cleared her throat. "It's all just a big set-up. Designed to get Joel Hunter into a whole heap of trouble."

Both Olbeck and Anderton were staring at her. Anderton's gaze fell to the newspaper article, which Kate had spread out on his desk before she started to speak. Then he looked back at Kate.

"Go on," was all he said.

"I don't exactly know why she did it," Kate said. "But I can probably have a good guess. Laura Ellis mentioned that Kiki had been abandoned by her father when she was young. I'd imagine that she's probably quite damaged by that. She acts brash and confident, but underneath it all she's vulnerable and needy. Probably unable to deal with rejection very well. So I imagine that if, for example, she'd had a brief affair with Joel Hunter and he'd then told her he can't keep seeing her, because he's married or for whatever reason he gave her, then Kiki's not going to take that very well. She's not going to take that *at all*."

"But," said Olbeck in confusion. "I thought Kiki was gay. Isn't she?"

Kate shrugged. "She might be. But from the sounds of it, she went after Laura and then just as soon lost interest. Is it too much to think that she might have been doing that as a smokescreen? Just to make sure that nobody realised she and Joel Hunter were ever an item?"

Anderton was shaking his head. "So you're saying that she did all of this just to get him into trouble? What about the rape?"

"There was no rape. She probably asked Joel to meet her out the back of Decadence for a quickie and then faked her injuries." She brandished the DNA report. "You can read it here. They swabbed her nails for DNA, as is usual in a rape investigation. They did find skin underneath them. *Her* skin. Not Joel Hunter's. The only DNA of his was found in her genital area, as you would expect if he'd had sex with her."

That shook them both, she could tell. Anderton reached his hand out for the report and leafed through it. "That's not enough evidence to suppose what – what it is you're saying," he said in a low tone.

"No, I know." Kate smoothed her hair back from her face. "And believe me, I would not be making these accusations lightly. But we've got a witness statement that tells us that nobody killed the cat. The witness hit it with a car, completely accidentally, and returned its body to the house where it lived. If nobody killed the cat, then why did Kiki – and only Kiki – receive a death threat? A death threat that was sent from a computer at her college?"

Both men were still staring at her. Olbeck said, after a moment, "But she was so distressed..."

He trailed off. Kate rolled her eyes. "She's a *drama* student, Mark. Probably the best in her class. She performs in front of a crowd for a living. I'm pretty sure that pulling this off would have been child's play."

Olbeck looked upset. "God, if what you're saying is true – Kiki is really disturbed."

Anderton snorted. "Disturbed? Bloody psychopathic, if you ask me." He shoved his chair back from the desk decisively. "Right, here's how we play this. Kate, go and interview Kiki. Tell her what you know and see if she'll confess. Mark, get down to this Joel Hunter guy and tell him you know he had an affair with Kiki. See if he confesses. I'll get the others to start pulling in any more evidence that we might have." He stopped and shook his head, staring at the photograph of Kiki Dee and her mother. "You know, this makes a lot more sense now." He indicated the picture. "Throw it all out in the open to make maximum trouble for the man."

"There's one thing I don't understand," said Kate. "Surely Kiki knew that there might not be a chance of a conviction. And she'd have to go through a full criminal trial, get dragged over the coals by his defence..."

"Oh, I imagine that she'd probably withdraw the charges, after a while," said Anderton, cheerfully. "In fact, I'd put money on it. By then, the damage is done. Joel Hunter's life, his marriage, his reputation is utterly ruined, and he's under a cloud of suspicion for the rest of his life."

"God." Olbeck was shaking his head.

"Come on," said Kate. "Let's get the evidence."

Chapter Thirteen

KATE PARKED THE CAR A few doors down from the large Victorian house. Kiki had returned home to the house she shared with her girlfriends, as Kate's phone call to Kiki's mother had ascertained. Kate sat for a moment, drumming her fingertips on the wheel. She was just opening the door when her phone rang. It was Olbeck.

"Joel Hunter's caved," he said with satisfaction. "Admitted he had a very brief affair with her – a two night stand. Then he came to his senses and told her he couldn't carry on because he was married. Usual rubbish. Why the stupid bugger just didn't come out and tell us all this before, I don't know."

"Great." Kate clenched a fist in triumph. "So how did Kiki react to being dumped?"

"Bombarded him with texts and calls. Threatened to tell his wife. Apparently the last text she sent him told him 'he'd be sorry'."

"I *see*," said Kate, with feeling. "So what happened on the night of the so-called rape?"

"Kiki called him and told him she urgently needed to see him. She must have sounded quite convincing, because he went haring off to the Decadence club after work and met her round the back."

"She *is* convincing," said Kate. "That's the problem."

"So anyway, she told him that she couldn't think of any other way of getting his attention and one thing led to another and bang – literally – they've had a quick knee-trembler up against the back wall of the club and she's got him right where she wants him. She's lucky you didn't come across her twenty minutes earlier or her whole plan would have fallen apart."

"Right." Kate looked over at the house, thinking. "I'll have a look at her phone in a minute, but I guess we can always pull the records from the phone company."

"Exactly. She's going to have a hard time explaining away why she was texting and calling the guy she says she's only met once before. Anyway, I'll let you get on with it."

"Thanks, Mark. See you later."

Kate walked up to the front door, rang the doorbell and stood back, smoothing her hair. The door was opened by one of Kiki's housemate's, a short, plump girl with long blonde hair. She indicated the living room door with a bob of her golden head.

"She's in there," the girl whispered, in a tone that suggested they were all treating Kiki as some sort of invalid.

Kate thanked her and opened the door to the living room quietly. When she entered the room, she saw that Kiki was curled up on the sofa nearest the bay window, a woolly throw over her lap, her head turned away. Kate saw that she was gazing out of the window, her face pensive and sad. Seeing her, Kate realised something.

It was a shock but it shouldn't have been, knowing what they knew about the girl. In some part of herself, Kiki Dee was enjoying herself immensely.

It must have been a challenge, thought Kate. A real challenge to her acting ability. And she was so good, wasn't she? It's easy to enjoy something that you're good at.

"Hello, Kiki," she said, out loud.

Kiki turned her head slowly, as if she'd been unaware before that Kate had entered the room. "Oh, hello, DS Redman," she said. Then she smiled sadly. "I'm glad you've come."

"Oh, yes?" said Kate, seating herself in a chair opposite.

Kiki looked serious. Her face contracted into a half wince, half smile. "Yes. I – well, I've been thinking. I want to drop the charges."

Bingo. Just as Anderton had said. Kate kept her face neutral but she allowed the faintest hint of surprise to enter her tone. "Really? Why's that?"

Kiki looked down at her lap. "I – I can't face the trial," she said, mournfully. "You hear it all the time, what the court is like for a rape victim. It's like being attacked all over again. I just can't face it. I can't!"

Kate took a deep breath. "We'd be there to support you every step of the way, Kiki. We'd be able to get you the help you need." She let a nuance of something infuse that last sentence and saw the flicker on the girl's face. She's wondering now, Kate thought. She wants to know if I know.

Kiki's voice hardened. "Well, I've made up my mind."

Although she knew she had no hope of changing her mind, Kate couldn't resist one last shot. "There's the matter of public safety, too, Kiki. You going to trial might help keep a dangerous man off the streets."

Kiki shook her head, the sharp edges of her bob swaying against her cheeks. The scratches were healing now. "No, I'm sure that's not the case. He's not exactly a danger to the public. He was obsessed with *me*."

Kate realised something then. Kiki Dee was never going to confess. She'd created the reality that she thought she had deserved, and nothing and nobody was going to persuade her to say otherwise. Had she got so caught up in the fantasy she'd made that she truly had lost hold of reality?

Kate made up her mind. "May I see your phone, Kiki?" she asked pleasantly.

Kiki looked at her warily. "My phone? Why?"

"I'd just like to have a quick look at it."

Kiki smiled a little tightly. "I'm sorry but it's upstairs somewhere. I don't know exactly where it is."

"Oh, come now," said Kate, smiling back. "I know you youngsters. You're surgically attached to your phones. It can't be far. Shall I help you look?"

She could almost see Kiki's mind ticking over the possibilities. Kate waited, patiently. If she knew Kiki, then she'd have thought so far ahead but not further – or perhaps she didn't realise that the police could access anyone's phone records or had thought that things wouldn't ever get that far. She was good, Kate gave her credit for that, but she was only twenty.

Kiki dug around underneath the rug and came up with an iPhone in a leopard-skin print case. "Oh, here you are. It was underneath my legs after all," she said with a light laugh.

Kate took it from her. "I'll need the passcode, please, Kiki." Kiki gave it to her and Kate tapped it in.

"Well, that's unusual," Kate said a minute later. "You don't keep many of your messages, do you?"

"I don't like clutter. Digital or otherwise." Kiki's voice was possibly harder than she'd intended.

Kate handed the phone back to her. She continued to regard the girl steadily. Very occasionally, this was sometimes enough. The weight of Kate's knowing stare got too much and the other party collapsed and confessed...

Kate knew it wouldn't happen now. All that Kiki did was stare back in an increasingly hostile manner.

"What?" Kiki said, eventually.

Kate kept her eyes on the girl's face. "Why did you do it, Kiki?"

Again, the tremor in the girl's face. She's not quite tough enough, thought Kate. Not yet. Give her ten years or so. A thought came to her that almost made her shudder. If Kiki had done this to a man whom she barely knew, someone who'd merely dumped her after a brief fling, what would Kiki do in the future to someone who had *really* wronged her? What would she do to a husband? A child? At least now, there was a chance of preventing that.

She stood up and began to speak the words of the arrest. Kiki said nothing but her pale face became whiter and whiter. She seemed to shrink a little, becoming even smaller under the woolly folds of the rug.

"Come with me, please," said Kate. Kiki made no protest but she stumbled, just once, on the way to the door. Kate took her arm and escorted her out. The last thing she saw, as she closed the living room door behind her, was the red illuminated mouth over on the far wall, smiling as if in gentle mockery.

THE END

Descent

A Kate Redman Novella

Chapter One

THE NEW YEAR CAME IN hard in Abbeyford, ushered in by weather so wintry it could have blown straight in from the Arctic. Fields ploughed up for the harvest several months ago froze into solid brown rutted waves of dirt. Puddles became opaque circles of ice staring blankly up at the white sky. The trees and grass were outlined with a glittering skin of frost crystals, so thick in parts that it looked as though it had snowed.

Snow would be better, Kate Redman thought as she sat in the toasty interior of her car in the police station carpark, trying to work up the willpower to plunge herself into the icy air outside. *At least if we had some snow we could go sledging*. But no snow was forecast yet – just more days of this intense, if seasonal, cold.

Kate squared her shoulders and pulled on the woolly hat that her friend and colleague DI Mark Olbeck had given her for Christmas. It had a giant red pompom on top of it, which Kate had eyed somewhat quizzically when she'd opened the parcel. "It's so *you*," Olbeck had insisted, and so, of course, Kate had thanked him nicely and worn it whenever she was going to see him, although privately she thought she looked as though she was walking around wearing a giant clown's nose on top of her head.

Still, it *was* a warm hat. She pulled on the matching gloves – smaller red pom-poms at the cuffs – braced herself and then opened the door, launching herself out into winter's frosty embrace.

She normally used the back door of the station, which opened with the electronic pass issued to all staff. Kate's pass didn't seem to be working today. As she waved it towards the sensor futilely, she had the guilty thought that perhaps she shouldn't have used it to scrape the ice from her windscreen this morning. Giving up, she trudged off towards the main entrance, pulling her clown-nose hat down more firmly around her ears.

The warmth of the main reception area of the station came as a welcome surprise. It was surprisingly quiet for a weekday morning. Perhaps the icy weather was keeping all the usual petty criminals indoors for a change. Kate stopped to say hello to PC Paul Boulton, who usually manned the desk, and they exchanged all the usual post-Christmas and New Year pleasantries.

"Oh, not bad, not bad. Quite quiet, actually. How about you?"

Kate paused. She'd spent Christmas Day with Anderton, the recently suspended DCI of the station. She paused because she wasn't certain just how far gossip about Anderton's suspension, or about his relationship with Kate, had gone. Besides, when your significant other was a man in his fifties, what were you supposed to call him? *Boyfriend* sounded ridiculous. *Lover* sounded, well, too saucy. Partner? Companion? Main squeeze?

Kate gave up. "Not bad, thanks. Pretty quiet too."

A blast of wintry air hit the back of her legs as the main reception door opened behind her. She turned just as a woman came into the station rather hesitantly, looking about her uncertainly.

"How may I help you?" asked Paul. Kate stepped away smartly, leaving him to get on with his job.

The woman came up to the desk. She looked to be in her late thirties, with a thin, pretty face and long, gently waving brown hair. "Oh, hullo – yes – I'm not sure if I'm in the right place—"

Kate, divesting herself of her many layers of outdoor clothing behind the counter, listened idly. Paul Boulton, highly experienced at helping hesitant members of the public, made encouraging noises.

The woman said "It's just – it's my friend. I think – I think she's missing. She's gone missing. "I don't know whether I should report it or not."

"Has she been missing for long?" Paul asked.

"Well, that's just it. I *think* so, but I'm not absolutely certain. It's just that a couple of days ago we arranged to meet for coffee and yesterday she didn't turn up. It's not like her, she's normally so punctual. And I've been trying to get in contact with her, and she's not answering her phone or her emails."

Paul reached for a notepad. "Let's just take a few details from you. Could I have your name?"

The woman clasped her hands together. Her fine leather gloves had a furry edging at the wrists and her woollen hat was obviously cashmere. Now why couldn't Olbeck have given her something like *that*, thought Kate, and then chastised herself for her ungratefulness.

"I'm Louise, Louise White. My friend's name is Karyn Denver. She spent Christmas Day with us and went home the day after Boxing Day. I haven't actually seen her since then but like I said, we were supposed to meet up for coffee yesterday, after New Year, and she just didn't turn up."

Losing interest, and conscious of her own work waiting for her, Kate headed off. She'd thawed out quite nicely by now and was positively glad to be back at work. Excluding Anderton, she'd seen little of her colleagues apart from spending New Year's Eve with Olbeck and his husband, Jeff. Practically bouncing into the office, she collided with DS Theo Marsh who was mid-yawn with his eyes closed.

"Ouch!"

"Oops! Sorry, Theo."

Theo grinned. "Kate, mate, I know it's been a while but there's no need to jump me. I'm glad to see you too."

"Ah, how I've missed your sexist banter." Kate gave him a just-this-side-of-friendly punch on the arm.

"Again, *ouch*."

"Oh, shush." Kate headed straight for the coffee machine that had finally replaced the ancient old kettle in the kitchen.

Theo followed her. "So, happy New Year and all that. How was your Christmas?"

Again, Kate paused. Then, feeling she should at least be honest with one of her colleagues, she tried for a casual tone and said, "Quite nice, thanks. Anderton and I spent it together."

There was just a fraction of a second's pause before

Theo answered in an equally casual tone, "Oh, right. Nice one. How is the guv?"

Kate paused for longer. How *was* Anderton? She wasn't entirely sure herself. Oh, he seemed happy enough, pottering around his cottage, going to the gym and catching up with old friends, but even so, Kate could sense a slight shrinkage in Anderton's normally ebullient personality. He must feel adrift – he *must*. So many years as a DCI. Managing his team, hunting down murderers and rapists and other violent criminals and all of a sudden – retirement. Because that was what he essentially was. Retired.

Kate sifted through all the possible answers before deciding on a minor lie. "Oh, he's fine." Because Theo looked as though he were waiting for more, she added, "Desperate for us all to get together for a drink. You know, catch up."

By now, DC Rav Cheetam had joined them in the little kitchenette. "Are you talking about Anderton?" he demanded. "How is he?"

Kate gave him the same non-committal answer and repeated the line about getting together for a drink.

"That would be great," said Rav. "It'll have to be a soft drink, though. You know, Dry January and that."

Theo snorted. "Yeah, I do Dry January too. Strictly no drinking – except at weekends, in the pub and if I get thirsty."

Kate rolled her eyes and left them bickering over the subject while she went over to her desk. Her desk mate, DS Chloe Wapping, was still on holiday, which was annoying. Kate relied on her fellow female officer to dilute some of the laddish tempo of the office. Although – a thought occurred to Kate and she looked to see if Olbeck was in his office. *Hooray* – he was. Kate got up to see him and, on an afterthought, pulled on her woolly clown-nose hat.

"Hi." She stuck her head around his office door and waggled it, feeling the pom-pom bounce.

Olbeck looked up and chuckled. "I *told* you. It suits you."

"Hmm." Kate walked in and found herself a chair. "Anyway, I wanted to ask you. Who's taking the lead? Who's our interim DCI?" A further thought occurred to her and she leant forward in excitement. "Is it you?"

Olbeck shook his head. "No. To be honest, Kate, I didn't want the job. Not that they asked me."

Kate was opening her mouth to ask *why not* when she shut it again. Olbeck had undergone a fairly traumatic couple of months recently, due to their last high-profile case. It had only been a few weeks since he'd returned to work from sick leave. She nodded, understanding. "So, who is it?"

"I got an email this morning. It's Nicola Weaver."

Kate was surprised at the jolt the news gave her. She only knew Nicola Weaver by name – the DCI had worked in Bristol and had obviously transferred to Abbeyford for the job – but her immediate reaction to the news was shock at the realisation that her new boss would be a woman.

A second later, she told herself that it was brilliant news. God knew there were precious few women in positions of high power in the force. Hadn't Kate just been bemoaning the blokey atmosphere in the team to herself? This could be great, she told herself, ignoring a flicker of disquiet.

Olbeck was speaking. "I know Nicky, a little. She seems very competent, and she's done really well for herself in a tough field."

"I can imagine." For a moment, Kate drifted off into a reverie where she herself attained the coveted position of DCI. Maybe even Superintendent?

She came back to reality with a start, realising that Olbeck's phone was ringing. He picked up the receiver and gave the usual greeting.

Kate knew, even without hearing whoever was speaking on the other end of the line, that something had happened. And by something, she meant a body. Something like that, anyway. She'd worked with Olbeck for so long that she could read his body language almost subconsciously; the slight stiffening of his shoulders, the almost imperceptible tension in his face.

She waited until he said goodbye and raised her eyebrows. "Something for us?"

Olbeck nodded. "Patrol called it in. They've found the body of a woman in Blackdown Woods."

"What a *lovely* start to the new year." Kate pushed herself upright and sighed. "Right, well, I await your orders. Or do we have to wait for our new DCI?"

She was half-joking but Olbeck looked serious. "I'm not sure when she's starting – I don't know. Perhaps I should—" He began hunting for something on his desk, gave up and looked at Kate. "No, we need to get going, Nicola Weaver or no Nicola Weaver." He handed a slip of paper over to Kate. "Here's the details, and they'll be on the system in a minute or two. Can you take Rav or Theo and head on over?"

"Your wish is my command." Kate inclined her pom-pom at him in acquiescence and waved a hand in goodbye as she left the room.

Chapter Two

Blackdown Woods was a local beauty spot; a hundred acre spread of thick, ancient woodland clustered around a natural stone gorge. Footpaths and bridle paths meandered throughout the trees, with one path running along the foot of the gorge. It was here that an early morning dog walker had found the crumpled body of a woman, splayed and broken, on the frosty mud of the path.

Kate and Theo had, by necessity, parked their car some distance away, in one of the two small carparks provided for visitors. As they walked towards the winding steps that led to the foot of the gorge, miniscule white flakes began to flutter down from the sky. Kate turned her face up to the clouds above. "Is that snow?"

"Looks like it. Bloody *hell*, it's cold." Theo banged his gloved hands together as they strode along. "I hope SOCO have already covered up the body."

"I'm sure they're on the case." Kate gripped the handrail as she made her way gingerly down the stone steps hewn out of the walls of the gorge many years ago. "Careful, it's icy here."

They reached the ground with no incident and hurried towards the other end of the footpath, where they could see a great deal of activity. Kate looked up at the steep cliffs either side of them. "Who owns this, anyway?"

"What?"

"The land. The woods. Is it private?"

"Nah. I think it's National Trust. We can find out later, anyway."

As they got closer, they could see the white forensic tent had been erected to hide the body. There were various people milling about: Scene of Crime officers in their white overalls, a few uniformed officers. Kate looked for the civilian who had discovered the body but couldn't see anyone. Perhaps they'd already been taken back to the station to give their statement. There were no curious onlookers, which made a change. It was obviously just too cold for people to be out and about as they normally would be in Blackdown Woods.

Kate and Theo gloved up, slipped on their shoe covers and covered their heads. Then they ducked, thankfully, inside the tent which was a fraction warmer than the frigid air outside.

Kate recognised the pathologist bending over the body immediately – it was Andrew Stanton, an old – very old – boyfriend of hers. It was one of the few triumphs of Kate's personal life that she felt that she'd managed to retain him as a friend.

He greeted her and Theo and added, "I'd say happy New Year but it doesn't seem very appropriate in the circumstances."

"No." Kate looked down at the body for the first time. With a slight shock, she realised that it was frozen solid, just as if it had been refrigerated. "What have we got?"

She could see for herself before Andrew began to tell her. A woman, fairly young, with blonde hair covering her face. She lay on her side, arms and legs in a tangle. She was dressed in running gear: Lycra leggings and a matching jacket, wearing trainers and thick sports socks. The circumference of frost crystals around her head glittered red.

"My first thoughts? She fell," said Andrew, simply. "But don't quote me on that. She's got significant traumatic head injuries and I suppose they could be from an assault. But she's also got several compound fractures – look, there and there—" He pointed to bulges in the Lycra on the woman's arms and legs and Kate realised, queasily, that the lumps were edges of protruding bone. "I'd say that's also commensurate with a fall."

Theo crouched down carefully for a closer look. "She's been out here for a while. Look, she's a block of ice."

"Yes, that could be a problem" said Andrew. "Once we thaw her out, the frost damage could hinder some of the findings. But we'll try our best."

Kate crouched down too. "Any ID yet?"

"Not yet." Andrew was beginning to exhibit the testiness that was customary when he began to feel pressured. "Look, this is all preliminary at the moment. Let me get on with it, and I'll see if I can find something conclusive. Otherwise you'll have to wait."

Kate and Theo exchanged a grin behind Andrew's back as he turned back to the body. "Right you are,"

Kate said, standing up with a groan. God, if she was like this in her mid-thirties, what was she going to be like at fifty?

Theo had sprung up with the ease of a man well acquainted with the gym. "Shall we have a look around, Kate?"

"Yes. I'm thinking up there to start with." Kate pointed to the top of the tent but she meant the top of the gorge. Theo understood.

"See if there's any obvious signs of falling off the cliff face or something?"

"You got it."

They ducked out of the tent again and both shivered as the cold air hit them anew. Snow was still falling, although not thickly and it didn't seem to be settling yet. There were still no onlookers at the blue and white police tape cordoning off the area – something of a first for a case, thought Kate. No visible press either. Good, that made things easier.

Kate walked back to the furthest side of the gorge where the woman had fallen and craned her neck upwards. The top of the ravine was just visible from here but she couldn't see if there were any signs of a disturbance, any grubbed up grass or flattened bushes. They'd have to walk up there. She gestured to Theo and they went to try and find the closest path to the top of the gorge.

It was a steep climb, and even Theo was puffing by the time they reached the top. Kate followed the gently winding path through the leafless beech trees. Undergrowth and bramble bushes hid the edge of the gorge from view, although here and there, they cleared enough for the sharp drop to be visible. Gingerly, Kate walked towards the edge, trying to see over to determine whether they were immediately above the body.

Theo followed her reluctantly and stopped well back from the edge. Kate could see the square white top of the forensic tent directly below her. She looked around carefully. They stood in a kind of natural clearing encircled with beech and hazel trees, thorny clumps of brambles and the dead brown stalks of bracken. The frosted grass was short beneath their feet and over on a tree-stump to the side, Kate could see rabbit droppings frozen into oddly beautiful little pearls.

"There's nothing here," muttered Theo, who had also been having a look.

Kate concurred. The edge of the cliff, whilst steep, was unmarked. No clawed-up grass around the drop, as there might have been if someone had been fighting for their life not to succumb to gravity. There were no footprints at all, apart from their own in the frosty grass. She walked backwards from the edge, sweeping her gaze from side to side.

"It would have *been* this side, wouldn't it?" she asked, looking up and across to the far side of the ravine. It was a good thirty feet across, possibly more, and the body of the woman lay close to the side they were currently standing on.

"Yup. Unless she was like that bird in the Matrix, you know, Trinity. There's no way she could have landed over this side if she'd jumped from the other."

Kate looked at him. "Jumped?"

"Well, it's a possibility, isn't it? We've had a few suicides here over the years."

"Really?" Although Kate phrased it as a question, she wasn't surprised. There was something about high spaces that attracted the desperate. Personally, she couldn't think of a more terrifying way to die. Well, she *could*, but she didn't really want to.

"Well, at least if that's the case we won't have to worry about it."

"True." Kate stood for a moment, looking down in the depths of the gorge. "But – I don't know. Would you get all dressed up for running if you were going to hurl yourself off a cliff?"

"Who knows?"

"True," Kate said again. "Anyway, let's split up and have a further look around. You take this side and I'll go back down to the bottom and see if Andrew's got anything yet."

"And who made you the boss of me?" Theo was only half-joking.

Kate grinned. "You'd better get used to being bossed around by a woman. I hear Nicola Weaver takes no prisoners."

"Yeah, well, if she's better looking than you, I might take it."

Kate stuck her tongue out at him before waving goodbye and heading back towards the path that descended into the gorge. She headed straight for the tent.

Andrew was supervising the placement of the body

bag when she walked in. Kate sidled up, hoping he was in a better mood.

"Hi. Any news?"

He turned and smiled. "Hi, Kate. I've got an ID for you. I found keys, a phone and a debit card in her jacket pocket."

"Fantastic. Thanks, Andrew."

Andrew held up an evidence bag containing the last item he'd mentioned. "The phone was smashed – well, the screen was broken anyway, and it's either completely dead or it's run out of battery. But the debit card has a name—"

Kate took it from him eagerly and turned the small black rectangle within it around so she could read it. "Ms K Denver." She stopped, hearing a faint bell ring. "I know that name." She closed her eyes momentarily, thinking back. "Oh, yes. Of course."

The missing woman – the one whose friend had reported her missing this morning. Could it only have been this morning? As was usual on a case, Kate felt as if she'd been working for days.

She looked up to see Andrew looking at her quizzically and smiled, sheepishly. "Sorry. That's great, Andrew. We already know who she is, so that's half the battle."

"Happy to oblige. I'll be in touch with details of the PM."

"Great. See you soon."

They said goodbye and Kate hurried outside, reaching into her pocket for her phone to call Theo.

Chapter Three

UNLIKE ANDERTON, THE FORMER ABBEYFORD DCI, DCI Nicola Weaver didn't enter the room with a crash of the door and a whirlwind of energy accompanying her. In fact, she entered the room so quietly that Kate, Rav, and Theo didn't notice her at first. Which was unfortunate, as they were currently engaged in playing that good old office game standby, 'Who can keep a screwed-up ball of paper in the air for the longest, using only their head'.

"Good morning," said Nicola Weaver's quiet voice, and Kate, who'd just achieved almost twenty seconds of triumph, jumped and lost her chance at the ball-in-the-air trophy. The paper ball fell to the floor and rolled towards Nicola, who bent and picked it up, two-fingered, as if it were a live mouse or a dirty sock.

"Sorry." Kate was aware of the colour of her cheeks. She felt the warmest she had been all day. Out of the corner of her eye, she could see Theo and Rav shuffling, torn between embarrassment and snickering. *God, how old are we all?*

They all sat down. Kate tried to sit up straighter in her chair, determined to make amends for her childishness. Nicola dropped the paper ball in the nearest litterbin with the faintest *moue* of disgust on her face.

Kate was conscious of a spurt of anger. All right, It was a stupid game, but really...

Nicola Weaver waited for a moment that stretched out well beyond the comfortable. The room was silent for at least thirty seconds, and she took the time to look at the three of them for a long moment in turn, before eventually speaking.

"As I said before, good morning." She paused long enough for Kate, Rav and Theo to mutter an embarrassed 'good morning' in return. "As you no doubt know, I am DCI Nicola Weaver, your interim manager for the foreseeable future, while DCI Anderton remains on gardening leave." She bestowed a rather meaningful smile at Kate as she said the last few words, and Kate, whilst mentally raising her eyebrows, managed to keep her face neutral and her expression only mildly interested.

Nicola paused again and then continued to speak. "Now, I realise that it's always something of a learning curve when a team manager is replaced, so I'm aware that some of you might well have some questions to ask. I will be in my office after this briefing for the next half an hour if you have anything in particular you'd like to discuss." She paused, only for there to be a brief, excruciating silence. Nicola smiled faintly and went on. "Now, let's begin on the briefing of our most recent case. Would anyone like to start? DS Redman, how about you?"

Feeling awkward, Kate cleared her throat. "We were called this morning by patrol to say they'd found the body of a woman at the bottom of the Blackdown

Gorge, in Blackdown Woods. Theo – er, DS Marsh – and I went there to survey the scene. SOCO were already there and the pathologist, Doctor Stanton, was, um, conducting his examination."

She ran out of breath and stopped speaking for a moment. Nicola hadn't taken her eyes off Kate's face.

"And?" Nicola asked, after a second.

Kate's jaw tightened for a moment. "Well, the preliminary medical findings seemed to conclude that she'd fallen from the top of the cliff. Theo – DS Marsh – and I went up to have a look, just to see if there were any signs of a cliff fall or similar, or – or anything pertinent to the enquiry. Um—"

Kate wasn't normally so inarticulate or hesitant, but there was something about Nicola Weaver's hazel stare that dried the words up in her mouth. For a horrible moment, her mind went completely blank.

Theo, bless his heart, leapt into the breach. "DS Redman and I took a good look around the top of the cliffs and the woods. Obviously we'll have to do a fingertip search if it turns out the death is suspicious, but on first glance there was nothing untoward to be seen."

By now, Kate had recovered her equilibrium. "Doctor Stanton recovered some ID from the body which gave us her name, Karyn Mary Denver. She's not been formally identified as yet, as we're just tracing her next of kin."

Nicola regarded her coolly. "Very well. Anything else? When's the post mortem to take place?"

"I'm just waiting on the details from Andrew – er, Doctor Stanton, I mean, but I'd imagine it would be in the next day or so." There was something about Nicola Weaver that made Kate adopt a spurious formality in her speech – very unlike her.

"Thank you. Please attend that, DS Redman, when you get the finalities."

Kate had actually been going to offer to do just that, but the cool way in which she was *told* what to do put her back up. Oh dear, she wasn't warming to her new boss at all. Was it just that Nicola Weaver was so different from Anderton? Or was it just that she appeared to be a stone-cold, grade-A bitch?

Sexist, Kate, sexist. She forced the thought from her head, smiled, and nodded. "Of course."

Nicola passed on without another glance at her. "Now, what about witnesses?" She looked enquiringly at Theo and her face softened, minutely. "DS Marsh?"

Theo shrugged, clearly less intimidated by his new DCI than Kate was. "I haven't had a chance yet to check with patrol, but I wouldn't hold your breath. It was minus four yesterday, and it's not very likely that many people would have been out for a walk."

"Hmm. Well, ask anyway. Once her next of kin have been informed, we can interview them to see if there are any circumstances surrounding Karyn Denver's death that we need to be aware of. Was she depressed, for example?" Nicola, who had been slowly turning in a circle, came to Rav. "DC Cheetam, I presume?"

Rav gave her a nervous smile. "That's right."

"Anything to add?" Nicola's tone was just the right side of patronising. Kate found herself clenching her fists. Okay, so Rav was the youngest but he wasn't *that* young – and he was a good and experienced police officer. Kate, through sad personal experience, was getting a bad feeling about DCI Nicola Weaver. She thought she sensed in her a bully – a bully who hid her bullying ways behind a polite manner and a calm and gentle voice.

Rav was suggesting they put a request for information board up at various entry points to Blackdown Woods. Nicola hesitated before answering in the affirmative. "I suppose it *might* do some good," was what she said, before turning away from them all and walking to the whiteboard at the back of the room.

She wrote up a summation of all they had just discussed in neat bullet points and assigned their various initials to various tasks. Then she turned back to face them, putting the top back on the whiteboard marker with a vicious little jab. Her calm smile didn't waver.

"Well, I'm sure we're all agreed that it's very likely that Karyn Denver's death was nothing more than a tragic accident. But, until we know more, obviously we are treating it as suspicious. Now, I know we have various other cases to progress but I think it would be more productive to go through those individually with the officers who are leading them. So, I'll see you all in my office at some point today – I'll have my assistant notify you with a time." Nicola's calm smile grew a fraction wider, although no less cold. "Thank you for your time, officers. Good morning."

Kate, Theo and Rav murmured some form of a thank you each. They remained motionless and silent until Nicola Weaver had left the room, shutting the door quietly behind her. Then, after a wait of several seconds to make sure she was out of earshot, they – as one – expelled their breath, blowing out their cheeks and giving each other appalled glances and raised eyebrows.

"What the hell—" Kate didn't need to say much more. She flumped back into her chair and looked at her two colleagues.

"Ice queen," agreed Rav.

"She matches the weather." Kate felt the urgent need for a coffee and walked over to the kitchen.

"Oh, come on," said Theo. "It's her first day here. And you know what you chicks are like."

"What?" demanded Kate in outrage. "We're like what?"

"Oh, you know, women in a position of power. You feel like you have to be a right ball-breaker, just to get some respect."

"I do *not*." Kate pushed aside the memory of a conversation that she and Chloe had had on just that subject.

Theo shrugged. "It's not so bad. Think about who we might have got instead."

"Like who?"

"Oh, you know. That useless fat git from Salterton, for one. What's his name. Chloe's old boss."

"George Atwell," said Rav, helpfully.

"Hmm." Kate could see his point, remembering what she did of Atwell. "I suppose you're right." She punched the buttons of the coffee machine with slightly unnecessary vigour. "Well, I suppose we'd better get on with it." She thought for a moment and added, with a grin. "Don't you agree, *DS Marsh*?"

Theo grinned back. "Oh, I certainly do, *DS Redman*."

"Coffee for you, *DC Cheetam,* I presume?" Kate glanced at Rav who was also smiling.

"Ooh, I say, that would be lovely, *Detective Sergeant Kate Redman*, if you would *be* so kind," Rav answered smartly, in a kind of put-on posh falsetto which made them all collapse.

***

ARMED WITH RESTORED GOOD HUMOUR and their hot drinks, the team wandered back to their desks. Kate only then realised that Olbeck hadn't been with them at the briefing. She looked into his office and realised why – he was clearly having a meeting with various other DIs from other departments. He certainly seemed to have a lot more meetings than he ever used to. No wonder he hadn't wanted the extra responsibility of a promotion. Not to mention the fact that he was shortly due to become a father – all being well. Kate knew that he and Jeff were well along the route to adopting a pair of siblings, a two year old boy and an eight month old girl. That was all she knew so far – both Olbeck and Jeff were keeping quiet of the details, for fear that something would happen to derail the whole process. "I don't want to jinx it," was what Olbeck had said, simply but with heartfelt sincerity, the last time Kate had enquired as to the progress of the adoption. And Kate, because she knew how very much this meant to both her friends, had done the kind thing and kept her mouth shut.

Once more crossing her fingers for a successful outcome, Kate turned back to her computer and checked her emails. There were three of interest. One from her friend Stuart announced his engagement to his long-term girlfriend. *Wedding invitation is in the post*, he had written, *but just wanted you to know anyway and save the date!* Kate sighed and smiled. She was happy for Stuart, of course she was, but every wedding and new baby announcement was, for Kate, bittersweet. Because she seemed so far from anything like that happening for her. But was that what she actually wanted? I don't know, Kate thought, staring blankly at her computer screen. *I genuinely don't know.*

Shaking her head and dismissing the thought, she turned to the second email, which was from Andrew Stanton, confirming the post mortem was scheduled for tomorrow afternoon. Kate replied in acknowledgement and also to confirm that she would be attending as the police representative.

The third email made her groan silently. It was from Linda Cumbald, DCI Nicola Weaver's new assistant. She *would* have to have an assistant, thought Kate resentfully. Anderton had never bothered, using the pool of administrative assistants in the station if he needed extra help. Linda had summoned Kate to a meeting with DCI Weaver at nine o'clock the next morning. Nine o'clock! *Jesus wept*. Kate gritted her teeth and wrote a short affirmative reply, unable to help herself by signing off with 'regards, Kate'. Everyone knew that when you wrote 'regards' it meant you weren't best pleased. Passive-aggressive, yes, but there you go...

She jumped as Theo tapped her on the shoulder. "What is it?"

"I've traced Karyn Denver's next of kin, it's her husband. Off to break the news now. Want to come, DS Redman?"

"That's stopped being funny. But yes, I will." Wanting to get out of the office, Kate leapt at the opportunity. "Come on."

"Come on, who?"

Kate gave him a look. "Come on, Detective Sergeant Theodore James Archibald Henry Sinclair George Ringo Paul John – um – Mick Ron – um – *Marsh*."

Theo's laughter followed her to the exit.

***

KARYN DENVER'S HUSBAND LIVED ON the border of the suburbs of Charlock and Arbuthon Green, a hinterland where the run-down estate of Arbuthon Green butted up against the slightly more prosperous and well-to-do inhabitants of Charlock. Kate had let Theo drive for once – she was no fan of driving on icy roads, and whilst Theo might be a cocky little so-and-so, he was also a very experienced and competent driver.

They found the Denvers' house easily – it was a nondescript semi-detached building, one of many built in their thousands after the Second World War. As they parked the car and walked towards it, Kate could see that there had been a few efforts made to smarten it up. The front garden was neat, with various shrubs and rose bushes planted around the edge of the small lawn, and there were colourful ceramic pots by the front door. The effect was slightly spoiled by the dead, brown plants contained within them.

Something else occurred to Kate as she went to open the garden gate. "Hang on a minute." Theo looked at her enquiringly. "I've just thought. Karyn Denver's friend was the one who reported her missing, not her husband. Don't you think that's odd?"

Theo frowned. "Well – kind of."

Kate persisted. "Her friend – oh, I can't remember her name – she said something about Karyn being with them for Christmas. Now I think back, I got the impression that it was just Karyn there with them, not Karyn and her husband."

"Well—" Theo lifted his shoulders. "We need to talk to this friend anyway. Let's interview this guy and see what we get."

Kate conceded that that was indeed the best course of action. They advanced down the paved garden path and Kate knocked on the door.

She had to knock twice more before it was actually answered. The door slowly opened to reveal a middle-aged man, dark-haired and bearded, wearing a frown that was almost as dark. "Yes?"

"Mr Thomas Denver? I'm Detective Sergeant Kate Redman, and this is my colleague Detective Sergeant Theo Marsh. May we come in for a minute?"

Kate was used to many different sorts of reactions to this type of visit, and it was never a situation that she relished. She braced herself automatically for tears, hysteria, and even violence.

There was none of that. Mr Denver stood regarding them both for a moment with a flat gaze that Kate found quite unsettling. Then he spoke. "What's this all about?"

"May we come in, sir?"

"No. What's this all about?"

Kate sighed inwardly. Rather shamefully, she became aware of how thankful she was that Theo's tall, strong, young presence was there, given how she could see how this interview was going. "I'm afraid I have bad news about your wife, sir."

Mr Denver's dark brown eyes regarded her steadily. "I don't have a wife," was what he said eventually.

There was a moment's silence. Kate cleared her throat and tried again. "I need to talk to you about Karyn Denver. You are down as her next of kin. Sir, may we please come in?"

Mr Denver didn't budge. "She's not my wife anymore. Whatever she's done, I'm not interested. She's nothing to do with me anymore. I haven't seen her for days."

"Sir, please—" was all that Kate managed to get out before the door shut in their faces with what was little less than a slam. Flabbergasted, Kate and Theo looked at one another. Kate raised her hand to the doorbell again.

"Don't bother," said Theo. "He's not going to listen. Let me try." He bent down and pushed open the letterbox to shout through. "Mr Denver? Mr Denver? We really do need to talk to you about your – your estranged wife. If you won't open the door, I'm going to leave you my card and my colleague's card. Please do get in touch with us or call the station."

Silence. The door didn't open. Kate blew out her cheeks and handed Theo one of her cards, which he dropped with his own into the letterbox.

They beat a tactical retreat back to the car and sat for a minute, wondering whether the door was going to open or their phones were going to ring. But there was nothing.

"Weird," said Theo. "Do you think he was in shock?"

Kate pursed up her lips. "I suppose it's possible. Hmm."

They waited another five minutes but Thomas Denver did not emerge from the house. Eventually, Theo sighed and started the engine. "We're wasting our time here. If he wants to know, he knows how to get in touch."

"Agreed." Kate leant her head back against the seat rest as Theo pulled away from the side of the road. All of a sudden, she felt exhausted. She still had reams of paperwork to catch up on, not to mention that bloody interview at silly o'clock the next morning... At least Anderton was going to cook tonight, that was something to be thankful for.

"Wake me when we get back to the station," she muttered to Theo and closed her eyes.

Chapter Four

KATE DREW HER CAR UP outside Anderton's cottage just after eight o'clock that evening. She'd already driven home, showered and changed, fed her cat Merlin and battled her guilt that she was leaving him again for yet another evening. Wearily, she hauled herself from the car, shivered at the cold air, and hurried towards the front door, clutching her overnight bag and a bottle of red wine. The door was slightly ajar and she could hear comforting sounds of music, pans clattering distantly from the kitchen and a welcome blast of centrally heated air. Quickly, she shut the door behind her.

"Do you know how much heat you're losing by leaving your door open?" she said to Anderton as she went up and kissed him.

"I left that for *you*. I was at a tricky stage with the roast lamb and didn't want to leave it to answer the door." Anderton's thick grey hair was curling in the damp steam of the kitchen.

Kate bit back the response she wanted to make. *So give me a key, then*. They weren't quite at that stage yet. Or were they? She accepted the glass of wine he held out to her and went and sat at the breakfast bar.

"You look tired." Anderton shot the roasting pan full of golden, crisping potatoes into the oven with a clang, shut the oven door with his foot and straightened up with a groan. "Busy day?"

"Yes. You know what it's like."

"I did." Anderton's tone was neutral, but Kate still felt a twist of unease. She was keenly aware that Anderton probably felt very left out of things, and she wasn't sure what the best approach was. Should she talk about work more than she felt she wanted to? Keep him in the loop, keep him feeling as though his contribution still mattered? Or should she shut up about it altogether?

She took a long sip of wine and sought for a less contentious topic of conversation. "Did you play golf today?"

Anderton straightened up again from the oven, wiping sweat from his face. His cottage was always warm but the kitchen was approaching tropical levels of heat, what with the oven, the gas burners and even the two candles burning on the dining table. "What's that?"

"Did you play golf today?"

"Not today." Anderton dropped the lid of a saucepan with a curse and a clang as he burnt his finger. "Bugger. Listen, Kate, I'm right in the middle of it here. Go and sit in the living room, and I'll get things under control and we can relax."

"All right." Kate obediently picked up her wine glass and made her way through to the cosy little front room, where the wood-burning stove was glowing and the curtains were drawn against the winter night.

"Oh, by the way—" Anderton's shout stopped her. "Have a look at the local paper. There's something in there I think you'd like to see."

Curious, Kate picked it up from the living room coffee table. Anderton had marked the page he'd been talking about with a yellow Post-It note. Kate opened it to that page, glanced over it and saw the article. *Charlie's Home-Grown Success*, was the headline. Kate read on, with a slowly dawning smile. The article featured Charlie Petworth, a man that Kate had once frequently arrested, when he'd been a homeless alcoholic and petty thief. Now, Charlie had obviously turned over a new leaf. Sober and with his gardening business back up and running, it seemed from the article that Charlie had won an award for his pioneering mentoring scheme, offering training and support to young ex-offenders who wanted to learn garden design.

"I thought that would please you," said Anderton, coming into the room and looking rather hot and dishevelled.

"It pleases me immensely," Kate said, grinning. "I'm so glad for Charlie. I always knew he had it in him."

"Yes, it's good news. He can't have been out of prison long."

They sat down to eat shortly after that and for a while, there was nothing but the sound of contented chewing, wine sipping and the mellow vocals of Ella Fitzgerald coming from the entertainment station in the corner of the room.

Kate put her knife and fork neatly together in the middle of her plate and thanked Anderton sincerely. "That was lovely. It's so nice to come home to a cooked meal." After a moment, she realised what she'd said and hastily amended, "I mean, it's lovely to come here to a cooked meal. Thank you."

Anderton said nothing but smiled. Kate, covering her confusion, told him of her early start. "A nine o'clock in the morning meeting! Even you weren't that bad."

"That's DCI Weaver for you," said Anderton drily. "She's nothing if not efficient." He looked as though he were about to say more but thought better of it. Kate had a sudden, paranoid flash of intuition that he'd slept with her – with Nicola. She had no evidence for it, but what had that ever mattered? She knew Anderton had had something of a reputation, which made her present situation slightly more uncomfortable than it perhaps could have been.

The moment passed and Kate and Anderton finished their wine and loaded the dishwasher and cuddled in front of the wood-burner and eventually made their way up to bed. It was an evening just like the others that had preceded it, save for those two moments of awkwardness and anxiety for Kate. Don't think about it, she commanded herself, as she lay in the crook of Anderton's arm, listening to his breathing behind her flatten out into sleep. Luckily, she was so tired herself that it was easy to think of nothing at all – just to fall forward into thankful unconsciousness.

***

"So, how was it?" Chloe asked cautiously the next morning at nine forty-five am, as Kate slumped down opposite her into her chair.

Kate rolled her eyes. "Crap. A whole lot of corporate flim-flam about being a team member and doing things by the book. I got the idea I was being warned not to go out on a limb or take a punt on things off my own bat."

Chloe grinned. "Your reputation clearly precedes you."

"So it damn well should." Kate wondered whether to mention the other bone of contention – the various hints and insinuations that Nicola Weaver had made on the subject of Anderton – all the while being just subtle enough for Kate not to be able to react negatively – or indeed, react at all. Kate had simply sat, trying to smile blandly whilst under the table she dug her fingernails into the palms of her hands. She regarded them now, little reddened half-moons dug into the flesh of her palm.

Chloe was occupied with something else, and Kate decided not to mention it. She had another paranoid flash that perhaps Nicola was speaking for the entire team in having a dig at Kate and Anderton's relationship. Perhaps they all disapproved? Perhaps they thought she and Anderton had been together for ages, keeping it quiet for years?

By now, Kate was biting her nails. She looked across at Olbeck's office. She and Olbeck hadn't yet really had a chance to talk about Anderton. She knew that he – Olbeck – knew, and she knew they'd have to address the elephant in the room at some point, but when? God knew Olbeck had enough on his plate at the moment...

Pushing the thought aside, Kate sat up and reached for her notebook. She was due at the post mortem of

Karyn Denver this afternoon, and there was still the interview with Karyn Denver's friend to be undertaken. Kate found herself wondering if Thomas Denver had emerged from his house yet – or even rung the station to be told the bad news. She frowned, thinking. Grief could do funny things to people, yes, but his reaction had been right at the extreme end. *She's not my wife, she's nothing to do with me...*

Calls were slowly trickling in to the incident room after Rav had arranged for the placement of incident boards at various points around Blackdown Woods. Probably most of the callers would have little of value to impart, but you never knew...

Kate made another attempt to contact Thomas Denver, which proved futile. Then she tracked down the contact number for Louise White – ah, *that* was the friend's name – and rang it. It was answered by a man, who confirmed he was Louise White's husband. Kate didn't mention why she was calling but she could hear a faint hoarseness in his voice that could have denoted grief. Or perhaps he just had a cold. Kate arranged to meet both the Whites at their home that afternoon. She'd call in on the way back from the pathology labs.

***

AFTER LUNCH, KATE MADE HER way to the station car park. For once it was sunny, but it was still bitingly cold. Kate pulled her scarf further over her face as she hurried towards her car and had a fleeting thought that she might try out a balaclava, except she'd probably then be mistaken for a terrorist. As she drove away, she twisted the dial of the car heater up to full.

Andrew Stanton was conducting the post mortem and Kate was quite glad. She knew he liked to work mainly in silence, punctuating the quiet with the odd, terse observation. This gave Kate a chance to sit down and catch her breath, to think about the rest of the working day ahead and what she should be doing. She looked at the body of Karyn Denver with practised dispassion. The woman had been superficially pretty, so Kate could see, with long, wavy blonde hair, dark roots showing through at the scalp. A closer examination showed a face rather long and slightly too equine for true beauty. Heavy hips and chunky thighs. But then, thought Kate charitably, nobody looked their best on the autopsy table.

She'd attended enough post mortems by now not to be squeamish. Even so, she never approached the situation with insouciance; it never became commonplace. She sat patiently, averting her eyes from the particularly grotesque bits, pondering the death of Karyn Denver and wondering what the conclusion would be.

At length, Andrew finished stitching, pulled the green cover over the corpse and straightened up with an audible groan.

"Hard on the back, your job," commented Kate.

"Tell me about it. You should see the money I spend on physiotherapists." Andrew balled up his gloves, threw them in the hazardous waste bin and turned to the sink to wash his hands. "Obviously I'll have the full report over to you in a matter of days, but I can tell you now that, like I first thought, the cause of death was traumatic brain injury, most likely caused by a fall."

"Right," said Kate, unsurprised. "Anything else?"

"She has compound fractures of the arms, legs and ribcage. Again, totally in line with what you'd expect in someone who's fallen – what would it be from the top of the Blackdown gorge? Fifty feet?"

Kate sighed. "Any signs of drugs? Alcohol?" She got up, picking up her bag. "I mean, anything that might point to it being an accident or a suicide?"

"What, as opposed to something else?" Andrew finished drying his hands and turned to face Kate. "No obvious signs of intoxication, no alcohol in the stomach. You'll have to wait for the blood tests to see if anything shows up but, off hand, I'd say no."

"Hmm." Kate looked back at the shrouded figure. "Anything that – that might indicate somebody else had a hand in her falling?"

Andrew smiled. "Well, I didn't find a bloody great handprint on her face or the middle of her back, let's say. I suppose, if you were clutching at straws, there's a very, *very* faint chance that she could have been hit over the head with something and thrown over the side. The impact injuries could have then covered the original trauma." Kate opened her mouth to respond, and Andrew added "But, seriously, Kate. You wouldn't get it to stand up in court. Not on its own."

Kate knew that. She sighed and thanked Andrew.

"My pleasure. How are you, anyway?" As always, once the examination was over, Andrew's manner switched back to his normal warmth and charm, which reminded Kate of why she liked him.

They chatted pleasantly for a moment, a little incongruously, Kate thought, given the presence of the dead body in the room with them. But then, Andrew probably barely noticed things like that anymore. After a few minutes' conversation, and after asking after his wife and son, Kate bid Andrew farewell and made her way back out to the car.

She spent a few minutes transcribing the essence of what Andrew had told her. She was starting to think that this case wasn't going anywhere. From the sounds of it, Karyn Denver had been out for a run and for some reason had slipped and fallen over the edge of the gorge. A tragic accident; no more. Kate pondered for a moment, put away her notebook, and started the car. She wondered whether she was keen to write off this case as non-suspicious because it would then mean she'd have to spend less time reporting to Nicola the Efficient. But then, what about the next case? Sighing again, Kate put the car into gear and drove away.

Chapter Five

LOUISE WHITE AND HER HUSBAND lived in a much bigger house than the one Kate and Theo had visited yesterday. It was detached, built of Bath stone – a handsome Edwardian building with the original stained glass panels in the front door and the bare, spiky branches of a climbing rose entwined on a trellis on the front wall. There was enough room in the driveway behind a large black four-wheel-drive for Kate to park her much smaller car.

A man Kate assumed to be Mr White answered the door. He was a good-looking man in his forties, with curly dark hair and a strong jawline. He looked serious but not unduly upset. Louise White, when Kate came across her in the living room, looked ravaged. There was no other word for it. Even as Kate was shaking hands, Louise began to cry, tears streaming down her face.

"I'm sorry, I'm sorry," she burst out, pressing a disintegrating tissue to her eyes. "It's still such a shock; I don't think I'll ever get over the shock. I still can't believe it."

Mr White, who had introduced himself as Paul, lifted a box of tissues from the sideboard and handed them to his wife. He made a move as if to put his arms around her but in the next moment, Louise had sat back on the sofa, as if all the strength had left her legs.

"I'm really very sorry," said Kate. She discreetly got out her notebook and pen. "I just wondered, if you're feeling up to it, if you could tell me a little bit about Karyn. It could help the investigation if I could just get a bit of background and it sounds as though you were pretty close. Am I right?"

Louise nodded, eyes downcast. Tears welled up again and spilled over. "How did – how did she die?"

Kate took a moment to answer. "I can't yet confirm that, Mrs White. I'm sorry. It may be that Karyn's death was nothing more than a tragic accident, but it's still too early in the day to say that. That's why I'm hoping you can help me."

"Yes. Yes, I understand. What is it that you want to know?"

Kate clicked her pen. "Have you been friends for long?"

Louise wiped her eyes again and sat up a little, clearly pulling herself together. "I suppose so. About three years – three or four years, I forget exactly. We – Karyn and I – met at a running club. We're both keen runners, and we were both training for the Abbeyford half marathon."

Kate knew that half marathon, having once had to train for it herself. Luckily, although it hadn't seemed so at the time, she was able to get out of running the actual race itself by reason of being stabbed nearly to death by a maddened killer.

Shaking off those thoughts, she concentrated on

what Louise was telling her. "Karyn moved down here from London about the same time as we did, so we had that in common too. She was so nice, so warm, you know, just a really nice person to be around."

There was more in this vein, the usual polishing-up of the recently deceased by their friends and loved ones. Understandable, but not particularly illuminating. Kate listened, nodded, and made a few notes. She watched Louise gradually become less upset and more animated, as she talked about her friend. Kate noticed Paul White watching his wife and there was something about his expression, the merest hint, that set her wondering what he was thinking. Did he look – angry? Or was that too emphatic a word? Had he been jealous of the obviously close friendship between his wife and Karyn Denver? Or was Kate just imagining things? She scribbled a 'P?' on her notebook, just to jog her memory if anything else came up.

"What can you tell me about Karyn's husband?" said Kate, once Louise had finally wound to a close.

Louise looked surprised. "Tom? Tom Denver? What about him?"

Kate wasn't quite sure what she was fishing for. "Well, did you guys all socialise together?"

"No," said Paul White firmly. "Tom isn't – he's not very sociable."

That tied in with what little Kate had seen of Mr Denver. "Right, I see."

Louise was looking tearful again. "Oh, poor Tom. Poor, poor Tom. I'd better go and see him, or – or write or something."

"Yes. Yes, we should." Paul White sat down beside his wife on the sofa and put a hand on her knee. Kate watched Louise's eyes drop to his hand but there was no expression on her face. She looked exhausted, if anything.

Remembering Tom Denver's reaction to their arrival on his doorstep, Kate paused in the act of packing away her things. "Were Karyn and Tom having problems with their marriage?"

Both Whites looked at her. Louise was the first to speak. "Problems?"

"Yes." Kate didn't elaborate. She remembered Tom Denver's words. *She's not my wife, she's nothing to do with me anymore.*

The Whites exchanged a glance. "Well," Louise began slowly – and with seeming reluctance. "They – they were arguing quite a lot. I don't know that it was anything serious but – well, I think things had been a bit strained. I don't really... Karyn didn't mention anything specific but when she was here for Christmas, and Tom wasn't – well, it was obvious that something was going on."

Kate had been scribbling busily. "Would you have said that Karyn was worried? Depressed?"

Louise bit her lip. "I don't know. It's funny at Christmas, isn't it? It's always a bit – a bit fraught." She looked down at her lap. "Karyn did seem a bit... subdued, I suppose is the word. Not depressed, exactly. Just maybe a bit quieter than she would normally have been."

Kate looked at Paul White. "What were your impressions, Mr White?"

"Me?" Paul looked startled to be asked directly. "Oh, well, I think Louise is right. Karyn was a bit quiet. But then, it was hectic anyway, with the children running around overexcited, and my parents were here too. I think Karyn maybe felt a bit left out, not being family."

"Did she normally spend Christmas with you?" asked Kate, curious.

"Not normally." Louise wiped her eyes again. "I just thought I'd ask her this time around because – well, I knew things were a bit strained with Tom and I thought she might like a break. That's all."

***

Kate drove straight home after her interview with the Whites, determined to spend an evening at her own house for once, keeping Merlin company. She parked the car and made her way to her front door, shivering in the icy wind. Luckily, she had plenty of firewood... Kate hurried inside, flicked the switch on the boiler to turn on the heating and began to lay a fire.

When she was home for the night, she normally tried to mentally switch off from thoughts of work. It wasn't always possible. In the most wrenching and stressful cases, Kate had sometimes found it preferable to go back to the office and continue working, rather than pretend she was trying to relax at home.

The Karyn Denver case wasn't one of those cases. But... There was something intangible about it that was making Kate uneasy. But what? She slowly paced up and down before the flickering flames in the grate, watching her socked feet move back and forth on the rug. What was it about this case that made her pause? Kate came to a stop and stared at the fire. It sometimes worked for inspiration, watching the dancing flames and the glowing coals.

Kate reviewed what she knew. It seemed likely that Karyn Denver had been out running and her death was the result of a fall from the top of Blackdown Gorge. Had she slipped? There was little physical evidence of that at the scene, although that didn't necessarily mean it hadn't happened. Had she deliberately thrown herself over? Kate thought back to the conversation she'd had with Louise and Paul White. From their words, it seemed as though Karyn had been a bit depressed. And clearly, things were not right with her husband. But was that sufficient motive for suicide?

Kate blinked and looked away from the flames. Then, before she could forget, and also so she could start to attempt clearing her mind of the job, she fetched her notebook from her bag and wrote *check medical records – any history of depression/mental illness?* She thought for a moment and wrote *interview Tom Denver*. Kate paused, tapping the pen against her chin. Merlin sauntered into the room and made a beeline for her lap, jumping up and curling up against her. Kate dropped an absent-minded kiss on his black head and, shifting slightly so she could still reach the notebook, wrote *Paul White?*

She capped her pen and sat back, stroking Merlin. She had no real idea of where the thought of interviewing Paul White came from again. It was nothing more than a feeling. She'd had cases like this before, cases where her intuition had served her well, whispering ever more strongly as the case progressed, flowing through the undercurrents of what had really happened. Then again, she'd had cases where her intuition had led her completely down the garden path, so it wasn't exactly a great substitute for normal police work.

"A feeling is not evidence," Kate remarked to Merlin, who flicked an ear in response. She smiled and sat back against the back of the sofa, stroking his silky black back and trying to think of something else.

Chapter Six

THE NEXT MORNING SAW KATE, Chloe, Theo and Rav waiting expectantly (and with not a little apprehension) for the ongoing debrief with their new DCI. Kate had made an effort to get in early, so early that even Olbeck, a notorious early riser, hadn't beaten her to her desk. Already primed with two strong coffees, Kate felt up to taking on whatever Nicola Weaver might throw at her.

As it was, DCI Weaver was late – not very late, just late enough for it to slightly inconvenience the rest of them, without being so late that it would attract comment. She didn't so much sweep as sidle into the room, catching them all chatting amongst themselves and not even about the case; about the current shambles that the British government was making of Brexit (Theo), how the wrong person had won Strictly Come Dancing (Chloe) and the latest triumph of Manchester United (Rav). Kate, uninterested in most of these topics, was watching the leafless branches of a tree outside sway in the breeze.

"Good morning," said the quiet voice of DCI Weaver, which somehow managed to penetrate everyone's consciousness in a way that almost made them jump. They all turned to face her. She bestowed upon them a smile that ran the gamut of warmth as it was turned about the room; from a fairly big beam at Theo, cooling rapidly as it swept over Rav and Chloe, before ebbing and failing altogether just as it got to Kate. Kate, conscious of this, breathed in sharply through her nose but kept her face in neutral.

She doesn't like me. Why? Kate pondered this just as she heard Olbeck's office door open and his footsteps come over to join them.

"Morning, Nicola," he said cheerily, seating himself by Kate as was his custom.

"Good morning – Mark." DCI Weaver flared her nostrils for a second before speaking again. "I understand that you're all used to a fairly informal debrief with your DCI. I work somewhat differently. From now on, we'll be having weekly individual meetings to ascertain how you're getting on and so I can monitor the progression of your cases." She paused as if to allow a protest or comment. When none came, she gave a tiny cough and carried on. "My assistant will contact you to arrange a time that's mutually convenient. We will also all have a more formal, minuted weekly group meeting."

"Um—" began Olbeck but Nicola forestalled him with a chilly smile.

"You and I will also meet twice-weekly, DI Olbeck, at a time that suits us both. I know how busy you are."

Nicola paused and looked about the room. Kate could see Chloe struggling not to say something and beamed a thought towards her. *Don't make her make you say it.* Chloe, like Kate, had a temper and Kate didn't want her friend's card further black-marked.

Chloe must have sensed what Kate was trying to

say – either that or she thought better of it. The silence in the room dragged out a few moments longer before Nicola cleared her throat and bent her head towards the clipboard that she held. "What else? Oh yes. As we're new to working with one another, I thought it might be rather productive to have some training together – some team building exercises and so forth. Again, my assistant will be contacting you with the details, to make sure we can all be available for the event I've got planned."

Again she paused, but the team stared stonily back at her and remained silent. Kate wondered whether Nicola Weaver actually knew how much they disliked her, and just didn't care, or did she genuinely think that they were happy to hear all this?

"Well, I'll let you get on with things. Look out for those emails, and I'll be in my office should you need me. Just make sure you check with Linda first."

She bestowed another wintry smile around the room and glided to the doorway, shutting it quietly behind her.

Kate held her breath, counting silently to ten. She'd reached seven before Chloe exploded.

"What the *hell*?"

"Now, now," Olbeck rebuked mildly. "She's got her own way of doing things. It doesn't necessarily mean it's a worse way."

Chloe paced up and down, shaking her hands in the air. "She keeps talking about teamwork but she won't let us debrief together as a team? What the f—"

"She did say we're going to be doing some team building exercises," Rav said hastily.

Chloe shot him a look. "Yeah. Because we've all got *so much free time* and *so little work*, we can take a few days out to go to some wanky conference centre to learn how to work as a team when we already bloody *do* work as a team!"

Kate, while agreeing with every word, thought it was possible that Chloe, right at the moment, wasn't prepared to listen to any kind of reason. She got up, went over to the coffee machine, and began to prepare everyone a hot drink. Biscuits might help. They always helped Kate.

By the time she came back with the drinks, Chloe had stopped pacing and had cast herself into her chair, pecking away at her keyboard in an irritated fashion. Rav and Theo had also started work. Kate distributed out her little hot beverage peace offerings. When she got to Rav, she thought of something.

"Has anything come in from the witness boards? Anything useful at all?"

Rav took the steaming mug from her gingerly. "Thanks for this. And yes, actually, something did come in. I was just about to run it past the boss when – well, it all kicked off."

Kate sat down on a nearby chair. "Tell me more."

"Right, well, time of death has been narrowed down to sometime around midday of Thursday twenty-eighth of December, right?"

"Has it?"

"Yeah, Andrew sent over the report earlier. I guess you haven't read it yet?"

"Next on my list," Kate said hastily. "Anyway, if that's the case, what's the deal?"

"Someone called in after seeing one of the boards in the forest. They were apparently walking their dog there on that day – the twenty-eighth – and they said they heard an argument and then a scream. But it was quite a long way off and so they thought they might have been mistaken. Anyway—" Rav stopped talking for a moment and began hunting around on his desk. "Where is it? Oh, here we go." He extracted a piece of paper from a cardboard folder. "This guy, the dog walker, he seems legit."

Kate took it and skim-read it. The witness, an Alan Abercrombie, seemed to be a frequent dogwalker in that part of the woods. Kate read through the rest of the notes. Apparently, Abercrombie had overheard raised voices over on the other side of the gorge to where he'd been walking. A few minutes later, he thought he had heard a scream but when he listened out for more, he heard nothing and had concluded that perhaps he'd been mistaken or, in his own words, 'it was just teenagers messing about'. Once he'd seen the police notice boards, he'd realised that he might actually have been a witness to a crime.

"I'm going to go and see him today," said Rav, taking the report back from Kate as she held it out to him. "It probably doesn't need two of us, unless you want to come?"

"Thanks." Kate was thinking of the long list of

things that she had to do herself. "I don't think I've got time, Rav. I'm sure you'll get all the information that could be useful."

Back at her own desk, Kate ran her eye down her 'to-do' list. Medical records, that was first on the list. Or should she interview Tom Denver first? Knowing from previous experience how difficult it was to try and catch a GP between patient appointments, Kate pondered and then got up, gathering up her bag and coat.

It was slightly warmer outside than it had been for a while and the patches of frost on the ground were shrinking. It felt very damp, though, and the sky sagged like a heavy grey blanket. Kate turned the car heater up and felt the welcome warmth on her face as she drove out of the station carpark. She was chancing her arm with Tom Denver, having not rung ahead to make an appointment, but perhaps that was for the best.

When she drove up to park outside the Denver house, she could see there was a car already in the driveway, a silver Ford. Perhaps he was home... Quickly, Kate pulled her coat on and got out of the car.

Tom Denver took so long to answer the door that Kate almost gave up and turned back. Eventually, after several rings at the doorbell and multiple knocks with the doorknocker, the door slowly swung open.

Tom Denver stood there silently, much as he had the first time Kate and Theo had visited him. He looked scruffier than he had done then, the grey sweatshirt he was wearing stained and marked. Kate could smell stale alcohol fumes even from three feet away. For a second, her mother reappeared in her memory; all those mornings before school, breathing whiskey fumes over Kate when she kissed her goodbye. That's when her mother was actually up and awake in the mornings. Half the time, it had been Kate getting her younger brother and sisters ready for school.

Pushing the memories away, Kate smiled neutrally and introduced herself again. She dropped the smile quickly, reminding herself that she was addressing a widower. Or was she? She needed to get to the bottom of the Denvers' relationship, but it was going to be tricky with this man.

"I'm very sorry to bother you, Mr Denver, but I was hoping to come in and speak to you for a few moments."

For a second, she thought he was going to refuse and then he stepped back a little, just as silently, and made a faint gesture with his hand to the open doorway.

"I haven't got long." His voice was deep, abrupt – he sounded as though those could have been the first words he'd spoken all day.

"Thank you."

Kate walked into the house, conscious of a prickle of unease. It was partly the darkness of the house – all the curtains and blinds that she could see were drawn – but it was mostly the brooding presence of Tom Denver, with his forbidding frown. Kate, swallowing her nerves, heading for what she assumed (rightly, as it turned out) to be the living room.

She seated herself on the edge of the leather sofa, taking in her surroundings whilst seeming to busy herself with the contents of her handbag. It was a room that had probably once been quite cosy and welcoming but now it had that indefinable air of neglect that characterised a house where nobody was making much of an effort anymore. Whilst not exactly dirty, it was messy, cluttered; dust was clearly visible on the blank screen of the television. Fluff, crumbs, and other detritus littered the carpet.

Tom Denver sat opposite her in an armchair. "Well?"

Kate cleared her throat and gave him the standard words of condolence. She deliberately used the words 'your wife', to see if he'd return the same, strange answer as he had when they'd first come to break the news to him.

He was silent for a moment. Then he said, "I told you, she wasn't my wife anymore."

"I'm afraid, in the eyes of the law, she still was, sir. I understand you'd recently separated."

He moved a little in his chair and Kate, nerves singing, managed not to flinch. "Who told you that?"

"I'm afraid I can't say, sir. Is it not true?"

Tom Denver looked at her. "Oh, yes, it's true. We split up a few weeks ago."

"I'm sorry." Kate looked down at her notes, giving herself time. "I'm sure you understand, Mr Denver, in the case of a suspicious death we have to look into all sorts of things. The personal relationships of the victim, their family background, their history."

"This is suspicious, is it?" Tom Denver sounded just a shade wrong – just a tiny bit too casual – in stark contrast to his previous mood.

"At the moment, we're proceeding on that basis, sir.

We'll know more as further evidence comes to light." Kate looked at him fully, realising he was actually quite good-looking, if you could see past the scowl. "I was wondering if you could tell me a little more about Karyn. Had the two of you been married long?"

Tom Denver clearly realised she wasn't going to give up easily. He sighed and sagged back in his armchair, his arms loosening in a gesture of defeat. "Almost fifteen years. It's our wedding anniversary next month."

"Did she have any history of depression? Any kind of mental illness?"

The scowl grew deeper. "No. Nothing like that. Karyn was always boringly sane."

The contempt was there, or was it anger? Did he care that his wife had died? Was he glad? Kate was beginning to feel more and more uneasy around him. She decided to stop pussyfooting around and asked him directly why he and Karyn had split up.

For a moment, she thought he wasn't going to answer. "We just drifted apart, that's all. We didn't have much in common anyway, and I suppose we just came to the conclusion that we were better off apart."

He looked directly at Kate as he said this but somehow, she knew he was lying. Or, if not lying, leaving out a significant portion of the truth. She hesitated, wondering whether to dig deeper. Then she decided not to. She did have one final question for him.

"Can I ask where you were on Thursday the twenty-eighth of December, around midday, sir?"

Tom Denver didn't ask her why she was asking that. He stared stonily at her and answered. "I was at work."

"Where do you work, sir?"

"At Reed Publishing." Kate knew it – it was one of the largest employers in the town. "I'm an accountant."

Kate thanked him and scribbled down her notes. It would be easy enough to check whether Tom Denver had actually been in the office that day. She dotted the full stop at the end of her sentence and capped her pen. Was he actually under suspicion? *Everyone's under suspicion, Kate*. Tom Denver was still clearly very angry at his wife for some reason. Just for leaving? But that didn't necessarily mean he'd killed her. If she had *been* killed.... With difficulty, Kate stopped herself from sighing out loud.

***

SHE DROVE BACK TO THE office feeling frustrated. It was turning out to be one of *those* cases: muddled, obstructed, full of feelings she couldn't quite put her finger on. Much like your relationship with Anderton, said the little gremlin who sporadically piped up with unhelpful mental comments. Kate gritted her teeth and pressed the accelerator down harder.

Chapter Seven

KATE WAS RUBBING HER EYES and yawning over her desk the next morning when Rav slapped down a folder in front of her face and made her jump.

"A good morning's always nice," she said grumpily, picking it up.

"Did you have a late night or something?" Rav looked far too chipper for Kate's liking. Dry January was clearly paying off. "Anyway, thought you'd want to see this."

"What is it?"

"We had someone call in yesterday, one of the Whites' neighbours. They reported seeing Karyn Denver leaving the White's house very late on Boxing Day, looking distressed. It's probably nothing but I thought you'd like to have a read."

That woke Kate up. She thanked Rav, who positively jogged back to his desk, and opened the folder to read.

The neighbour, who had asked to remain anonymous, had said pretty much what Rav had just told her. That Karyn Denver had been observed leaving the home of Louise and Paul White at about 1am on the morning of the 27th of December. The report mentioned that Karyn had seemed visibly upset and distressed and had walked quickly off down the road, clutching her handbag and a second, larger bag. Nobody had followed her and it seemed the White house remained dark and with no signs of a disturbance. The neighbour hadn't thought much of it until the report of the finding of Karyn's body had made the local news.

Kate read it through once more and frowned. Then she got up and fetched the witness statement from Alan Abercrombie, the dog walker who had apparently overheard an argument in Blackdown Woods on the day of Karyn's death. She read through it again, more slowly this time. There was little to go on. Abercrombie had been too far away to overhear what was said, or even if the voices belonged to a man or a woman – or both – but he had definitely heard raised, angry voices and a minute or two later, what he'd thought was a scream. "I listened hard after that for a few moments but heard nothing. It was getting cold and so I decided to go home." Kate read through to the end of the paragraph, her eyes focusing on one particular sentence. "I did think I saw a man on the opposite side of the gorge walking quickly in the opposite direction. He had on a red and black coat which caught my eye, but it was literally just for a moment before he went behind the trees and out of sight."

Kate sat back. The two pieces of information were so thin, so little to go on, but... But... After a moment, she pulled up details of Paul White, noting down his workplace and Googling the number. She'd been meaning to interview him for a while, and this would probably be a good time. She'd call into Reed Publishing too, on the way, and find out whether Tom Denver had actually been in the office at the time of his wife's death.

It was still cold when Kate made her way to the car park, but nowhere near as frosty as it had been. As Kate unlocked the driver-side door, her eye Was caught by something heartening, the early green spikes of what looked like snowdrops, poking out from the mud on the verge. Spring was hopefully just around the corner...

***

Reed Publishing was nearer to the police station than Paul White's workplace. Kate parked in the spacious visitor car park and made her way to the reception area. She ascertained from the helpful, if slightly alarmed, receptionist who Tom Denver's supervisor was and was quickly ensconced in their office. It was perhaps fortunate that because of the time of year, things were less busy than they could have been.

"Oh, yes, Tom was here on the twenty-eighth. I must admit I was slightly surprised, because he normally takes that Christmas week off but he didn't this year." Norman Frankl, Denver's boss, was a portly, cheerful looking middle-aged man. "Yes, he was definitely here."

"For the whole day?" Kate scribbled busily in her notebook.

"Well, I suppose so. I didn't exactly have him under *observation*." Frankl twinkled at her from behind his thick glasses. "With the building being what it is, we're not exactly open plan." Kate could appreciate that; the Reed Publishing company being located in an old, renovated building, full of wood panelling and wall beams.

"But he was definitely here. I saw him to say goodbye to at the end of the day."

"Right. Thank you." Kate stood up, wondering whether it was worth asking her next question. "Could you just show me where his office is, exactly?"

"Of course, my dear. I'll take you there myself." Frankl courteously indicated the door of his office and stood back to let Kate go first. "He's not actually there, you know, today. Poor man, we've given him compassionate leave for a fortnight."

Kate nodded. "You were aware that he and his wife had actually separated before she died?"

Frankl looked faintly shocked. "Had they? No – no, I had no idea. But Tom's very reserved, you know. Keeps things close to his chest. He never used to talk about his private life."

Frankl led Kate along a bewildering series of corridors and small, rickety staircases before indicating a small room tucked away at the end of a dark passage. "Here you go."

Kate thanked him and took a look inside. It was cramped but neat, with a modern desk and chair rather starkly contrasting with the almost medieval surroundings of the actual building. More pertinently, it wasn't overlooked and had only one small window, which looked out onto the wall of the opposite building. Kate stood for a moment, thinking. Could Tom Denver have slipped out, that day? Crept out to track down his wife on her run in Blackdown Forest? Kate remembered that seething undercurrent of anger that she'd sensed running through him at both their meetings. She pondered for a moment longer and then turned towards the door. Then she froze. Hanging on the back of the door was a man's jacket, black with a red collar.

Norman Frankl was still babbling on about Tom and the way the office had clubbed together to send flowers and if he could help in any more ways, then he'd be happy to. Kate gave him a professional smile, held a hand up as a visual brake to his verbal diarrhoea, and told him she'd seen all she needed to see and would be in touch if anything else came up.

Striding out to her car, Kate pondered her next move. Okay, so the victim's husband had a similar coat to the one seen by the only witness to the crime. But did that actually mean anything? So had probably hundreds, if not thousands, of people in this town. Kate reached her car and flung herself into the driver's seat, reaching for her notebook. *Coat,* she scribbled. *Worth impounding? Check CCTV around building to see if Denver ever left on the 28th.*

The trouble was, as Kate knew full well, that none of the evidence was solid enough to even risk an arrest warrant, let alone a charge. And where was the motive? Okay, so the Denvers had split up, but that didn't normally warrant a murder charge. Frustrated, Kate threw her notebook over on the passenger seat with her gloves, handbag and coat and started the engine.

She heard her mobile phone start ringing as she negotiated her way across Abbeyford to Paul White's workplace but didn't have time to pull over to answer it. She knew it was probably Anderton – he'd taken to ringing her during the day, not for anything in particular but just for a chat. Kate sympathised – she knew he was probably a bit lonely stuck at home, not to mention the fact that a man of Anderton's energy and intellect didn't take kindly to boredom – but it was getting more and more difficult to find the time to talk to him. I'll phone him later, she promised herself, trying to concentrate on the sat nav's directions.

Chapter Eight

PAUL WHITE'S PLACE OF WORK could not have been in greater contrast to that of Thomas Denver's. The office buildings containing the solicitors' practice of Chipstead, Denham and White were almost brand new; built of angular cream-coloured stone, black cladding and some rather startling but undeniably effective strips of copper. Their burnished hue reflected the struggling rays of the sun, which were just creeping out from behind the cloud.

Kate had rung ahead, if only by ten minutes, to ascertain that Paul White would be in the office. She was quickly shown through to where he was located, and he opened the door to her himself, shaking hands courteously. For all that, Kate could sense an undercurrent of anxiety in his slightly too casual small talk, just a tiny thrum underneath the superficial normality. But that was actually quite normal when interviewing people who didn't have a lot to do with the police in day-to-day life. It didn't necessarily mean he was hiding something. As Kate sat down, she took a surreptitious look at the back of his office door but the only coat there was a dark-grey, pinstriped suit jacket, matching the trousers Paul White was currently wearing.

"Where was I?" Paul White sounded almost

shocked to be asked. "On the day – I presume that was the day Karyn – well, died?"

Kate smiled neutrally. "If you could just let me know, sir, where you were from half eleven am on the twenty-eighth of December last year?"

Paul White frowned. "Well, um – it was Christmas week, wasn't it? So I took the week off, I normally do – spend time with the family and all that. So, um, I would have been at home."

"I see. What were you doing at that particular time, Mr White?"

Paul White was looking slightly more relaxed now. "Oh, gosh. Half eleven on a holiday day? Probably just watching TV, something like that."

"Did you go out at all that day?"

Paul White looked hard at her and then smiled. "No. No, I don't think so. I didn't have any reason to go out, and I like relaxing at home."

"Was your wife at home?"

The hunted look came back, if only briefly. "Louise? Yes, of course she was. She was doing a big declutter of the whole house in time for New Year."

Kate nodded. Was there actually any point to this? What did she have to go on, apart from a vague feeling that something wasn't quite right?

She cleared her throat. "We have a witness statement that says they saw Karyn Denver leave your house at one am on Boxing Day – so, actually, on the twenty-seventh but very early – in a distressed state. Can you tell me anything about that?"

Paul White stared at her. "What?"

Kate met his gaze calmly and repeated her question. Paul White blinked and then said, somewhat reluctantly, "Well, she had been upset, a bit, earlier in the evening. Both Louise and I were trying to help, you know, calm her down. I think the situation with Tom had been getting at her and you know what Christmas is like. But I didn't think she'd actually left. Not that night."

"Really?" Kate looked down at her notes and then up again. "You didn't notice that she wasn't there in the morning."

Paul's face cleared. "Oh, no, we didn't actually, because she'd already said she'd have to leave early, she had some sort of appointment the next day."

"What was this appointment?"

Paul White shrugged. "I've no idea, sorry. She didn't go into details. But she said it was first thing so she'd slip out early in the morning without disturbing us." He rubbed a finger along his jaw and added, "This is just an impression – I don't know – just an *inkling* that she might have been going to see a divorce lawyer. But I really don't know."

Kate pressed him for more details, but he continued to repeat that he knew nothing else, that Karyn Denver had been distressed earlier but that both he and Louise had succeeded in calming her down and that they'd all gone to bed at the usual time. He stressed again that Karyn had told them she'd had an early morning appointment and they hadn't expected to see her in the morning.

At length, Kate knew she'd got everything from Paul

White that she was likely to get. It seemed straightforward enough but... Kate was thinking hard as she took leave of Paul White and headed back to her car. What was this mysterious appointment of Karyn's on the 27th December? If, in fact, it had actually existed? Had she actually left at one am? that morning and, if so, why? What exactly had she been upset about? Paul White had been vague, saying that Louise had done most of the comforting, and he'd merely made hot drinks before retiring and leaving the women to it.

Kate drove to the White's house, taking a chance that Louise would be in. In fact, she was, looking calmer but no less unhappy. She led Kate into the sitting room and offered tea.

"I still can't really believe it," Louise said, bringing in two steaming mugs and handing one to Kate. "I mean, I know it's happened, I mean logically I know it's happened, but I still can't really *believe* it." Her voice had that same note of bewilderment that Kate had heard so many other times when talking to the recently bereaved.

"That's very normal," Kate said sympathetically. She sipped her tea with gratitude – breakfast seemed a long time ago. "It's a curve, and you have to move through the stages. It's just incredibly hard, and I do know how you feel."

Louise pressed her lips together and her eyes grew glassy. "I just miss her so much. We spent so much time together and now—" She broke off, blinking hard and raising her own mug to her lips.

Kate allowed her a moment and then began. "I'm

just trying to build up a picture of what happened on the twenty-eighth of December, Mrs White. I'm sure you can understand how valuable that is to us in this kind of investigation."

Louise nodded. "I can. I've been obsessing over it myself, you know, going over and over and over it… I suppose just seeing if I can get my head around it, what happened." She looked pleadingly at Kate, who nodded reassuringly.

"Again, Mrs White, that's completely normal. Once you've been through the trauma of a bereavement, it's completely normal to try and piece things all together again and again. I suppose it's the brain's way of trying to process it." Kate put her tea mug down to pick up her pen. "I've spoken to your husband, who tells me that Karyn was upset the night before she left here. So, Boxing Day. Is that right?"

Louise stared at her for a moment blankly and then her face cleared. "Oh – oh, yes, she was, a bit. You know I'd said before she was a bit down generally, because of Tom and, well, her marriage falling apart, really. That's enough to get anyone down, let alone with Christmas thrown in as well." She paused for a breath and Kate nodded encouragingly. "Well, we'd all had a bit to drink on Boxing Day, and we were watching TV – there was that really good BBC adaptation of that Agatha Christie book on – we both loved Agatha Christie – anyway, and Karyn just started crying." Kate saw Louise's own eyes fill with sympathetic tears. "We didn't really talk much about it, I could see she didn't want to. I mean, I tried, but she just didn't want to. So I just gave her a hug, and Paul made her a hot drink and well, that was it, really."

Kate was busy writing all this down. She looked up from her notepad. "And you don't know why she left in the middle of the night?"

Louise's eyes widened. "Left in the middle of the night?" She looked astonished. "Did she?"

"Yes, apparently," said Kate. "One of your neighbours saw her going down the street at about one am."

Louise looked even more astonished and then tearful. "Oh – I thought she left really early in the morning. She'd said she had an appointment and she would go early so as not to disturb us. Oh, God, she must have been feeling even worse than she let on—" Her voice wobbled and she stopped speaking, pressing her fingers to her mouth.

"You don't know what this appointment was, I suppose?" Kate asked.

Louise shook her head slowly. A tear rolled down one cheek and she brushed it off almost angrily. "No. No, she wouldn't say. I didn't want to push her. To be honest, I was pretty tired and a bit drunk myself by then, so I just wanted to go to bed. Oh, I should have listened—" She broke off and then spoke again. "I wonder – I wonder if she was going back to Tom? You know, whether she thought she'd made a mistake, or that she wanted to see him or – or, I don't know—" She looked across at Kate, smiling painfully. "I'm sorry, I'm babbling. I'm just really upset."

Kate said various soothing things and gradually Louise began to sound a little more in control. Kate flexed her hand, aching from writing quickly, and pressed on with her questions.

"Can you tell me what you got up to on the twenty-eighth of December, Mrs White? From, say, late morning onwards."

Louise tucked her hair behind her ear on one side. "I was here, all day, I think. I was doing the normal – I mean, every year between Christmas and New Year I try and do a bit of a clear-out of the house, you know, start the new year with a fresh start, that sort of thing. So I was doing that."

"All day?"

"Yes. I mean, I stopped for lunch and everything, but I was here."

"And how about your husband, he was here too?"

"Oh yes, he must have been."

"You're sure?" Kate said it as casually as she could.

"Yes." Louise wiped her eyes again with a tissue. "Oh, wait, he did pop out actually. Not for long, just to get some milk, I think, we were almost out after Christmas."

"When was that?" Kate asked, in an equally casual tone.

Louise puffed out her cheeks in a considering fashion. "Oh, I can't remember exactly. Not that early. Mid-morning? I can't remember to be honest, it wasn't late, that's all I know."

"Right," said Kate, feeling a slow burn of excitement in her stomach but determined not to show it. "Did either of you speak to anyone that day? Go on social media? Anything like that?"

Louise looked a bit nonplussed. "I don't do Facebook, I'm afraid. Um – oh, I did speak to my brother. I remember because I was halfway up the attic ladder when he rang, and I nearly fell off. That must have been late morning."

Kate nodded. "And Paul had left by that time?"

Louise shrugged. "I think so. I hadn't seen him for a while so I'm really not sure. He was back by about one o'clock though, because that's normally when we eat lunch at the weekend and he was home by then."

"Thanks, that's very helpful." Kate, to throw Louise off the scent, asked a few more innocuous questions and then asked if she could use the facilities.

"Of course, I'll show you the downstairs loo." Louise led her to the downstairs cloakroom, located as were most in these Victorian conversions, under the stairs.

Kate closed the door and locked it. She'd hazarded a guess that this cloakroom would contain the bulk of the family coats and her hunch had been correct. Quickly, running the tap to hide any noises, she flicked through the different garments. There were raincoats and children's jackets, waxed Barbour coats and – yes – Kate pulled it from under a pile of other coats – a black and red coat. It was large, obviously a man's. Kate stared at it for a moment and then hung it back up and put the other garments on top of it. She was getting a glimmering of understanding – just a glimmer – but it was enough to go on, for now. She felt like this in most cases; as if the solution was hidden behind a thick bank of fog and gradually, as the clues were uncovered and the evidence mounted, the fog thinned and eventually cleared, leaving the *why* and the *how* and the *who* in clear sight.

Chapter Nine

"You want what?"

Despite DCI Weaver's incredulous tone, Kate refused to be cowed. "I'd like to pull the phone records of Paul White and Karyn Denver."

"And your reason for doing so?"

Kate resisted the impulse to answer along the lines of *because it's police work, Nicola baby. Didn't anyone ever tell you that*? Instead, she took a deep breath, smiled and said "I have a feeling that we might find something of interest there."

Nicola Weaver stared at her with her lip curled. Then, probably because she couldn't be bothered to argue, shrugged and looked away. "Do as you like, DS Redman. Please don't make extra work for our IT department just for the sake of it, though."

"Of course not." Kate kept the smile on her face, damned if she was going to let the other woman see how much she riled her.

"Keep me up to speed if you do find anything." Nicola Weaver turned to face her computer screen in a dismissive fashion.

No, I thought I'd keep it all to myself, you stupid cow. Kate smiled until she felt her cheeks begin to ache and then quietly left Nicola's office, shutting the door behind her.

She thumped down into her chair with such force that Chloe, opposite her, looked up, startled. "What's the matter?"

Kate kept her voice low. "Nicola *sodding* Weaver."

Chloe rolled her eyes in a sympathetic fashion. "Don't let her get to you. It's not worth it."

"I know," said Kate, sighing. She picked up the phone and dialled the IT department. Chloe overheard her conversation with interest.

"You think there'll be something there, then, do you?"

"I do. Don't ask me how I know. It's really just a hunch – no more than that."

"That's good," Chloe said absently, her eyes drawn to her computer screen. Then she looked back at Kate. "God, I miss the boss, don't you?" Then she laughed. "Oh, wait, you don't have to."

Kate smiled a little awkwardly. She and Chloe hadn't really spoken about the fact that Kate and Anderton were in a relationship. In fact, Kate realised, it was some time since she'd spent time with any of her friends: Chloe, Olbeck, Hannah. All her spare time lately had been spent with Anderton. Perhaps that wasn't very healthy. She made a promise to herself then that she'd try to find a bit more balance in her personal life. It wasn't that she didn't want to spend time with her friends, it was just that, currently, Anderton seemed to need her more...

"How's that going?" Chloe asked. She sounded honestly interested, rather than catty.

"Oh, fine." Kate shuffled some papers on her desk.

"I bet he misses being here. Or maybe he doesn't. Maybe he'd had enough."

"I don't know," said Kate, honestly. "I really don't know how he feels about it."

"Don't you talk about it?"

Kate was uncomfortable with where the conversation was going. "Well, we do and we don't. Anyway, I've got to go and get those numbers, Chloe. See you later."

"Bye, bird." Chloe gave her a grin and returned to her own work.

As Kate headed towards the stairs to the IT department in the basement of the building, she heard her mobile ringing. Retrieving it from her pocket, she saw Anderton's name flashing from the screen and suppressed a sigh.

"Hello?"

"Hello, it's me. How's your day going?"

"Fine." Kate, conscious of the time, was about to tentatively suggest she call him back at a later point when he surprised her.

"I've been thinking. I think you should retake your inspector exams."

That brought Kate to a standstill. "You do? Really?"

"Yes," Anderton's voice said firmly. "It's time for you to take the next step, Kate. You need to keep moving up."

"Well—" Kate considered the idea. She'd failed the exams some years ago and that had really stung, although the hurt was in the past now. "Well, I'll think about it. I'll certainly think about it – if you think I've got a good chance of getting them."

"I do. We can talk about it later, anyway. I know you're busy." Was that a wistful note she could hear in his voice? "Anyway, are you coming round to mine later or shall I come to you?"

"To me, please," Kate said, thinking of poor Merlin. "But we might have to get a takeaway because I haven't got any food."

"Leave it with me."

Kate, pleased with his confidence in her, said she'd look forward to that and said goodbye. She also felt a little relieved – and guilty at her relief – that she hadn't been side-tracked into a long conversation. Quickly she ran down the stairs, thinking that if she could get those numbers by the end of the day, that might mean she could leave on time for once.

***

With the promise of the phone records to be on her desk by close of business, Kate skipped back up to the office and thought about lunch. She took a quick look out of the window; the sky was grey and mist clung to the distant shape of the hills beyond the edges of Abbeyford. It wasn't actually raining, though. Determined to get a bit of a break, Kate grabbed her coat and bag and then hurried over to Olbeck's office to see if he wanted her to get him a sandwich.

"I'm just popping out—" she began and then stopped dead, her head around the door. Olbeck was sitting at his desk, staring into space with tears rolling down his cheeks. Kate gasped. "Oh my god, what's wrong? What's wrong?"

Olbeck smiled at her, brushing at his wet cheeks. "That was Jeff, on the phone just now. The adoption order's signed. They're ours. Both of them. They're our children now."

Kate sagged in relief and found herself smiling back. "Oh, my. Oh, *Mark*." She found herself near tears and swallowed painfully. "Oh, *Mark*. What a relief."

Olbeck rubbed his face with his hands. "I can't believe it. I'm going to be a dad. I can't *believe* it." He stood up and Kate, honestly delighted for him, ran over and flung her arms around him.

"That is such wonderful news! I am so, *so* happy for you."

He hugged her back tightly and they stood like that for a moment, swaying together in the middle of the carpet.

"What the hell's going on here?"

Kate and Olbeck broke apart and turned to see Theo in the doorway with his hands full of folders, regarding them both with astonishment.

Kate opened her mouth to tell him and then shut it again. It was Olbeck's good fortune to tell.

He did so, and Theo's handsome face broke into a broad grin. "That's amazing, mate. Seriously, congratulations. I'm really pleased for you. Blimey, when I first came in I thought you'd crossed to the other side, you know what I mean?"

Kate laughed. "You *would* think that."

Theo winked at her. "Well, if anyone could turn a gay man, mate, I'm sure you could."

Kate rolled her eyes but she was feeling too happy

for Olbeck to make much of it. Instead, she suggested they all go out for a proper lunch, to celebrate, and Olbeck concurred. Theo regretfully declined, having an interview to take.

They went to the café rather than the pub, and Kate sat back and let Olbeck talk and talk and talk; a veritable flood of words, both delighted and apprehensive. She couldn't help a small tremor of grief; the regret and the sadness about what had happened in her past, but she knew that there would be time for her to examine that at leisure on her own that evening. For now, she owed it to her friend to listen and celebrate with him.

They walked back to the office in a very good mood, and Kate's was further improved by a sheaf of papers left on her desk with a little note from Joel in IT. Good, she could make a start on analysing those phone records. And if nothing came of it, she would at least know that she'd covered all bases and could move forward onto a new case with a clear conscience.

Chapter Ten

THE FIRE WAS REPLENISHED WITH a good supply of logs. Mozart played softly on the music system in the corner of the room, Merlin was curled in a half-moon on her stomach, and Anderton had her feet in his lap, rubbing her toes. All was well – or it should have been. Kate, staring up at the ceiling and trying to relax, was feeling more and more uneasy.

"What's up?" Anderton said eventually. "Am I doing this too hard?"

"No, no, it's lovely." Kate raised her head to look at him. "It's fine."

"So, what's wrong?"

Kate sighed and sat up, dislodging Merlin who leapt indignantly off her stomach to the floor and stalked from the room. "Just something at work."

"Our Nicola not annoying you further?"

Kate rolled her eyes. "Well, yes obviously, but – it's the Denver case, actually."

Anderton looked interested. "Come on, then. Spill."

Kate got up and retrieved her briefcase from the hallway and came back to sit down again, withdrawing the phone records from within it. She handed them to Anderton, fighting down a qualm that perhaps this was unethical in some way. After all, Anderton was technically still a police officer – he hadn't been *sacked*.

Anderton took them from her without comment but he raised his eyebrows.

Kate pointed to the highlighted parts of the record. "See those? Those are texts and calls from two phones. Karyn Denver's – and Paul White's."

Anderton's eyebrows rose higher. "That's a lot of contact. Daily. Multiple texts daily."

"I know. Far more than Paul White was sending to his wife, for example."

"Do you know what the content of the texts is?"

"Not yet. That'll mean some extra digging for IT. But I can guess."

"You think they were having an affair." Anderton quickly flicked through the rest of the sheets. "I'm thinking you're probably right."

Kate sighed. "So, given that someone like Paul White was seen in the vicinity of where Karyn Denver died, at the time when she died..."

Anderton put up his eyebrows again. "But if he's having an affair with her, why would he want to kill her?"

Kate shrugged. "What if she was pressurising him to leave his wife and he didn't want to? Or she was blackmailing him?"

"What about his wife?" asked Anderton. "She's surely got the best motive of all, if she discovered what was going on?"

Kate shook her head. "She's clearly devastated by her friend's death. You can't fake that kind of shock. And I checked her phone records. She never left the house that day. And that's the other thing. Paul White said *he* didn't leave the house that day. But his wife said he did. She said it quite unselfconsciously, in fact, it was like she'd almost forgotten that he had, but if she's telling the truth and he isn't..."

"Right." Anderton shuffled the papers together into a neat pile and handed them back to Kate. "So, what's your next move?"

"Bring Paul White in for questioning. I'll talk to the DCI tomorrow." Kate rolled her eyes again. "Although I'm sure she'll try and tell me I'm wasting my – and her – time." She sat herself down in Anderton's lap and kissed him. "I wish you were back there."

"Do you?" Anderton didn't say any more but returned her kiss with enough emphasis for Kate to realise, with a leap of pleasure, that the time for talking shop was now over.

***

KATE TOOK CHLOE ALONG WITH her to the White's house the next morning, thinking that perhaps she would make a more empathic officer than Theo. This was going to be a difficult arrest, no two ways about it. Chloe and Kate were silent in the drive to the house, perhaps thinking that very same thing.

Paul White opened the door, dressed in a suit and with a briefcase in his hand. Behind him, Kate could see the chaos of a family readying themselves for school and work and cursed under her breath. She hadn't thought about the children being here, although God knew she should have, seeing as it was only eight o'clock in the morning. All she'd wanted was to intercept Paul White before he left for work. She could tell, by the slight stiffening of Chloe's shoulder behind her, that her friend was thinking the same thing.

Paul White looked shocked and then angry at seeing them. "Yes?" he asked impatiently.

"Mr White, we'd like you to accompany us to the station this morning to answer some questions, please." Kate avoided saying police station in a hope that the children wouldn't overhear and be frightened.

Paul White looked even more annoyed. "Accompany you? Don't be absurd. I've got a meeting in half an hour—"

Chloe's limited supply of patience had worn thin. "Paul White, I'm arresting you on the suspicion of the murder of Karyn Denver. You do not have to say anything, but it may harm your defence if you do not mention when questioned something you later rely on in court."

There was a gasp from the corridor behind Paul White. Kate could see Louise White in the doorway of the kitchen, frozen, one child's school shoe in her hand. Thankfully the children weren't in sight and were hopefully out of earshot.

Louise came forward, the shoe dropping on the floor. "What's going on? What's the matter?"

"Your husband is just coming with us to answer some questions, Mrs White," Chloe responded smartly. She stepped forward with the cuffs in her hand. Paul White's eyes bulged at the sight.

"We don't have to use these," said Kate, "But we will do if we have to."

Still staring, Paul White spoke, failed, tried again. "That won't be necessary."

Chloe nodded approvingly. "Come with me to the car then, sir."

She led him away. Kate turned to watch, just in case Paul White decided to try something foolish. Chloe tucked him into the back of the car with practised ease, and Kate turned back. Louise White had come outside, onto the top step. Kate's eyes went to her face.

She'd expected to see horror, alarm, anxiety, confusion. Instead, Louise's gaze met hers.

The strangest thing happened; something that Kate had only experienced before with people she knew well. She had it many times with Anderton, several times with Olbeck, a handful of times with Chloe and her friend Stuart. It was almost like telepathy – a shared glance and somehow, you knew what the other person was thinking. It was a time when words were superfluous. One glance was literally all it took.

Kate had it now, as her eyes met Louise White's. As the implication hit her, she gasped and she could see by the contraction of Louise's face that the other woman felt something too.

"Come on," said Chloe, standing by the driver-side door. "Let's get back."

"Leave me here," murmured Kate, hardly aware of what she was doing. As she watched, Louise White turned sharply to head back inside her house.

"What—" was all that Kate heard from Chloe before she walked away, heading for the front door of the White house that had just been sharply closed.

Kate wasn't expecting Louise to answer her knock. She felt oddly dreamlike, as if someone else was raising her knuckles to the red paint, rapping once, twice on the wood.

Slowly the door opened. Louise stood there, shaking. Not just trembling but actually shaking, as if giant hands had her by the shoulders and were roughly agitating her back and forth. She said nothing but pulled the door wider, and Kate stepped inside.

They faced each other across the hallway.

"You knew," was all Kate said.

Louise's face contorted. For a moment, Kate thought she wasn't able to speak; wasn't physically able to form the words, the adrenaline coursing through her was so strong.

"I didn't." Louise's voice juddered. "Right up until Boxing Day. I had no idea. Wait, that's not right." She was the only moving thing in a silent space. "I knew something was wrong, I knew something was badly wrong, but I didn't know what. I didn't know what."

Kate opened her mouth to say something but Louise gave her no time.

"I confided in her. In Karyn. I cried in her arms about the state of my marriage." Kate flinched, unable to help it. Louise looked as though she had some kind of disease, a palsy, malaria; something to galvanically twitch every muscle in the body. "And all the time, she was it. The problem." Louise turned her head sharply to look across at the living room. "I came down on Boxing Day, after putting the kids to bed and they were there, kissing in the living room."

Kate took a deep breath. She began to say something, something comforting, something sympathetic, but Louise didn't give her the chance. She spoke on, bitterness flattening her voice, making an old woman out of her.

"The second I saw them, I knew. I knew I hadn't been mad, hadn't been paranoid, all the things that Paul told me I was when I confronted him. Of course, I had no idea it was *her*. I couldn't believe it. I *just couldn't believe it*." She stared at Kate with haunted eyes. "There's a part of me that still doesn't believe it. Not *Karyn*. Karyn wouldn't do that to me. Karyn wouldn't treat me like I would treat my worst enemy. She was my friend."

"I think—" began Kate, but it was useless. Louise spoke on, as if there was something in her compelling her to speak. Perhaps there was. Kate had seen this before; the wish for confession, perhaps for absolution.

"I don't know what hurts worse – the fact that either they both hated and despised me so much, that they thought this would be a suitable punishment. Or the fact that I mattered so little, that they didn't even give me a second thought. Both of them thought that a few orgasms were worth the – the rupture of my family. The heartbreak of my children when they don't have a father living with them anymore. They thought fucking each other was worth causing me the most excruciating pain I've ever had to experience in my life." She pressed the back of her hand to her mouth for a moment. "Do you know what it's like to look back at your life for the past few years and realise that it was all a lie? All of it? All those memories and things that you've done as a couple and as a family – *it's all lies*. It's all tainted, every single bit of it. Do you know how painful that is?"

Kate shook her head helplessly. For the first time in her life, she felt that, perhaps, a murder victim had had it coming.

Louise still fixed her with that burning gaze and for the first time, Kate saw something in her eyes that wasn't quite sane. Perhaps it was understandable, but it was there. She tensed, wondering what would be more inflammatory to the situation; allow Louise to continue to speak or to risk interrupting her.

Kate risked it. "So, what happened, Louise?" She was keenly aware that she hadn't cautioned her and mindful of the fall-out of the last case where Anderton had done the same, she wondered what to do.

Louise took a deep shuddering breath. She hadn't yet cried but her eyes glittered with something that wasn't tears. "Paul made her leave. I told him if he didn't, then I'd hurt her. I couldn't have stopped myself."

Kate thought back to how Louise had acted, through this entire case. She was a better actress than Kate had even dreamed. But then, thinking about it, Kate realised that she hadn't been acting at all. The shock, the psychological trauma – it had all been real. It was just that the cause of it had been different, that was all.

"So Karyn left your house early on the twenty-seventh," Kate said, phrasing it not really as a question. That would tally with what the neighbour had observed. She had a feeling that the next revelation from

Louise would be crucial to the success of a charge. She really must caution her, come what may. Bracing herself, she said, "Louise, I'm sorry. I'm more sorry for you than you might think. But I must do my job. I'm arresting you on the suspicion of the murder of Karyn Denver. You do not have to say anything, but it may harm your defence if you do not mention when questioned something which you later rely on in court. Anything you do say may be given in evidence." Kate took a deep breath and said it again. "I'm sorry."

Louise had stilled. Kate, nerves singing, resettled her feet slightly to give herself more stability. Then Louise sighed. She said, dully, "There's nothing more to say. Paul went out to meet her on the twenty-eighth of December. He knew she'd be out running and he said he wanted to tell her that it was over."

"And?" Kate held her gaze steadily.

Louise didn't drop her eyes. "And – Karyn died."

Silence fell. Kate broke it eventually by telling Louise that she had to accompany her to the police station.

"What about the children?" was all that Louise said.

"I'll call someone," said Kate. "They'll be fine."

She expected resistance but Louise merely nodded, her eyes downcast. They sat in silence, waiting for Social Services.

Chapter Eleven

"So, which of them is telling the truth?"

DCI Nicola Weaver stood with Kate, Chloe and Theo in the viewing gallery of the IT department in Abbeyford Station. On two separate screens in front of them, they could see Paul White and Louise White, both sat at an interview table with a solicitor beside them. Neither of them were talking – they were staring ahead, mute and miserable.

Kate was beginning to develop a substantial dislike of answering any of Nicola Weaver's questions. She was aware that this wasn't quite rational, but there you go... As it was, Theo spoke up.

"White's sticking to his story that he never left the house on the day of the murder. His wife maintains that he did go out, for about forty minutes, around the time that we think Karyn Denver died."

"That doesn't answer my question, DS Marsh." The half-smile that Nicola gave Theo was flirtatious enough to soften the criticism. Kate mentally raised her eyebrows.

"Yeah, right. Sorry." Theo didn't seem phased by either the comment or the smile. "We'll have to continue to interview them and see what we come up with."

"Good. You can take Paul White. DS Wapping, you take Louise White."

Kate waited to be given her orders. She could feel both Chloe and Theo's awkwardness as the silence stretched on. "And what about me?" she asked, as lightly as possible.

Nicola smiled sweetly. "Oh, you just take the one that suits you best, DS Redman."

The three of them watched her walk off. Kate wondered whether she'd been the only one to hear the needle in that deceptively innocent remark and she thought, from the puzzled look on Chloe's face, that perhaps she hadn't.

Nobody remarked on it. Instead, they headed for the interview rooms. Kate, in a spirit of *screw you, DCI Weaver*, decided to sit in on both of them and joined Theo first.

***

PAUL WHITE'S SOLICITOR WAS SOMEONE Kate hadn't seen before; a young-ish Asian man dressed in a suit who introduced himself as Kaleem Naswar. Paul White didn't take much notice of the introductions. He was staring at the top of the table, looking white and ill.

Theo didn't waste much time. "Right, Paul, you understand why you're here?"

Paul White didn't raise his head. "Not really," he muttered.

Theo glanced at Kate. "You've been arrested for the murder of Karyn Denver and cautioned for the same offence. Do you have anything to say?"

Naswar looked as if he was about to say something but Paul White didn't give him a chance. He lifted his head and fixed Theo with a glare. "I had nothing to do with Karyn's death, nothing."

"Nothing, Mr White?" Kate leapt in before Theo had a chance to speak. "You were having an affair with her?"

Paul White didn't blush but his face twisted for a moment. "No, I wasn't."

Theo slapped down a bunch of paper on the table, making both Paul and his solicitor jump. Kate, despite the gravity of the situation, bit back a laugh. "Phone records, Mr White. Shall I explain them to you?" Without waiting for an answer, he began to read from the paper. "'My gorgeous girl, it's been ages since we've been naked together.' 'Hey sexy lady, you still okay to meet up tonight? Can't wait to throw you on the floor and have my wicked way with you.'" Theo stopped reading and looked up. "Texts from your phone to Karyn Denver's. There are more. A lot more. Want to read them out?"

Now White did blush, a rosy hue that contrasted oddly with the hint of dark stubble on his jaw. He shook his head.

"Do you have anything to say?" pressed Theo relentlessly.

After a moment, White spoke, as if his throat hurt him. "All right. I was – we were – we had – it was a fling, that's all. It didn't mean anything."

Remembering the naked pain on Louise White's face, Kate was conscious of her fists closing under the table. Theo spoke again. "It didn't mean anything? So why were you in the woods where Karyn Denver's body was found, on the day of her death, at the time of her death?"

Paul White was beginning to look desperate. "Look, I wasn't there. I never left the house that day. Please – you have to believe me. Look, Karyn and I – what we did was wrong but it wasn't serious. I wasn't – I was never going to leave Louise and the kids, I couldn't do that, it would kill me."

"So you thought you'd just have a bit of fun on the side," said Kate, unable to keep the contempt from her voice. "And chose your wife's best friend with whom to do so."

White flinched. "It wasn't – it wasn't like that. It wasn't calculated. It just happened."

"Just happened?" Kate could feel the fury growing. "You just *happened* to have sex with your wife's best friend? Just like that? You didn't ever think of stopping?"

Theo shot her a glance and, with difficulty, Kate subsided.

Theo cleared his throat. "Was your wife with you all the time you were at the house on the twenty-eighth of December, Paul?" Kate knew that some officers, Olbeck in particular, liked to keep things as formal as possible for as long as possible, only using first names of suspects when they wanted to unsettle them, but Theo had once told Kate that, "They don't deserve the compliment of having a title, mate, know what I mean?"

Paul White's eyes flickered minutely. "Yes. Yes, of course she was."

"She didn't leave the house at any time?"

"No, she didn't."

"But you did?"

White frowned again. "I told you, *I didn't leave* the house."

Theo and Kate said nothing but let the silence grow in a meaningful way. Paul White shifted uneasily. His solicitor leant over and murmured something in his ear, to which he nodded.

Theo eventually spoke. "Did you meet Karyn Denver in the woods on the twenty-eighth of December, Paul?"

Paul White's jaw tensed. "No comment."

"Did you cause Karyn Denver's death?"

"No comment."

Kate sighed inwardly. *Here we go*. Once the 'no comments' started, the interview was effectively over. She tapped Theo's foot with her own and gave him a meaningful glance, meaning, *I'm out of here.* He nodded and said, for the benefit of the video tape, "DS Redman has left the interview."

***

KATE SHUT THE INTERVIEW ROOM behind her and stood for a moment in the corridor, wondering what to do. After a few minutes, she walked up to the other interview room, where she knew Chloe was interviewing Louise White. Kate stopped just outside the door, wondering if there was any point in her entering. Chloe was a good and experienced interviewer. And really, what was there to discover? Louise White may have had a motive, but her phone records showed she hadn't left the house on the day of Karyn Denver's death. Her husband had provided an alibi, for what that was worth. Paul White, on the other hand, had left the house – both his phone records and his wife had confirmed that. His distinctive jacket had been spotted in the vicinity of the ravine. Was that enough for a charge? Kate bit her lip. She realised that the interview room in which Louise White sat was one of the ones with a viewing mirror and hurried to the room where the mirror was located and stared in.

The sight of Louise White gave her a pinch of alarm. The woman looked close to a nervous collapse: her fingers twisted and writhed around themselves and she was compulsively turning her wedding ring around and around on her finger. Her eyes had a glazed stare that made Kate very uneasy. She could see now how thin Louise was, even thinner in the face than she had been the first time Kate had ever seen her, coming into the police station to report Karyn Denver missing.

Inside the room, Chloe had clearly come to the same conclusion as Kate – that Louise was very nearly at the end of her tether. Kate watched as Chloe manipulated the controls of the recording device and leant forward over the table, saying something to Louise to which the other woman barely responded.

Kate waited, watching. Chloe left the room, and a moment later she came into the viewing room, looking unsurprised to see Kate there.

"Alright, bird?"

"Yes. What do you think?"

"Of Louise?" Chloe's voice held a sigh. "She's – she's not in a good way."

"I thought that." The two of them watched Louise's hunched figure through the glass, her frantic twisting of her wedding ring. "Have you got anything useful?"

"Not really. She still insists that Paul White left the house that day, but that's all she'll say."

Kate reached out and rested her finger on the cold glass. "He insists he didn't. And he's adamant that Louise didn't either."

"Yeah, well, he's lying," said Chloe matter-of-factly. "He was there at the ravine when Karyn Denver died."

Kate kept her fingers resting on the cold glass. She could see her reflection, the slight frown on her face. "That's all we got though, isn't it?" she murmured. "Phone records and a witness sighting…"

She let the sentence drift away. Chloe was looking at her curiously. "What's up, bird?"

Kate took her fingers from the glass, sighing a little. "It's back to front."

"What is? The mirror?"

Kate half-laughed. "No. It's not that—" She broke off and looked at Chloe. "Listen, can I talk to her for a moment? I've got something – an idea…"

Chloe shrugged. "Be my guest."

***

LOUISE LOOKED UP DULLY AS Kate entered the interview room, which was something. The nervous movement of her hands stilled for a moment.

Kate sat down opposite her and gave her a sympathetic smile. It wasn't false; Kate had rarely felt so sorry for anyone as she had for this woman. Perhaps Louise sensed that as the desperation in her face lessened, just a little.

Kate leaned forward. "Louise," she said. "I want you to know that I get it. I'm on your side. I want to help you. Do you realise that?"

There was a moment's silence and then Louise gave a very faint and tremulous nod.

Kate spoke again. "You do realise that this could be the end of your family. Both you and your husband are under suspicion. Both you and your husband could be charged. And, I'll be frank, I'm worried about you. I think you're dangerously close to a nervous breakdown. So I suggest – I urge you – to tell me what really happened."

It was a long shot, but Kate had faith in herself. She'd seen this work with others, not least in Anderton's last case where he'd effectively got a serial killer to own up to things even the police weren't aware of having happened.

Louise stared at her for so long that, for a moment, Kate worried whether her sanity had finally broken or that she hadn't heard what Kate had said to her. Then suddenly, to Kate's intense astonishment, Louise leant forward and took Kate's hands.

Her hands were cold and trembling. Kate had the impression that Louise not so much wanted to feel another person's warmth as actually needed to – as if Kate's hands were the only thing keeping her from falling.

Louise's eyes were huge in her face. "I didn't kill her," she said, in a voice barely above a whisper.

Silence hung in the room. Kate nodded, slowly, unwilling to startle the other woman.

Louise spoke again. "It was an accident. A genuine accident. I – she—"

Her voice broke and she stopped speaking. Kate, speaking low and clear, tightened her grip on Louise's hands and said, "Can I tell you what I think happened, Louise? You can tell me if I'm wrong."

Louise, after a moment, nodded. Her eyes never left Kate's face.

Kate began. "I think it was you who went to the ravine that day. I think you contacted Karyn through your husband's phone, and it was you who took that phone with you." A pause and then she asked softly, "Am I right?"

Louise nodded again. She began to speak and her voice sounded as though she had a bad cold or as if she hadn't spoken aloud in weeks. "You have – you have to understand, I wasn't thinking properly, I wasn't – I wasn't in my right mind. Since I found out, I hadn't eaten anything, literally nothing. I couldn't. I was sick when I tried. I hadn't slept for two days. And I had to try and be normal for the children and that took – that took everything from me. I was – I was mad."

Kate nodded. Slowly, she stroked her thumbs over Louise's bony hands, trying to comfort her.

Louise gulped and carried on. "I knew I had to see her. I just couldn't *not* see her. I think I wanted her to deny it. I still now don't believe it, not really. Not

Karyn." She took a deep, shuddering breath. "I knew – I knew she wouldn't come if it were me asking her, so I sent her a text pretending to be Paul. She said she was going out running that morning. The psychopathic bitch was actually going running. She'd ruined my life and she's out *running—*" For a moment, her face contorted with rage. "I took Paul's coat because it was the warmest one we've got. I was so cold – I couldn't stop shivering."

Silence fell again in the room.

Louise took another deep breath. "She got such a shock when she realised it was me. And she wouldn't talk to me. She was such a coward. She just wouldn't meet my eye. She wouldn't even look at me."

"So what happened?" murmured Kate, hoping not to break the confessional spell.

Something strange happened to Louise's face then. It emptied, as if the life within it had been suddenly wiped away. "She was running. She was scared. She fell."

Kate paused for a moment. "Louise, was she running away from you?"

"Not in the way that you think." Louise still looked as though her consciousness was far away from her body. "She – we were arguing. Or I was shouting. I think – it's a blur. In some ways I feel like it didn't really happen." She looked at Kate, who nodded. *Disassociation*. Not unheard of in times of extreme trauma.

"Did you push her over the edge, Louise?"

Louise's haunted eyes met hers. "No. She fell."

"Did you cause her to fall?"

"No. She fell."

And that was all that she would say on the matter. Kate pushed – a little – but there was something stony and implacable in Louise's face now, something that would not yield.

Kate cleared her throat. "Did Paul leave the house that day?"

Louise said nothing but Kate could feel the jump in her hands.

"Did he?" Kate persisted.

Louise looked down at the table. "No," she muttered.

Kate breathed in. "But you wanted him punished."

Louise said nothing. After a moment, her head bobbed, just once.

They sat in silence for a minute. Kate, eventually, gave Louise's hands a gentle, supportive squeeze and then drew her own hands back.

"Louise—" Kate began, but the other woman began speaking over her.

"You asked me to confess because my family was under threat. That's what you said to me at the beginning." Louise held her gaze. Kate waited, knowing there was more. "You were right, in a way. But not right, really, because my family doesn't exist anymore. The two of them saw to that. They saw my family and they destroyed it, and it can never be put back together. Not really. And the worst thing of all?" Kate tensed, waiting. Louise's voice broke a little. "The worst thing of all? It never existed. Not really. My life – the life I thought I had – it just didn't exist. It wasn't there. I thought it was, but I was wrong. *They stole my reality.*" Her voice thickened again. "That's why I don't care what happens next. At least whatever happens next will be *real*."

Kate blinked, her eyes suddenly hot. Never before had she wished so much that the outcome of a case could have been quite different. She got up from the table, slowly, feeling exhausted.

She was almost on her feet when Louise spoke again. "It was a mistake, anyway."

"What was, Louise?"

Louise looked away. She sounded oddly tranquil. Perhaps the rage and hate and pain had been burned away by her confession, if only for a time. Kate found herself strangely glad. "It was a mistake, to wish her dead."

"I'm glad you feel like that—" Kate began. She sat down again.

"Oh, no, it's not that. It's not that I regret her dying, or not in the way you think. No, it's that death's too good for her. Now she's dead, she can't suffer any more. Whereas I've got to suffer every day of my life for what they did to me. I should have kept her alive to *suffer*." For a moment, rage suffused her voice.

There was a moment's silence. Kate was gathering herself to get up when Louise spoke again and this time, there was a brightness in her voice, a glittery insane brightness that sent a cold chill down Kate's spine. "Still, at least I can remember the look on her face when she fell over the edge. At least I have that. I think about it all the time, you know. It comforts me." Her gaze met Kate's and the brightness dropped away. Louise's mouth trembled.

"Come on," Kate said gently. She took the other woman's shaking arm in her hand. "Come with me."

Carefully, as if Louise White was an old, frail woman, Kate led her through the door and away to the cells.

***

IT WAS A SUBDUED KATE that knocked on the door of Anderton's cottage that night. Anderton's beaming smile as he opened it to see her dropped away in a hurry.

"What's wrong?"

Kate sighed and stepped forward into the welcoming enfold of his arms. "Bugger it all," she said into his shoulder, muffled.

"Come on in and tell me about it."

They went through to the cosy kitchen and Anderton poured Kate a glass of wine. She sat down with a thankful sigh, unzipping her boots and throwing them and her overnight bag into a convenient corner. She told him all about what had happened, watching him move around the kitchen preparing their meal.

"Well, they're not going to charge her with murder," said Anderton, poking at the joint in the roasting tray. "They wouldn't have a hope of making it stick. Manslaughter, at the very most."

"You think so?" Kate brightened for a moment and then slumped.

"Maybe not even that. Perverting the course of justice, maybe. Preventing a lawful burial. Concealing a body. I don't know—" Anderton shot the roasting pan back into the Aga and shut the door with a clang. "Anyway, you did what you could."

"I know. It's just – I suppose it's one of those cases in which nobody wins." Kate held her wine glass out for a refill.

"Well, they're all like that, Kate. Really."

"I suppose so." Kate rotated her newly filled glass in her hands, watching the lap of wine against the curved bowl of the glass. "You know, I will never, never understand a man – or woman – who throws their family away for the sake of a shag. Never."

Anderton looked uncomfortable. "Well – you know, I'm probably not the best person to talk to about that."

"Yes, well," Kate said, darkly. "I hope you've changed."

"Shush, now," said Anderton soothingly. "Have some more wine, some dinner, and you'll feel better."

Kate sighed again and attempted to sit up out of her slump. "Yes. Yes, you're right." She cast about for some positive news. "Oh – I've decided to take my inspector exams again, just like you suggested."

Anderton looked genuinely pleased. "Good. Good show. I'm very pleased to hear that." He began to take plates out of the warming part of the oven. "Oh – and I've got a present for you."

"You have?"

"Yes. Hold on." Anderton put the plates down and hunted for his wallet on the breakfast bar. "Now, where is it?" He located the item and opened it up, extracting something that gleamed silver under the lights. "Hold out your hand and close your eyes."

Grinning, Kate did so and felt something small and

cold being placed in her palm. She opened her eyes to find a silver key lying there. Quickly, she looked up to see Anderton smiling at her.

"Your key to the front door. I think it's about time you had one, don't you?"

Grinning even wider, Kate tried to conceal the delight on her face. Then giving up, she got up and kissed him. "Thank you. That means a lot."

Anderton tipped her face back and smoothed a thumb along her jaw. "You mean a great deal to me, Kate. I hope you know that."

"Well, it's always nice to hear it." Kate kissed him one more time. "Come on, let's eat. I'm starving."

He released her and she carried the plates to the table for him. Before it could be lost, she transferred the key to her keyring and tucked it away safely in her handbag. Then she went to join Anderton at the table, feeling happy.

THE END

Tasteful

A Kate Redman Novella

Author's Note

As some of my readers may know, I used to live in the beautiful Georgian city of Bath in the UK (if you haven't been, I urge you to go – it's lovely).

In 2016, no fewer than three severed human feet were found in and around Bath, very close to where I actually lived at the time.

It's not an exaggeration to say that for *years*, I wanted to somehow include these bizarre happenings in a Kate Redman story, but for the life of me, I couldn't think how to do it. Finally, inspiration struck (at six in the bloody morning!) and fingers crossed, I *think* I've managed to create a credible story.

I hope you enjoy it ☺

For Izzy Siu, what a w*nker ☺
(Joking. With love and thanks, doofus.)

Chapter One

THE COTSWOLD WAY, AN ANCIENT walking track in the south west of England, stretched for just over a hundred miles from Chipping Camden to the Georgian jewel that is Bath, winding through green valleys. Its chalky path ran along the tops of hills, skirting the edges or striking through the very heart of several ancient towns and villages. It was popular with ramblers, walkers and those with dogs demanding exercise and adventure, but on a dull, grey March day, two ramblers had it mostly to themselves. Occasionally a horse rider passed them, greeting them in the customary country way with a raise of the hand as the two people pressed themselves into a hedge to accommodate the snorting, steaming animal.

"How much further?" Margery Cook asked her companion, who was consulting Google Maps on her phone.

"Hang on a minute." Cathy Watford squinted at the screen. "The signal's not very good out here... Oh, wait, here we are." She looked up at her friend. "Not far at all. We just follow this path down the hill, take a right, and then we should be on the outskirts of Abbeyford."

"Thank goodness," sighed Margery, turning and beginning to walk again. She was fifty-eight and an experienced rambler, evident by the walking poles she planted confidently on the ground as she strode along. Though fit, she was certainly feeling the fifteen miles they had covered that day.

Cathy, eight years her junior but less fit, fell behind a little, and she was the first to see the object that Margery had missed in her eagerness to reach Abbeyford. She was so far ahead, in fact, that she nearly missed Cathy's shout, but the wind carried it in the right direction and Margery turned, half surprised, half exasperated.

"What is it?" she shouted back in return and then sighed, walking back to her friend who was staring at something on the ground. "What?" she repeated irritably as she reached Cathy.

Cathy hadn't taken her eyes off the thing on the ground.. Margery peered closer and frowned.

"What is that?" asked Cathy, quietly.

Margery was a no-nonsense type, but one glance at the object on the grass verge made her look more closely and then recoil. Cathy gave her a worried look.

Margery's heart thudded a little faster. She risked another look, crimping her mouth. Then she looked directly at Cathy. "It can't be, but...it looks like a foot." The absurdity of the situation, not to mention the gruesomeness, almost made her giggle for a second.

"That's what I thought," Cathy said uncertainly. "But it *can't* be. Can it?"

They both looked again. The foot—if that was indeed what it was—was swollen, yellowish and blotched here and there, with blue and purple patches. But there were toes and pale curling toenails.

"It must be fake. Or—or..." Cathy ran out of ideas. She took a step back.

Margery put a hand on Cathy's arm. "Dear, I think we're going to have to call the police. They'll be the ones to decide what to do." She glanced around her, at the new budding trees, the occasional glimpse of sun behind pallid clouds and then down at the foot, incongruous and menacing on the grass. She pulled her backpack off and began rummaging about for her phone. "I just hope we can get a signal to call them."

Chapter Two

IN THE INCIDENT ROOM OF Abbeyford Police Station, Detective Inspector Kate Redman put down the phone on her desk and stared blankly across the room.

"What is it?" Detective Sergeant Chloe Wapping asked from her desk across from Kate's. "Something bad?"

Kate shook her head, still staring ahead.

"Well, spit it out then, bird."

Kate came back to life. "Apparently, they've found a foot."

It was Chloe's turn to stare. "A *foot*? *Just* a foot?"

"Oh, come off it," was Detective Sergeant Theo Marsh's contribution from across the room. "April Fool's is next week, mate."

Try as she might, Kate could not break Theo from the habit of calling her *mate*, formed through years of working together as equals and then as her subordinate. She didn't really care anymore, anyway. *Much.* "I'm being serious. Two walkers up on Hydon's Hill reported it. The uniform that went to see thinks it's human."

"Blimey," was Chloe's considered opinion.

"It'll be a fake," scoffed Theo.

Chloe had turned to her computer and clicked the mouse. "Actually, it *could* be human. Isn't the teaching hospital around that side of the town?"

"So?" asked Theo

Kate had caught Chloe's drift. "Medical students? Arsing around for a joke? Playing a prank?"

Chloe had already clicked and forwarded the link of the hospital's page to Kate's computer. She heard the ping of the notification and vowed, once again, to change her computer settings to stop her hearing that bloody sound approximately a thousand times a day (it felt).

"Right," she sighed. "Let's get started." It was an unusually quiet week for the normally busy Abbeyford force, and despite the fact they were a team member short in numbers, there had still been plenty of time to catch up on emails, file their expenses and drink plenty of coffee. "Chloe, could you get SOCO on it, please?"

Theo snorted. "SOCO? For a bloody foot?"

Kate started to laugh. So did Theo. "It's hardly gonna need an evidence tent, now, is it?"

Kate, gasping by now, pinched her fingers together. "Only if it was a *tiny, tiny* one."

Everyone rocked with laughter at the ridiculous image. Kate looked over to where Detective Inspector Mark Olbeck should have been sitting in his office, wanting her friend to share the joke, but he was clearly out at a meeting. She turned back. Detective Constable Ravinder Cheetam, Rav to his friends and colleagues, walked into the room and regarded them all with astonishment.

"What's going on?"

Chloe told him, still giggling. Rav shook his head. "A foot?"

Kate sobered up. "Okay, okay, come on, team. Chloe, seriously, we'll need *one* SOCO up there. We'll see what they say before we send a path doc." Giggles threatened to return and she forced them down. "I'll go and see for myself."

"Oh, come on, mate," said Theo. "It's way beneath your rank."

"I know. I'm just intrigued. And, for once, not particularly busy." Kate began to gather up her stuff, preparing to leave. She tipped Theo a wink. "Besides, as the most senior officer currently here, I order myself to go."

She said goodbye and turned to leave before she remembered and hit her forehead with her palm. "Oh damn. I've left my car at home. Rav, can you drive me?"

"Sure."

"Thanks. Come on, get your stuff. There's something I need to ask you on the way."

"So, what is it, guv?" Rav asked as they drove towards Hydon's Way.

"Don't call me that," Kate said automatically.

"Sorry, boss."

"*Rav*—"

"Sorry, ma'am."

Kate raised a threatening arm, and Rav grinned and shut up. For a second.

"Seriously, what was it you wanted to ask me?"

Kate snapped back into work mode. "Sorry, right.

When's Jarina due again?" Jarina, Rav's wife, was expecting their first child.

"April fourteenth. But you know what they say, they never come on the actual date, do they?"

"Well, logically, *some* babies must do, but I know what you mean. It's just I've got someone in to cover you for paternity leave and hopefully stay on when you get back." Kate suddenly became aware of how that might sound and hastily added, "Obviously, I'm not *replacing* you—"

"Obviously," Rav said, grinning again. "I'm just amazed Those Upstairs deemed us worthy enough of the funds. We've been trying for bloody years."

"I know. Well, anyway. He starts on Monday next week. Martin Liu. Seems a nice bloke."

"DC?"

"Yes. He's transferring from Bristol. Anyway, we'll get the paperwork for your leave sorted out over the next few weeks, just in case Baby Cheetam does decide to come early."

Hydon's Hill was approaching. Kate was again struck by the absurdity of the situation, but she kept her thoughts to herself as Rav sought a parking space in the narrow country road that led to it.

Chapter Three

It was a steep climb to the top of the hill, and Kate, if not Rav (a dedicated gym goer), was puffing by the time she got to where the activity was. The two ramblers were nowhere to be seen but the uniformed officer, who she recognised as PC Dai Williams, was talking to the scene of crime officer. Kate, despite her skill at facial recognition, could never tell them apart, clothed, gloved, booted and masked as they were. The SOCO stood up as they approached and pulled down the mask, revealing a middle-aged woman's face. Kate was still none the wiser.

They introduced themselves (Kate cunningly let the woman go first) and took their first look at the foot. Kate blinked again at the surrealism of the scene; a decomposing body part framed against the fresh green of the new spring grass sprouting around it.

"What can you tell us—er—Jackie?"

Jackie shook her head. "Very, very little, I'm afraid, DI Redman. As you can see, it's a human foot, cut off just above the ankle. It's decomposing. I'm assuming it's from a Caucasian, but the skin's degraded so far I could be wrong about that."

"Man or woman?"

Jackie shook her head again. "I'm sorry but it's just impossible to tell."

"Right." Kate looked down again at the sad little piece of someone's body. Who would chop off a foot? She said it out loud. "Who would chop off someone's *foot*?"

The very second the words left her mouth, an extremely horrible thought came to her. She turned to Rav with a gasp.

He seemed to instinctively realise what she meant. "Oh God..."

"There might be other...other pieces." Kate felt like hitting herself. How had that possibility not occurred to her before? She reached for her phone, calling the office. She listened to the ringing at the end of the line, heart hammering.

Chloe answered.

"Chloe, is Mark out of his meeting yet?"

"Not yet. What's the prob—"

"We need a search team up here right away. She looked at Jackie, who looked apprehensive. "And a full SOCO team. Both Rav and I think there might be more body parts."

"Shit," said Chloe. "I'll tell Mark to call you. Leave the rest to me and Theo."

"Thanks, Chloe. Hurry—as fast as you can," Kate said, looking around at the darkening skies. The clocks had not yet gone forward, and daylight was draining away around them.

"We should start to look," said Rav.

"No. We don't have any scrubs. We could contaminate a much wider crime scene."

"It's OK," said Jackie. She pointed to her large bag

lying some feet away. "Some spares in there. I always like to keep a few."

"I can imagine," Kate said, imagining the kind of conditions techs were required to crawl around in. She and Rav dressed and gloved up and began to look, dreading what they might find.

DI Mark Olbeck did better than phone up. He arrived in person, just as Kate was doing her best to avoid being attacked by a particularly vicious bramble. "Kate?" he enquired anxiously, as she swore at the thorns snagging at her scrub suit. "Have you found anything? Are there more body parts?"

Kate tore her sleeve from the bramble's grasp. "Not so far. We're all looking." At the bottom of the hill she could see white vans parking behind Rav's car. "But we're still searching. There's nothing so far, at least."

Soon, the crime team had arrived and were setting up their powerful arc lights to illuminate the rapidly darkening path and the woodland that straggled alongside it. Uniformed officers armed with large torches began strafing the damp ground with powerful beams.

Kate was glad to stand up and stretch out her aching back, eager to hand over the search to people who were trained to do this for a living. She stripped off her scrub suit and put it in an evidence bag, just on the off chance that she might have picked up something important in her hunt through the undergrowth. Olbeck came over as she shrugged her jacket back on; the sun was retreating and it was growing very cold as the night crept in. Kate gave him a strained smile and he returned it, before saying, quietly, "Kate, do you remember the Butterfly Killer?"

Kate looked at him with incredulity. "Mark, is it likely that *I* would have forgotten that case?" It was too dark to see if he actually blushed, but he shifted on his feet, exclaiming at his stupidity.

"It's ok," said Kate. "It *was* a while ago." Just the same, she felt her hand involuntarily move to the scar on her back, a ridged remnant of a long-forgotten case.

"I know it's rare. But it does happen. It's not like we haven't had serial killers in this country."

"I know. Fred and Rosemary West. The Yorkshire Ripper. Harold Shipman. To name but three—I mean four." Kate stopped herself from shivering, as much at names she uttered as the cold wind that flapped her light coat. She clutched it closely around her.

Olbeck noticed her discomfort. "Look, shove off home, if you like. I'll finish up here and leave these guys to their jobs. I'm not staying much longer anyway. Jeff will need a hand with bath time."

"Well, if you're sure. See you tomorrow, and kiss the kids and Jeff for me."

"Of course. Come over to dinner soon."

"Would love to." Kate wasn't being polite. Jeff, Olbeck's husband, was an excellent cook. She gave him a grateful pat on the arm and turned to stride off into the darkness, following the faint white line of the chalk path with her little keyring torch.

Chapter Four

THE NEXT MORNING, KATE FACED her new recruit across the table in one of the interview rooms and rose to shake his hand. He was Chinese in heritage but with a pleasing Bristol burr to his voice and handsome brown eyes.

"Welcome DC Lui. Can I call you Martin? We're pretty informal here."

"Of course."

Kate estimated he would be about thirty-five. As way of introduction, she filled him in on the extraordinary events of the previous day.

He looked confused. "Does that sort of thing happen often around here?"

Kate pushed her chair out and stood up. "Martin, I can't recall it ever *once* happening around here. Anyway, come with me and meet the rest of the team." They entered the incident room and she made the introductions. Martin shook hands and said the usual words of those starting a new job, but he had a confident, warm manner that made her pleased about her judgement in hiring him.

As Theo assigned Martin a seat and took him through the usual introductory procedures, apparently including, as standard, an IT password and key pass—that never worked properly first time, Kate thought, grinning, as she looked around the rest of the room. *What a diverse bunch we finally are,* she thought, with some surprise and pride. Theo was half-black, a fact of which he was frequently and vocally proud, Rav was of Indian descent, and now there was Martin. Chloe and herself represented the female side, as they were both—well, women—*and badasses,* Kate added retrospectively. She herself was half—maybe more than that, as her mother hadn't been exactly specific, possibly because she didn't actually know herself—Irish. In fact, as Olbeck was gay, Kate was struck by the lack of a straight white male in such a small, close-knit team. So, who would do?

Anderton. The name immediately jumped into her mind, of course. Anderton had been the DCI who had greeted Kate upon her arrival; he had delivered her first ever case as a newly qualified detective sergeant. Her attraction to him had been instant, but it had been years before they had both acknowledged it, with a lot of stumbles and misunderstandings along the way. And there they were, an established couple, about to buy the perfect house together. Their first home. Kate shook her head at the wonder of time's ability to rocket past, scarcely noticed. Then she recollected herself and called everyone to the morning meeting.

"Right, first. Of course. Our foot." She added a few details for those, like Martin, who hadn't had a chance to review the case file yet. "Any news from our friends at the path lab yet?"

Rav had rung them. "Nothing yet. They're a bit swamped with cases from other districts."

Theo scoffed. "It's hardly going to take a long time, is it? "Ooh, look, a foot. It's dead.""

Everyone laughed. Kate shook her head at Theo. "All right, well, someone follow up on that. Rav? Like Theo says, it won't take long," she added, mindful of the approaching Cheetam baby.

"I will."

"I'll do MISPER," Chloe offered and then laughed again. "But perhaps we'd better wait for the DNA first to do that database. I highly doubt anyone's reported a foot missing."

Kate couldn't help smiling. "Probably not. God, I'm a bit stumped. How do you go about looking for a foot's owner?"

"Ha, ha," said Theo, smirking.

Kate looked at him. "What?"

"Oh, I thought you were making a joke. Stump, you know."

Kate stared blankly at him. "No."

"Oh." After a moment he added, "It wasn't funny anyway."

Kate rolled her eyes. "I think, realistically, that the only thing we can do is wait for the path lab results and the DNA test. Theo, you may as well get on with whatever's more urgent." Right in the nick of time, she remembered their new recruit. "Martin, can you do a search of all the bases and search engines just in case anyone else has had this type of thing? It's a faint hope but—" Martin nodded eagerly, and Kate smiled at him. "Right, anyone gets anything, let me know. If the press call, just give them the bare facts and a 'can't comment further' type of thing." She pushed herself away from table she'd been leaning on and added, with an ironic tilt of the head towards her desk. "I'll be in my office."

K ATE WAS GREETED BY THE welcome smell of roast chicken wafting from the kitchen as she got home that night. Since his 'retirement', Anderton had turned into something of a gourmet chef, and Kate was never less than grateful. As she put it to him once, she could burn water.

"Hi," she called, unzipping her boots and placing them in a neat pair by the coat rack. Her cat, Merlin, came to greet her, twining like a black ribbon around her ankles. Kate bent to rub behind his ears.

"Hi," Anderton said, appearing in the kitchen doorway.

Kate groaned. "Do you *have* to wear that?"

"Yes," Anderton said with a dignity that was ill-deserved, given he was wearing an apron that said 'Kiss the Cook'.

With a theatrical sigh, Kate did as the apron told her.

"Bad day?" Anderton asked. "Come into the kitchen, I've got a few things left to do."

KATE SAT AT THE KITCHEN table, thankful to be off her feet. She told Anderton what she could about the case while he basted the chicken and turned the roast potatoes. Kate's stomach rumbled.

"Bad day?" repeated Anderton.

"Not bad," said Kate, pouring herself a glass of wine. "Just...frustrating, I guess. I mean, a *foot*. For God's sake..."

"It's a first," Anderton said drily.

"Rav's got the PM tomorrow." An image of the foot marooned in the middle of a hospital gurney in the autopsy room occurred to Kate. It was almost sad, in a way. "So we might know more then." She took a long, grateful sip of the pinot noir. "Still, we didn't find anything else, thank God, so there's that to be thankful for."

After dinner they retired to the living room. Although the day had been warm, the nights were still very much the opposite, and Kate was grateful for the warmth and the comforting glow of the fire Anderton had built in the grate.

"Oh, by the way," Anderton said, pulling Kate towards him, "That house we liked is already under offer."

Kate looked at him in dismay. "Oh no! I loved that one."

"It might not go through. Also, it *was* a bit over budget."

"I know, I said that myself, but... Damn." Kate snuggled her head into his broad shoulder. "Why is house buying in this country so stressful?"

"Because estate agents are bastards."

Kate laughed. "That's not why." She paused and added, "Well, we're so quiet at the moment, apart from this bloody foot, we could do some more viewings?"

"I'll set some up." Anderton paused to kiss her, lingeringly. "And now, if your dinner has settled, why don't we go up to bed?"

"Good idea."

Chapter Five

SPRING WAS BACK WITH A vengeance the next day; blue skies, whipped-cream clouds, sunlight refracting off the dew jewelling the grass on the lawn. Kate drank her coffee, kissed Anderton goodbye and set off for work on foot, determined to make the most of the good weather.

It was another quiet morning in the office. Rav was attending the PM, Theo was off interviewing witnesses, and Olbeck was in another meeting. Kate asked Chloe to take Martin through the various systems the team had in place in the meantime, and she actually managed to clear her in-tray for once. She was regarding its emptiness with satisfaction when Rav returned.

"Anything?" asked Kate.

Rav shook his head. "Not much. Apparently it's been treated with some sort of preservative—formaldehyde or something like that. Kirsten's running some more tests but she said we wouldn't be able to get any DNA because of that."

Kate frowned. "Oh. That's a bugger. Is she sure?" She dismissed the speculation a second later. Dr Kirsten Telling was very good at her job. "Okay, well if she says we can't, we can't, I suppose. Damn."

Rav was already wandering back to his desk. "She'll

send the report over later." He added over his shoulder with a grin. "It'll be quite short."

"Won't it just." Kate rolled her eyes.

"Only a foot long," added Rav, grinning.

Kate did a very unladylike snort of laughter. "You've been working on that one for a while, haven't you?" she asked, giggling but Rav, chuckling himself, was interrupted in his reply as the office phone rang. Kate reached out for it but Rav beat her to it, so she shrugged and looked again at her emails, still smiling.

She was reading one from HR regarding some dreadful sounding team-building day, no doubt dreamt up by administrators who organised these things and failed to realise they were entirely counter-productive—nothing made you despise your fellow co-workers more than being forced into some feeble role-play and 'trust' exercises in a grim little council hall in the middle of nowhere—when she heard Rav exclaim loudly and looked up.

"You have got to be kidding me," he said, churning his thick black hair in a way that reminded Kate of Anderton. She sat up, nerves buzzing, and waited impatiently until he'd finished the call.

"Well?" she asked, the second Rav put down the receiver.

He looked at her and half laughed. "You won't believe it."

"*What?*"

"They've found another foot."

It was Kate's turn to churn her hair. "What?" she said again.

"I'm serious. Some kids playing in the recreation ground at Atherton Park found another foot. Just the one, cut off at the ankle."

"You're kidding me." Kate unconsciously echoed Rav's exact words. She got up, throwing her hands in the air. "What the hell is going on?"

"I have absolutely no idea. Someone's idea of a sick joke?"

"But where are they getting the feet, if so? Who just has *feet* lying around?" Kate and Rav regarded each other for a moment and then collapsed into giggles.

"I shouldn't laugh," said Kate, collecting herself after a moment. "I know we haven't found anything else, but these are human—I mean..." She trailed away, not sure of where her thoughts were taking her.

"Do you want me to go?" asked Rav.

"Yes, you'd better." Kate regarded the empty office and shrugged. "Chloe's busy with Martin, and I really should get on with things."

"No problem." Rav reached for his jacket just as his mobile phone buzzed and clattered on his desk. He reached for it, opened up the message and gasped. "Oh my god."

"What is it?"

"Jarina's gone into labour! Oh my god, oh my god—"

"Oh, Rav..." Kate absorbed his excitement and anxiety as if by osmosis. Her stomach flipped. "Oh, that's so exciting!"

"Shit, shit, I have to go—"

"What did she say? If she's texting you, it can't be that urgent..." Rav held out his phone in a shaking hand

and Kate read the message. "Look, you idiot, she's telling you not to rush. She's not even going to the hospital yet." Looking at Rav, dancing from foot to foot, Kate could see she was wasting her breath. "Look, head on home, why don't you?"

Rav looked at her, pleadingly. "Can I?"

"Of course, silly." Kate knew he'd be absolutely no use to her now, in this state of mind. Not that she could blame him. "Go on, go home and keep me posted. I'm so excited for you!"

Rav barely stayed for the fleeting hug she gave him before grabbing his stuff and running from the office. Kate yelled after him, "And drive *safely*! Jarina wants you there in one piece."

Shaking her head and grinning, she returned to her desk and tried to concentrate on work. Another foot? This was getting more bizarre by the day. After a moment's thought, she went to find Chloe and Martin, catching up with them in the evidence room.

"*Another* one?" were Chloe's first words, after Kate explained the situation. Martin said nothing but raised his eyebrows.

"I know. Bizarre isn't the word." Kate wondered about mentioning Rav's news but decided it could wait, for the moment.

"Shall we go?" Chloe asked, motioning to her companion.

That had been Kate's original thought but then she had a swift change of mind. "Actually, Chloe, I'll go and I'll take Martin with me. Can you man the office?"

"I can *woman* it," said Chloe, with a grin.

Kate held up a fist in feminist solidarity. "Good woman. Right, Martin, come along with me."

Chapter Six

JOSH KIRKWOOD CROUCHED IN THE shadow of the laurel hedge, propping himself against the garden wall. He was cold, damp and uncomfortable. This was the second time he'd hidden himself there—the first had been three days ago, when he was scoping out the house, checking out the security, looking for weak spots, gazing through the ground floor windows at the treasures within. He knew money when he saw it, and this house, a monolith of golden Bath stone, reeked of money; it positively *oozed* it. Josh shifted position, inhaling the night scents; the damp earthy smell of the rotten leaves beneath his boots, the sharp tang of cat piss beneath the laurel hedge. As he waited, he thought he saw a cat trot across the dew-silvered lawn but another glance showed him it was a fox, sharp-faced and smaller than he expected. It turned its head quickly towards him and he caught the glint of moonlight off its eyes as it looked into his, although he hadn't moved or made a sound, as far as he was aware.

The porch light of the house clicked on, spreading warm golden light across the gravel driveway and over the car parked there, an old but beautifully kept Jaguar. Josh wanted that car—wanted it very badly—but it was no use. He was no car thief and something like that was far, far too noticeable to sell on. He pressed himself back into the shadow as he heard the front door open and the owner of the house step out.

"I'll be back before midnight, Mother," the man called back into the depths of the house. Josh strained his ears but couldn't hear any reply. No matter; he'd watched the old lady from this vantage point on several occasions and knew she always made her way up to her bedroom at nine o'clock sharp. He just had to sit tight for a few more minutes, let that bloke get far enough away, and then sneak in through that dodgy window round the side. There was some lovely stuff in the living room and dining room, and Josh knew a fence or two who'd be able to make good use of anything he got.

After ten minutes, he knew matey in the Jag wouldn't return. Stifling a groan, as he pushed himself into a standing position, he stretched for a moment, rubbing life back into his legs. Then, hefting his small backpack, he crept across the dark lawn towards the side of the house, where the window with the broken latch lay hidden from view by an overgrown bush. This whole garden needed a good seeing to, thought Josh, and felt a surge of righteous dislike for the house's owners. People shouldn't be allowed nice stuff if they weren't even going to take care of it.

Cautiously, he crept back to the front of the house again and peeped through the window of what he knew was the living room. Again, he was struck by the beautiful design, the plushness of the velvet curtains, the Persian rug covering the well-polished old floorboards, the mellowed leather of the Chesterfield that stood facing the dying fire. *Tasteful, very tasteful.* Josh appreciated good taste, especially when he could avail himself of some of it for cold, hard cash.

A guard had been placed in front of the hearth and as Josh watched, the overhead chandelier was switched off, the soft light extinguished in a blink. That meant the old girl was making her way up to bed. Josh crept forward a little more, straining his ears. He was sure he could hear the creak of the stairs as she made her slow, uncertain ascent. He looked at his phone, noting the time. Give it twenty minutes for her to get properly settled and then on we go...

Twenty minutes in the cold and dark dragged. Josh was desperate for a fag, even for a pull on his vape, but no dice---he couldn't risk anyone smelling either smoke or blueberry flavoured vapour. Shifting from foot to foot, trying to keep warm, the thought occurred to him that there was possibly an easier way to make a living. But then, what did he know about that? He'd been brought up in crime, tutored in it by his father and uncles. There was literally nothing else he knew how to do.

He prided himself on his work, though. Nobody ever got hurt. No smashing the place up or leaving something disgusting behind. He knew a few guys who thought nothing of stealing women's underwear, taking a shit in the bathtub or worse, on the floor. *Gross.* Junkies, most of them. Josh wouldn't give most of them the time of day. He wasn't like that. He preferred not to steal jewellery—it was sentimental, even if it weren't valuable, right? He had something most in his trade didn't: morals. There *was* such a thing as having pride in your work, even if you were a burglar.

Eventually, the time ticked by and Josh pulled out his tools, inserting the screwdriver into the minute gap between the bottom of the window frame and the sill, greened with moss and lichen. He'd tested this out before, without going inside, and again, the window went up fairly smoothly and quietly. He only opened it enough for him and his backpack to slip inside. Luckily, he was slim—too thin, really; he needed to go to the gym more, but that was difficult when he worked nights and slept during the day.

Inside the house, he paused, listening. He could hear the very faint sound of a television overhead, which was good—it would act as cover for any noise he made, although God knew he was experienced enough now not to go blundering into furniture or tripping over cables or suchlike. He knew for a fact that the owners did not have a dog. Josh wouldn't dream of burgling a house with a dog; a) because dogs barked at and sometimes attacked intruders and b) Josh liked dogs and would never want to be a situation where he'd have to hurt one.

He crept through the house cautiously, making for the living room. His backpack was deceptively capacious and he carried several other fold up bags in which to stow smaller treasures. He paused at the entrance to the living room—or would it be that old fashioned term, drawing room, in this stately place? Who cared? Josh longed to turn on the light, to gaze at all the wonderful things inside the room, but knew he couldn't. So tasteful. What he wouldn't give to live in a house like this, surrounded by beauty. *As if.* He couldn't even afford to move out of the council house he still shared with his parents. His mum kept it neat and clean as a new pin, but it was cramped and tatty, all the same. The chances of him ever owning—or even renting—a place like this was laughable. Not unless he pulled off some huge, daring heist, like Brink's Mat or the Hatton Garden robbery. Why hadn't his old man ever organised something like that? He didn't think big, his dad. That was the problem...

Shaking off his intrusive thoughts, Josh moved slowly and carefully through the room, picking the choicest pieces, or those that he could carry, anyway. He longed for the grand piano in the corner but what was the use? Stealthily, he opened drawers, hoping perhaps for cash or credit cards, but there was nothing useful in the chest of drawers that he searched, only a few bottles of spirits which, after a moment, he added to his backpack.

At the back of the room was a set of double doors. Josh approached, checking all the while for alarms and cameras. There was nothing. Carefully, he opened one of the doors and looked through, shining the thin white beam of his torch into the room. It was a study, walls lined with books and a heavy mahogany desk sat square in the middle of the Persian carpet. Josh slowly swung his torch light across the room, checking for anything to steal. Then he froze.

In the middle of the desk, there was a large glass jar, very large, the kind that Josh had seen when his dad started making home brew. Something floated within it. Josh, holding his breath, approached closer, unaware that the torch had begun to jitter. He stared at the jar, illuminated now by the strobing light in his shaking hand. He hadn't been mistaken, not at all.

In the jar on the desk, was a human head.

Chapter Seven

KATE AND MARTIN DROVE BACK to the station after viewing the crime scene in thoughtful calm. Kate was pleased to find that Martin was one of those rare people with whom she could share a comfortable silence, even though she barely knew him. Compared to Theo's restlessness (not to mention his penchant for playing appalling drum and bass through the car stereo) and even Chloe's sometimes wearying intensity, it made a pleasant change to be able to drive in restful silence. Her mind replayed the events of the last hour.

It had been eerily similar to the examination of the first foot. The limb, blotched with decay, garlanded by flies, laid like a macabre exhibit on the fresh green grass. Even Jackie, the SOCO, had been the same. At least Kate had managed to remember her name this time. What *had* been different, none of them could have predicted.

Kate glanced across at Martin, sitting quietly with his hands folded in his lap. "So, I don't think either of us was expecting it to be from a totally different person, were we?"

Martin half-smiled. "Well, I know *I* wasn't. I just automatically assumed it was the matching pair to the first foot."

"Same here." Kate flicked the indicator on to join the dual carriageway. "It just gets weirder."

Martin nodded in acknowledgement but said nothing. After a moment, Kate reflected that she probably should try to get to know him a little better, draw him out of himself a bit.

"How long were you with Bristol, Martin?"

"About seven years. Ever since I started." Martin unlaced his fingers and Kate caught a glimpse of a wedding ring on his right hand. She decided to leave the personal questions until later.

"What was your last case?"

Martin glanced at her. "The Poppy Taige case. We were working with Missing Persons on that."

Kate nodded. Poppy Taige was a twenty-year-old Bristol University student who had disappeared after a night out with her friends over two months ago. "I don't know much about that, just what the press have been reporting. It's gone a bit quiet on that now, though, hasn't it?"

Martin nodded. "We were only involved in a preliminary capacity. Obviously loads of students go missing after heavy nights out, for one reason or another. It's just... Well, as you know, they tend to turn up again—alive...or not." It was Kate's turn to nod. "Well, with Poppy, she just vanished."

Kate shook her head. "Her poor parents."

"Yes." Martin was silent for a moment. "Anyway, I transferred before anything really happened. Well, nothing *has* really happened. The case is ongoing."

"And now you're investigating stray feet."

They exchanged smiles. "It's fine," said Martin. "It's different, isn't it?"

"That's one thing to be said for this job," agreed Kate. "It's never boring." They were coming into the town centre of Abbeyford, passing brick office blocks and the two high-rise towers that the planners of the 1960s had been permitted to build. "Can you imagine working somewhere like that instead?"

"I did, for a bit."

"Really?"

Martin chuckled. "Yes. Town planning department of the council. God, it was tedious. I stuck it out for two years, after university, and then decided life was too short to be stuck behind a desk."

"Good plan." Kate swung the car into the station carpark. "Now, let's go and wow them all with the little fact that we now seem to have feet from *two* unidentified people, God help us."

***

JOSH KIRKWOOD LAY IN HIS bed, covers pulled up to his chin, staring at the ceiling. There was a crack in the plaster that looked like a dragon; it had been there ever since he was a little boy. When he was younger, a child, he'd imagined the dragon coming to life at night, flying around the room, swooping at him as he lay in bed. The only way he'd conquered his fear of that happening was to reframe the dragon as a friendly one, a pet who'd keep the other monsters at bay, breathing fire to dispel the bogeymen who always lurked in the dark corners of a child's bedroom.

Dragons were not his worry now. Over and over again, Josh relived the moment he'd discovered that jar in the study and seen the horror contained within it. He'd stared and stared, convinced that he'd been mistaken, until, unable to help himself, he'd crept closer, shaking all over, directing the beam of his torch onto and through the thick glass walls of the jar. He could see the ragged ends of flesh where the neck had been cut, pale pink in the jittering light of the torch. The eye-sockets were empty, cavernous holes, just visible beneath the drooping eyelids. Short dull black hair floated in whatever fluid preserved the head. It was impossible to say if it were male or female; the features were bloated, distorted by decay, age or just the convex surface of the curving glass walls of the jar.

In his bed, Josh turned over, pulling the pillow over his head. He'd fled the house, of course, hefting his backpack with the already purloined treasures, throwing it onto the lawn beneath the dodgy window, sliding that back down onto the windowsill as quietly as he could. He'd been almost panting as he did so, the air whistling in and out of his lungs in what were very nearly sobs. A quick check to see if he'd left anything incriminating and then he was off, over the back wall and down the lane, running now, barely caring if he was heard.

Fuck, what was he going to *do*? Josh sat up abruptly and reached for his phone. For the hundredth time, he opened up his picture gallery and looked at the photos of the jar that he'd taken. The quality wasn't good—the only light he'd had to see by was his torch and the flash of his phone had reflected off the glass, but you could see the head. Sort of. Enough to know that he hadn't imagined it.

He could hear his mum calling him from downstairs, something about walking the dog. He ignored her. What was he going to do?

His gaze fell on the local paper, crumpled up and stuffed into the bin over by his chest of drawers. *Local girl still missing* was the headline. After a moment, Josh got up, moving like an old man, and pulled the paper from the bin. There was a picture on the front of the bird who was missing, pretty trim she was, dark-haired and smiling. Josh didn't fancy her—she reminded him of one of his cousins, Hayleigh. Nausea twisted his stomach and he dropped the paper back in the bin before climbing back into bed.

What if the head was hers, the missing girl? Poppy someone. Like almost everyone else in Abbeyford, Josh was well aware of the feet that had recently been found. Were they *her* feet? Poppy's? Was that her head in the jar?

Oh, Christ. Josh felt even sicker. What if there was a serial killer going about? It had happened before here—Josh had been too young to be really aware of it but he remembered his mum and dad talking about the killer who'd murdered those hookers, years ago. He thought of his younger sisters and his female cousins, Hayleigh amongst them. *Shit, shit, shit.*

He knew what he *should* do. He should report it to the police. But how could he, knowing that he'd have to say how he'd seen the jar, because he was in the process of burgling that house? People like Josh just didn't get involved with the police. At all. Ever. Not to mention what his old man would do when he found out. For a start, Josh would be out on his ear, nowhere to go, onto the streets, and probably with a broken jaw to go with it. *Shit*.

He risked a glance at the paper in the bin. He could see Poppy Taige's large dark eyes regarding him from the picture, just peeking over the top of the bin. She looked as though she were pleading with him.

"Fuck, I can't. Don't ask me." He blushed at actually having spoken aloud. Groaning, Josh rolled over to face the wall, pulling the covers over his head.

Chapter Eight

"So, how many unidentified limbs do you think you'll find today?" Anderton asked, setting a steaming cup of tea in front of Kate. She noted with satisfaction he'd used her favourite cup and saucer, the vintage one with the delicately painted violets and gold rim.

"Ha, ha. There can't be any more, surely? I mean, it's odd enough to have *two* feet in your possession..." She let the thought hang in the air as she sipped her tea.

"Oh, by the way, I've set up a few more viewings for us this weekend." Anderton applied himself to his own breakfast: bacon, eggs and toast.

"Are you sure you should be eating that at your age?"

"Cheek. I only have it occasionally." Anderton pointed a buttery knife at her. "Besides, when was the last time you went to the gym, missy?"

"I hate the gym," Kate said absently. She was thinking ahead to work, planning her day. "Anyway, email me the links to the houses when you get a moment, and I'll have a look. Providing I don't have to deal with any more feet."

"Do you know what I think?"

Kate indicated with raised eyebrows that Anderton should go on.

He did so. "I think it's someone who has one of those weird Victorian collections. You know, like stuffed animals, curiosities, things like that. Perhaps they'd been bequeathed them in a will or something."

Kate pondered. "Possibly. But...why get rid of them? Why plant them all about town?"

Anderton shrugged. "People are weird."

"Don't I know it." Kate finished her tea, got up, and kissed him goodbye. "Have a good day, darling. I'll try and get home on time."

It was another glorious spring day. As Kate pulled the front door shut behind her, her mobile chimed and she dug it out. It was a message from Rav. *It's a boy!! Born at 4am this morning. Jarina and baby well. So knackered but so happy.* He'd added about a hundred smiling and love-heart-eyed emojis after the words.

Kate pulled in a deep, pleased breath. She texted back appropriate congratulations and love to Jarina and as yet unnamed baby, and she even added a few emojis of her own. Making a mental note to get some flowers and a card arranged and sent to the hospital, she strode off to work, feeling happy.

Her good mood at Rav's delightful news buoyed her all the way to the station. Running up the front steps, eager to let the reception staff know the news, Kate realised she'd have to wait for a moment or two. PC Paul Boulton was currently booking someone in, a thin young man, dressed in a grey hoody and skinny jeans. He had a look of such misery on his face that it stopped Kate in her tracks.

Paul Boulton looked up and saw her and she saw a flash of relief cross his face.

"Everything all right, Paul?" Kate asked, approaching the desk.

"Yes. Yes. Actually—" Paul inclined his head towards the office behind the reception desk. "Could I have a quick word?"

"Sure." Kate stepped behind the desk as Paul handed over the booking in to his companion, PC Nevis and gestured to Kate to come into the office.

"What's the prob?" asked Kate, once they were inside with the door firmly closed.

"Bit of an odd one." Paul sat down and Kate did likewise. "That young lad out there. Do you recognise him?" Kate shook her head. "He's Josh Kirkwood."

Kate *did* recognise the surname. "Ah," was all she said.

"He's only twenty eight but he's got a rap sheet as long as your arm." Paul paused and added, somewhat reluctantly. "Anyway, he came in to confess to another burglary."

Kate raised her eyebrows. "*Confess*? Is that usual with him?"

"No. Not at all. The thing is...he said, well—the circumstances are a bit unusual." Paul seemed as though he was going to say more for a moment and then shook his head. "Perhaps it's best if you talk to him directly."

"Me?" Kate didn't normally handle burglaries, but she knew Paul Boulton well enough to respect his opinion.

"You're handling this foot case—cases—aren't you?"

"That's right. Has this got something to do with that?"

"It might do. Sorry to sound so mysterious, but Kirkwood's story is...odd. Probably best you hear it from the horse's mouth."

Mystified but intrigued, Kate nodded. "Okay, I'll take him in. Has he been cautioned?" Paul nodded. Kate went on. "Ok, great. What interview room is free?"

When she and Josh Kirkwood were sat down opposite each other in a free room, Kate took a fresh look at him. He was tall but very thin. His face would have been good looking if he'd put on a little weight but his skin was awful; greyish, marked with spots, his eyes ringed with dark circles and his jaw darkly furred with what was probably three-day-old stubble.

"Can I get you a cup of tea, Josh?" asked Kate.

He shook his head. "Can I vape?"

"I'm afraid not." Kate gestured to the no smoking sign on the wall, with the addendum beneath: *including e-cigarettes*.

Josh scowled. Kate waited a moment and gently asked, "Could you tell me what happened, Josh?"

Josh was silent for so long that Kate was about to repeat the question, when he spoke. "I was doing this house, on Park Lane. This big place."

"Do you have the number or the name of it?"

Josh shook his head. Kate persisted. "Have you seen it by daylight?"

"Yeah, course. That's how I saw all the stuff."

Pondering for a second, Kate grabbed her phone and brought up Google Earth. She homed in on Park Lane, scrolling inward until the road was revealed and the houses that were ranged along it. They were huge properties, Georgian townhouses that were more like mansions. "Which one is it, Josh?"

He pointed. Kate scrolled in even further to view the house number. Number 18, Park Lane. She scribbled it down on her notebook and excused herself from the room a moment. Using the reception phone, she called the office and got Chloe, asking her to check on the Land Registry for details of the owners of the house.

Back in the interview room, Kate apologised again for leaving. Josh didn't look as though he cared much.

"Now," said Kate. "What happened?"

***

Josh's confession took a long time. Kate listened patiently and only raised her eyebrows once, when he described the first moment of seeing the head in the jar. She noted how his hands shook as he recounted the memory and felt the first surge of pity for him. Eventually, his faltering narrative came to an end and he lapsed into silence.

Kate was equally silent for a moment. She was thinking hard, not so much about the grotesque finding in the jar—if indeed, it even existed. Mind you, so many strange things were happening in Abbeyford at the moment, anything was possible. Even so, she found it hard to believe a serial killer would be quite so bold as to leave a body part of one of his or her victims in plain sight.

No, what Kate was thinking was that this young man, this habitual thief, this ex-offender (she'd checked his rap sheet and seen that Josh had already served two short sentences for burglary), this hardened criminal had known what punishment he would face for admitting to his crime. And he'd *still* come in to the station and confessed, because he wanted them to know that they could be facing something far, far worse. Say what you wanted, but that took guts. And character.

Kate said as much. Josh blinked, clearly unaccustomed to any form of praise or positive reinforcement, however faint.

"What?" was all he said.

"You should feel very proud of yourself," Kate said gently. "You did exactly the right thing, Josh. That took real courage."

A tear tracked its way down his cheek. Josh swiped angrily at it but said nothing.

"I'm going to ask the duty solicitor to sit in with you for a briefing," said Kate. "Unless you already have a solicitor?" Josh shook his head. She paused for a moment, wanting to impart some words of comfort but unable to think of what to say. "It's possible... I mean, I don't want to get your hopes up, but it's very possible that—given the circumstances and your mitigating behaviour—you might not get a custodial sentence. It could be suspended." Josh looked up hopefully, and Kate forced herself to add, because the last thing she wanted to do was deceive him, "I'm not saying it's definite. But I will certainly be putting something in my report that hopefully the judge will interpret as a reason to be more—more *lenient* in sentencing."

Josh hung his head again. Kate sighed inwardly but pressed on, aware of how fatuous she sounded. "Even if you—you go to prison, could you perhaps look at it as... oh, I don't know, perhaps as something of a fresh start? There is support, you know, in prison. You just have to ask for it."

Josh looked at her, sullenly. "Yeah. Yeah, all I've got to do is avoid the rapists, the smack dealers and the ISIS recruiters and I'll be peachy fucking creamy."

Kate splayed her hands helplessly. "I'm sorry, Josh. I really am truly sorry." Not for the first time in her career, she had run up against one of the unpalatable truths about crime; sometimes, the perpetrator was as much of a victim as the innocent bystander. What chance had Josh had, brought up in such a family as his? For him to have retained or developed even a *tinge* of empathy— amply born out here by his actions—was something of a miracle. For a moment, she remembered Rosa, the drug dealer and prostitute from an earlier case[1] who'd somehow managed to straighten herself out and make a new life for herself. She still messaged Kate occasionally on Facebook, letting her know how she was getting on.

"Listen," said Kate. "This will go to trial. You know that, Josh. There's nothing I can do about that. But I have a friend—he's an ex-offender himself—who runs a scheme for young people who've been to prison, to

---
1 *See Chimera (A Kate Redman Mystery: Book 5)

train them up and to help them get back to a normal life. It's a real support, there's therapy and work and everything. I'll ask him to come and visit you."

She paused, but she could see Josh wasn't listening. As she watched, another tear slid down his grimy face, disappearing into the stubble on his still-boyish jaw. Inwardly, she sighed again, but all she could say out loud was "I'm sorry," once more. Because she truly was.

Chapter Nine

"'Terence Buchanan,'" Chloe read from the print-outs in her hands. "He's co-owner of number eighteen, along with a Mrs Mary Warner."

Kate glanced over at her companion in the passenger seat. "Married couple?"

"Doesn't say. We'll soon find out, anyway." Chloe glanced at the sat-nav on Kate's phone, clipped to the dashboard. "Only ten minutes away."

The glorious spring sunshine of the morning had held. Kate had rolled down her driver-side window, but it was still warm, almost too warm for the cashmere jumper she'd put on that morning. The daffodils' brief moment of glory was almost over, but as Kate drove along the narrow road, heading for the outskirts of Abbeyford, where town met countryside, she could see the nodding blue heads of the bluebells and the white stitchwort of the daisies dotting the grass. Buds were finally beginning to unfurl on the hedgerows, misting the tangled branches in pale green.

"God, I love spring," she said to Chloe.

"Me too. You doing anything nice this weekend?"

"House-hunting with Anderton. Again. What about you?"

Chloe grinned. "Couple of dates."

Kate chuckled. "Haven't you exhausted Tinder yet?"

"No chance. There's a never-ending supply of new men."

"Blimey. Oh, well, have fun." Kate thought for a moment and then added, "Safe fun."

Chloe rolled her eyes. "Okay, Mum."

"I mean it."

"I know, but you don't have to worry. I'm always careful."

"Okay. Good. What about that Roman chap you were seeing? The one you met at my Halloween party. He seemed keen."

Chloe ran a hand through her hair. Usually, she wore it up in a neat twist but today it was loose, falling in golden waves to her shoulders. "I'm still seeing him. I'm just seeing other people as well." She glanced over at Kate. "He knows that, it's all above board. I'm not lying to him. I'm just not quite ready for exclusivity yet."

"Well—" began Kate and then realised they'd arrived at their destination.

Park Lane was easy to find, clearly marked on the sign at its entrance as a 'Private Road, no parking, turning or cold callers'. Inwardly, Kate rolled her eyes. She pulled up outside number eighteen and pulled on the handbrake.

Chloe was regarding the high golden walls of the house. "Now, is it just me, or does it seem somewhat unfair that one person should be quite that rich?"

"You don't know that they're actually rich," Kate said, getting out of the car.

Chloe scoffed, slamming her own car door. "Come on, that's a cool three million pound house there, at least." She shook her head. "How does *anyone* in this country actually have that kind of money?"

"I don't know." Kate checked she had her warrant card and notebook. "Come on, they're expecting us."

"This is going to be an interesting conversation," Chloe murmured as they walked up to the massive front door and Kate raised the brass doorknocker and dropped it with a thump.

THE MAN WHO ANSWERED THE door was tall, fairly distinguished looking, with plentiful but greying dark hair and tortoiseshell-framed spectacles. Kate estimated his age at about forty-five. He shook hands with them both, introducing himself as "Terence Buchanan. I confess I'm not sure what this is all about, but I hope I can help, officers." He stood back to allow the two women to enter the hallway. "Please do come through to the drawing room."

Kate and Chloe followed him. Kate, observing silently, thought she had scarcely seen a more beautifully furnished house. Surreptitiously, she allowed her fingers to brush against the plush grey velvet of an armchair as she walked past it.

Once they were seated, Terence Buchanan offered them refreshments. Normally, Kate would have accepted (it was always useful to have a nosy about without the house owner being present) but she decided against it this time. Succinctly, she explained what their issue was, silently thinking it sounded even more ludicrous when put into words.

Terence's eyes widened. "A head?" He started to laugh. "Oh, I know exactly what you mean. Sorry, it's just—" He got up and gestured towards the double doors at the end of the room. "It's in my study, please do come through."

Exchanging glances, Kate and Chloe followed him. Immediately, Kate saw the jar and the head within it. Still chuckling, Terence picked it up and held it out to them.

"It's a prop," he said, smiling. "I work in the film industry and I borrowed this from a friend of mine. Quite macabre, isn't it? I can promise you it's not real, though."

Inwardly rolling her eyes, Kate took the jar. She could see how Josh Kirkwood would have been fooled, particularly in the dark and under the influence of heightened adrenaline. In broad daylight, it was obvious it was not a real head. She looked at Terence. "Would it be all right if I just took it out of this jar for a moment?"

"Of course. Be my guest."

Whilst Kate was unscrewing the lid to the jar, Chloe asked Terence whether he could shed any light on the feet that they'd recently found. He shook his head. "I'm terribly sorry but that's absolutely nothing to do with me. You're welcome to have a look around the place if you want but, no, this funny little head is the only body part lying around here." He chuckled again. "So bizarre, isn't it? I can see why you're flummoxed."

As he was speaking, the door to the drawing room opened, admitting a very old lady who bent over a polished walking stick. She advanced slowly across the carpet, smiling in a hesitant manner.

"May I introduce my mother?" Terence indicated with an incline of his head. "Mrs Mary Warner." Kate and Chloe shook hands with Mrs Warner and explained the reason for their visit.

"I did say to get rid of that ghastly thing, Terry." Mrs Warner pursed her wrinkled lips up in disgust. "I don't know why you'd even want such a horrible thing on your desk."

"I know, it's a bit odd," said Terence, cheerfully. "I suppose it just makes me laugh. And now it apparently scares burglars off."

Kate, having examined the fake head more closely, dropped it carefully back into the water in the jar—or preserving fluid or whatever it was—and screwed the lid on tight. She handed it back to Terence. "I meant to say you might want to review your security arrangements. You have a lot of valuable things here, Mr Buchanan. I'm assuming you have insurance?"

"Oh, gosh, yes, we're insured up to our eyeballs, aren't we, Mother?"

Mrs Warner nodded. "My late husband was quite a collector," she said by way of explanation.

"Well, you've certainly got some lovely pieces here," Kate said, taking another appreciative look around. She was almost ready to leave but she had to ask the question. "Mrs Warner, Mr Buchanan, can you shed any light on the...on the feet that have recently been found in the area?"

That they knew exactly what she was talking about

was obvious. Mrs Warner shook her head, scrunching up her already wrinkled face. "Oh, goodness me, no. Nothing at all to do with us."

Kate smiled but directed her question to Terence. "You don't use anatomical specimens to build your special effects, by any chance, sir?

Terence shook his head, half-smiling. "I see what you're getting at, DI Redman, but I'm afraid the answer is no. I don't do much body-work anymore, anyway, to be honest. There's far more work goes on with CGI now than with actual models." He gestured to the head in the jar. "This chap's probably about five years old at least. He was in some god-awful British horror film that sank without trace at the box office."

"I see. So, you've got no, um, teaching aids or curiosities or anything like that? I'm not saying if you have that you planted the feet," Kate added, quickly, seeing him frown. "But I think you can agree that security in your lovely house is possibly not the best. If you did have something like that here, is it a possibility that a burglar could have taken it?" Into the increasingly chilly silence, she added, "I'm sorry, sir, but I'm just thinking aloud. I don't mean any offence."

Terence spread his hands. "None taken, officer, but I'm afraid I really can't help you. You're more than welcome to look around, but I can assure you that neither Mother nor I keep anything like that around here." He favoured his mother with an affectionate glance. "As you can see, we prefer the slightly more tasteful ornaments."

"Yes, thank you. I don't think a formal search will

be necessary at the moment, sir." Kate handed over her card and added her usual caveat of not hesitating to contact her or Chloe if new evidence or anything pertinent came to light. Both Terence and Mrs Warner nodded solemnly.

"Anyway, thank you for your time," finished Kate. "We'll see ourselves out. Sorry to have disturbed you."

They drove back to Abbeyford station in thoughtful silence.

"God, what a house," said Chloe, eventually.

"I know. Amazing." Kate changed gears as she approached a T-junction. "What I wouldn't give for a place like that."

"Fat chance on our wages." Chloe rolled her window down a little.

Kate was thinking. "Do you think we ought to search the place?"

Chloe shrugged. "On what grounds? He has a fake head in a jar, which is a bit odd but not illegal. I can check on his background, see if he really does work in films."

"Thanks, bird. I'll talk to Mark, see what he says, but you're right." Kate thought back over their meeting with the owners of eighteen, Park Lane. "He offered twice to have us go over the place, I'm pretty sure he wouldn't have done that if he'd had anything to hide."

"So, the search for the mysterious foot thief goes on."

"That it does." Kate thought, but didn't add, *at least*

it's just feet, not a missing girl. Where *was* Poppy Taige? *Come on, Kate, that's not even your case, it's not even Abbeyford's problem.* Pushing the thought from her mind, she drove herself and Chloe back to the station through the warm spring sunshine.

Chapter Ten

DS THEO MARSH CLICKED THE MOUSE on the 'send' button on his email account and sat back in his chair, rotating his stiff shoulders. Last email for the night, he decided, glancing at the clock. Eight o'clock. He dug his phone from his back pocket and peered at the screen. A message from Nicola, his girlfriend, popped up. Well, *girlfriend...* she was almost fourteen years older than he was, and she had actually been his former DCI, but they'd been seeing each other for a few months now, so... Disappointed, he saw she was working late again tonight. *Sorry sweetie, developments in the Taige case so am stuck in the office. I'll make it up to you*, with a winking emoji that made Theo raise his eyebrows in pleasurable anticipation.

Still, that left him with a free evening. Gym? But he'd already been that morning before work. He looked around the office, hoping to persuade one of the others to join him for a pint. Rav was nowhere to be seen—oh, yeah, Jarina had had the baby, hadn't she? Huh, no fun for Rav for a few months... Theo looked hopefully across at Chloe, tidying up her desk in preparation for her exit.

"Oy, Chloe. Fancy a swift one?"

"Can't, Theo, mate. I've got a date."

"Oh." Theo observed Chloe for a moment. "You're not wearing that, are you?"

"Why not?" Chloe looked down at the tailored black suit that she habitually wore. "They can take me as they find me, Theo."

"Right." Theo turned back to his desk, muttering under his breath, "It's not like you're going to be in it for long, right?"

"What?"

"Nothing," Theo said, grinning. "See you later, then. Don't do anything I wouldn't do."

"That'll leave me with plenty of scope, then," said Chloe, patting his shoulder as she walked by. "Good night, me old mucker."

"Night." Theo watched as the door shut behind her. Martin Liu, the new constable, was the only one left in the office. "Martin. Hey, Martin. D'you fancy a pint?"

Martin looked for a second as if he was going to refuse. He glanced down at his hands for some reason and then half-laughed and nodded. "Sure. Might have to be just the one, though."

We'll see about that, thought Theo, whose capacity to lead his fellow officers astray, especially on a school night, was legendary. "Come on then, mate. We'll go to The Arms. You'll need to know where it is anyway."

The Arms, as most of the Abbeyford nick referred to it, was a local pub. It served as both an informal office and decompression chamber for the team, and Theo was not surprised to see a few of the other officers from the station there when he and Martin pushed open the saloon door.

Two hours and four pints each later, after Theo had pushed for a fifth but Martin had stuck to his guns, they left the pub and began the walk back to their respective houses, conveniently located near to each other. They both trudged through the suburbs, towards the outskirts of Abbeyford, bantering slightly tipsy remarks as they went, breath pluming white in the cold air.

"This is stupid, we should have got an Uber, mate," Theo said eventually. They passed a small area of parkland, separated from the pavement by ancient iron railings. In the park, a small children's playground lay quiet and deserted, the two swings creaking slightly in the wind that was beginning to whip up.

Martin shivered. "I think we're almost at my place anyway. I don't know this area very well yet. Why don't you come in for a cuppa?"

A hot drink was sounding increasingly good to Theo. "Yeah, sure."

"I think—" Martin began before Theo's arm shot out to quiet him. Without speaking, Theo drew his companion back into the shadow of a tree, staring intently across the dark parkland. Martin obediently fell silent. Copper's senses, thought Theo, thinking of a conversation he'd had with Kate once. *They never let you down.* Someone was in that parkland, and that someone was up to no good, he could just tell.

The two men waited, watching the darkness.

"What do you reckon?" Martin murmured close to Theo's ear.

"Dunno. Drug deal, maybe." Theo watched as a dark figure crept across the grass of the park, seemingly heading for the children's playground. He frowned, peering intently at what was unfolding. There was only one person in the park that he could see. He strained his eyes, looking for another figure, but there was nothing. What the hell was the guy—he assumed it *was* a guy, he couldn't actually make out any features—doing? Theo glanced along the railings, looking for a way in. He didn't fancy vaulting over the high, sharply-tipped railings and impaling himself on the way. With relief, he saw the outline of a gate ten feet or so away, back in the direction from which they had come.

"Come on," he said to Martin and began to run, as quietly as he could.

They caught the guy with almost ridiculous ease. He—it *was* a man—had been putting something on the ground by the children's slide, concentrating on whatever it was he was placing so carefully. Theo, putting on a last burst of speed, thought for a moment about warning him with a shout and then thought, *fuck it, I've got him under behaving suspiciously*. He barrelled into the back of the crouching dude, who gave a single shout of alarm and toppled over. *Then* Theo made his profession clear, pinning the guy to the playground floor. It was made of that weird spongy concrete designed to stop little kids breaking their arms when they fell off the climbing frame, Theo thought irrelevantly, and then he and Martin were hauling the man to his feet.

"What—what—" The guy stuttered like anything, probably terrified out of his wits. That suited Theo. He cautioned him using the drug laws, although he was beginning to wonder if that was really what had been going on.

"What are you up to then, mate? Hanging around a children's playground at this time of night?"

The man he and Martin held between them looked no older than twenty. He was tall but thin, had a scrub of beard and those tragic ear-stretcher earrings in both ears. Millennial he might be, but Theo had no time for hipster fashion.

"I—I—nothing! I was just—"

"Come on, mate. You're coming with us to the station." Theo looked across at Martin, who he noticed was looking intently at the ground.

Just then, the moon sailed out from behind the thick blanket of cloud that had covered it so far that evening. White radiance flooded the playing fields and the blackness of the tarmac. Theo heard Martin gasp and looked himself at what his colleague had been staring at. Then, with a muttered aside to Martin of "*Hold him,*" he reached for his phone and flicked on the torch setting.

"Well, well," said Theo, regarding the human foot lying on the ground. He looked at the shivering man drooping in Martin's hands. "Now that *is* interesting."

Chapter Eleven

KATE BURST INTO THE OFFICE early the next morning, looking around wildly for Theo. He was just packing up his bag, yawning hugely.

"Why didn't you call me? I've missed it all."

"Mate, Mark told me not to. He was going to handle it."

Kate baulked, flinging her handbag under her desk. "Why?"

Theo yawned again. "I dunno, maybe 'cos he wanted you to get a decent night's sleep, for once? Besides, he said to go and see him, you can take over. We've still got the guy here for another twelve hours."

Slightly mollified, Kate nodded. "So, he was planting another foot, then? Seriously? In a children's playground?"

"Yeah, I know. Tell me about it, the sick bastard. Anyway, go and see Mark, he'll bring you up to speed." Theo slung his leather jacket on and picked up his rucksack. "I'm off home, I'm cream-crackered."

"See you." Kate spoke absently. She looped her neck with the lanyard that held her office pass and hurried for the interview rooms.

The suspect and Olbeck were in Room 5, accompanied by a duty solicitor Kate hadn't seen before, a rather mousy, middle-aged woman with lank brown hair. Kate knocked on the glass panel and raised her eyebrows as Olbeck caught sight of her.

A moment later, he exited the room, shutting the door behind him.

"What's the story?" asked Kate.

Olbeck smiled. "Good morning to you too." Kate flicked a hand impatiently, smiling back, and he went on. "Well, as Theo no doubt told you, we arrested this guy last night in Atherton Park. Theo and Martin saw him planting another foot in the playground there."

"What's his name?"

"Oliver Neville, apparently. We've confirmed that."

Kate peered through the glass panel. "God, he looks young."

"He is. He's only nineteen."

"Has he confessed to anything yet?"

"Not yet. No commenting himself all the way, at the moment."

Kate rolled her eyes. "What do you want me to do?"

Olbeck rubbed at his jaw, where the dark tips of stubble were just beginning to surface. "Keep at him. I'm going to head home before Jeff divorces me."

"Has Neville had a break?"

"Of course. What do you take me for? We got him up again at eight for questioning."

"Okay, leave it with me."

Kate gave him a quick goodbye kiss on the cheek. As Olbeck walked away, Kate had a thought. "What does he like drinking?" She gestured to the boy inside the room.

"Black coffee, I think."

"Righto. See you later."

Before she entered the interview room, Kate got a steaming mug (a mug, not a plastic cup) of black coffee, some of the nicer, wrapped biscuits and a pack of tissues. Then, carrying these things on a tray, she manoeuvred her way into the room. It was time for Good Cop, to see if that made a difference.

She smiled kindly at both Oliver Neville and his solicitor, proffering the drinks and introducing herself in a slightly breathless, scatty way. It was very much not her usual *modus operandus*, and almost the antithesis of her personality, but she had a feeling it might work in this case. Up close, despite his hipster trappings, Oliver looked like nothing so much as a grubby-faced boy with suspiciously red eyes. Kate knew that Olbeck was a sensitive and careful interviewer but if this lad had gone a few rounds with Theo, as seemed the case, he would probably definitely be feeling a little psychologically tender.

"So, Oliver, could you just take me through what happened last night?"

Oliver dropped his eyes to the shimmering black circle of his coffee mug. "No comment," he muttered.

Kate nodded, not letting her impatience show. "You're a student, aren't you, Oliver?"

The question clearly took him by surprise. "Yeah," he answered, before he could think to give his usual answer.

"Where do you study?" Kate kept her tone as casual, friendly and non-threatening as she could.

Oliver looked her full in the face and she saw his

pupils widen as he looked at her properly for the first time. *Well, well,* thought Kate, amused. *That could help.*

"Um—um...at Abbeyford Arts." It was the town's premier art and drama college; Kate knew it quite well. Her younger brother, Jay, had studied there, and there had also been a series of suicides there some years before[*2]. Kate thought of that time with an inner shudder and then dismissed the memory. She nodded at Oliver encouragingly. "What exactly are you studying, Oliver?"

"Art."

"Oh, my brother did the same," Kate said, allowing some gentle enthusiasm to enter her voice. She smiled at Oliver, holding his gaze for a moment longer than was strictly necessary. Tentatively, he smiled back, and she clenched her fist in triumph, out of sight, under the table. "He had some great teachers there. He was doing hyper-realism—you know, when the paintings look like a photograph? What about you? What kind of things are you doing?"

Hesitatingly, and with many an encouraging nod and smile from Kate, Oliver began to tell her about his course, the exhibition he was hoping to hold, the fine art degree he hoped to go on to after he finished at his college. The feet and his arrest were never mentioned, either by Kate or by himself. She didn't even make notes, knowing that the entire interview was being recorded. It was much more like a therapy session than an interview.

---

2 *See Creed (A Kate Redman Mystery: Book 7)

If only she could get rid of the bloody solicitor! Kate had a feeling that a confession might be imminent, but with his brief sat there, what chance did Kate have of encouraging him to come clean? She let no hint of her thoughts show in her face, keeping her expression arranged in a gentle smile, holding it until her face began to ache.

Then, seemingly as a gift from the heavens, the solicitor asked to be excused for a moment. Comfort break, Kate thought, remembering Theo's rather more ribald term for it. The memory threatened to make her giggle, and she turned it into a cough, indicating with her head that the woman should go on ahead.

Once she and Oliver were alone, she knew she'd been right. He was bursting to tell her, and he immediately leaned forward. Kate mirrored him, keeping that kindly smile on her face.

"I didn't mean any harm," Oliver said, almost whispering. "But it was for my show, you see. I just thought it would be so...so *powerful*. You know, like, really meaningful."

A little lost, Kate just nodded. Oliver continued, clearly encouraged by her interest. For the first time, she wondered whether there might be something... Well, whether he might have some *additional needs*.

"It's called *Disintegration*. The show, I mean. Like, the decay of everything—society and politics and the environment—only I'm using kind of everyday objects to highlight it. You know, juxtapose decay against a living backdrop."

Kate wouldn't have termed severed human feet as

'everyday objects', but she said nothing, nodding again. She was beginning to feel like one of those silly novelty dogs that sat on the parcel shelves of cars, their heads dipping back and forth with every bounce of the suspension. Should she ask him where he got the feet? But no—he was finally talking freely now, and Kate kept her mouth shut, even as the mousy solicitor came back into the room and sat back down again next to her now loquacious client.

Chapter Twelve

"A bloody art exhibit," grumbled Theo later that afternoon. "I've heard it all, now, I seriously have. And you've let him go."

"I had to, you know that. Besides—" Kate paused, thinking of the conversation she'd had with Olbeck before Oliver Neville's release. "What exactly *were* we going to charge him with?"

Chloe, who'd been listening in as she packed up her desk, spoke up. "Surely—well—unlawful disposal of a body? Something like that?"

Kate shook her head. "No. The CPS would laugh us out of court."

"Well, what then?"

"I've got it," announced Theo. Kate and Chloe looked at him. "Littering."

That made them all snort. Shaking her head, Kate looked down at the notes she'd made. "I had to let him off with a caution. There is one interesting thing, though."

"*One* interesting thing..." Theo ambled over and perched on the edge of her desk. "What's that?"

"Well, remember how we were all debating where on earth anyone would be able to have three separate human feet in their possession?"

"Yeah."

"Well, now we know. Oliver got them from an online auction. They were scientific exhibits. Medical curios, I suppose you would call them." Mentally, Kate saluted Anderton, who'd been bang on the money with that one.

Chloe looked puzzled. "Well, that's an explanation of sorts, but I don't quite see—"

Kate flicked over a page of her notebook. "The auction was selling off a lot of stuff from a closed-down art gallery. Anyone heard of it? It was on Bridge Street, in the Old Town. *Granello Fine Arts*?"

Chloe and Theo were looking blank. To be fair, Kate had never heard of it either; she didn't exactly have cause to patronise fine art galleries particularly often.

She went on. "Anyway, I did a bit of digging and called the auction site. The sale was because of probate. The owner of the art gallery had died."

"Come on," said Theo. "There's obviously more."

"You are the world's worst at the big reveal," agreed Chloe, grinning.

"Huh." Kate pushed her hair back and went on. "Anyway, the co-owner of the gallery, along with the dead guy is…guess who?" Over their audible groans, she smiled and added, "Okay, okay. It's Terence Buchanan, the guy with the head in the jar."

"What?" Chloe raised her eyebrows.

"I know. Odd coincidence, hey?"

"Seriously?" asked Theo.

"Yes. He and his partner, the guy that died—his name was Matteo Granello, by the way—opened it in the late nineties."

"So, why didn't he tell us about the feet?" Chloe asked.

"Well, to be fair, he may not have known about them. But I'm going to go and ask him, just to wrap things up." Kate threw her notes into her handbag and picked up her coat. "So I'll be out for the afternoon." She paused before she left, her eyes sweeping over Rav's empty desk. "Can someone organise some flowers and a card for Rav and Jarina?"

THE GOOD WEATHER HELD. KATE drove along the rapidly greening lanes, enjoying the sight of the spring flowers and the leaves on the trees opening into that fresh green colour that lasts so little time before darkening. She'd called ahead to ascertain that Terence would be at home. What a strange little case this had turned out to be...

He greeted her politely at the door and ushered her once more into the drawing room. Kate explained, quite simply, why she was there. "It's a matter of tying up loose ends, Mr Buchanan. Thank you for seeing me."

"That's quite all right, DI Redman. How can I help?"

Kate brought up the gallery and his partnership with the late Mr Granello. "Were you aware that he stocked this kind of...well, curiosity?"

Terence shook his head. "I'm sorry to disappoint you, but I had no idea. I was very much what they call a 'silent partner' in the business. It was Matteo's baby—he was the artist and collector." He smiled rather sadly. "I was, I suppose, the money. Anyway, we dissolved the business partnership a few years ago, and Matteo took it on by himself. He was making enough money by then to do so."

Kate caught the change of expression. "May I ask what Mr Granello died of? I'm sorry if it's a painful subject, I'm just trying to get the whole picture, if that makes sense."

"Yes of course. Poor Matteo. He had pneumonia." Terence hesitated and added, "Actually, sorry, I don't know why I'm fudging it—it hardly matters now. But Matteo, well, to put it bluntly, he had AIDS. The pneumonia was a complication of that."

"Oh, I see," said Kate. She was a little shocked. Did people really still die of AIDs in this day and age? She'd thought the drug treatments were really effective now. But, of course, there had to be exceptions. Looking at Terence, she wondered at the extent of his partnership with Matteo Granello. Had they been in a relationship? She could hardly ask him if he were gay...

Terence was still speaking. "Anyway, he bought all sorts of things. Fine art, yes, but he loved the more... *quirky* collectables."

"Like your head in the jar."

The sadness dropped from Terence's face and he actually chuckled. "That he did. He actually used to call it Graham." Kate laughed and Terence shook his head. "I'd forgotten that." He paused, the laughter dying away, and added, "I miss him."

"I'm very sorry," Kate said, reflecting that she had seemed to say nothing much else over this case. "Anyway, thank you for your time, Mr Buchanan. I'll leave you in peace now."

"Let me show you out."

At the front door, Kate hesitated and held out her hand. Terence shook it, saying goodbye courteously, before shutting the door behind her.

Kate walked down the entrance steps to her car. She sat for a moment in the driver's seat, looking up at the house. A tiny thread of disquiet ran through her, so tiny as to almost be dismissible. Was it the case? She saw, for a moment, Terence Buchanan framed in the window of the drawing room. Their eyes met, and after a long moment, he smiled.

Kate smiled back, forcing it. *Come on, woman. There's nothing more you can do here.* She lifted a hand in farewell and drove away, putting that momentary flicker of unease to the back of her mind. *Home time.*

Epilogue

Terence Buchanan watched as the inspector drove away, the smile dropping from his face. He waited for several long minutes until he was sure DI Redman wasn't coming back. He hadn't liked the look on her face when she'd met his gaze.

After twenty minutes, he knew he was safe. He went into the corridor. The ceiling hatch was hidden in darkness at night, unless the hall lights were put on. Terry flicked the switch to illuminate the hatch, making very sure that the plush red velvet curtains draped across the hall's only window were tightly shut. Then he fetched a dining room chair—these Georgian ceilings were so high—and reached for the hatch, catching the interior ladder before it fell on his face. He moved the chair and settled the ladder, climbing up to the dark heights with the usual growing excitement and anticipation. It had been too long. Should he wait? The sensible thing would be wait until all this ridiculous foot business died down. No, he wanted to do it—he *longed* to. Mother would be out for hours...

He climbed the ladder and stepped carefully onto the boarded floor of the attic. He felt for the keys in his pocket and opened the two heavy-duty padlocks that kept the treasure inside the large chest freezer safe from view. As he raised the lid, frosty air swirled out, hiding the contents for a few seconds. Used to this, Terence blew warm breath over the coils and the fog abated. He gazed down at the beautiful things inside.

"The police are fools," he said, because he often talked to her. "As if I'd have anything to do with those disgusting old feet." He picked up one of the icy packages and regarded its contents with a smile. "Whereas *your* feet, Poppy my darling, I think I could stomach. Yes, I think I could." He replaced the package into its neatly ordered place and added, "Soon. Soon we'll be together. Even more of you." He blew what was left of her a kiss and closed the freezer lid reluctantly, securing it fastidiously again so as to keep his special girl safe.

THE END

ENJOYED THIS BOOK? AN HONEST review left at your favorite retailer and Goodreads is always welcome and *really* important for indie authors. The more reviews an independently published book has, the easier it is to market it and find new readers.

You can leave a review at your favorite retailer.

Want some more of Celina Grace's work for free? Subscribers to her mailing list get a free digital copy of **Requiem (A Kate Redman Mystery: Book 2)**, a free digital copy of **A Prescription for Death (The Asharton Manor Mysteries Book 2)** *and* a free PDF copy of her short story collection **A Blessing From The Obeah Man.**

Requiem (A Kate Redman Mystery: Book 2)

WHEN THE BODY OF TROUBLED teenager Elodie Duncan is pulled from the river in Abbeyford, the case is at first assumed to be a straightforward suicide. Detective Sergeant Kate Redman is shocked to discover that she'd met the victim the night before her death, introduced by Kate's younger brother Jay. As the case develops, it becomes clear that Elodie was murdered. A talented young musician, Elodie had been keeping some strange company and was hiding her own dark secrets.

As the list of suspects begin to grow, so do the questions. What is the significance of the painting Elodie modelled for? Who is the man who was seen with her on the night of her death? Is there any connection with another student's death at the exclusive musical college that Elodie attended?

As Kate and her partner Detective Sergeant Mark Olbeck attempt to unravel the mystery, the dark undercurrents of the case threaten those whom Kate holds most dear...

A Prescription For Death (The Asharton Manor Mysteries: Book 2) – A Novella

"I HAD A SURGE OF kinship the first time I saw the manor, perhaps because we'd both seen better days."

It is 1947. Asharton Manor, once one of the most beautiful stately homes in the West Country, is now a convalescent home for former soldiers. Escaping the devastation of post-war London is Vivian Holt, who moves to the nearby village and begins to volunteer as a nurse's aide at the manor. Mourning the death of her soldier husband, Vivian finds solace in her new friendship with one of the older patients, Norman Winter, someone who has served his country in both world wars. Slowly, Vivian's heart begins to heal, only to be torn apart when she arrives for work one day to be told that Norman is dead.

It seems a straightforward death, but is it? Why did a particular photograph disappear from Norman's possessions after his death? Who is the sinister figure who keeps following Vivian? Suspicion and doubts begin to grow and when another death occurs, Vivian begins to realise that the war may be over but the real battle is just beginning...

A Blessing From The Obeah Man

DARE YOU READ ON? HORRIFYING, scary, sad and thought-provoking, this short story collection will take you on a macabre journey. In the titular story, a honeymooning couple take a wrong turn on their trip around Barbados. The Mourning After brings you a shivery story from a suicidal teenager. In Freedom Fighter, an unhappy middle-aged man chooses the wrong day to make a bid for freedom, whereas Little Drops of Happiness and Wave Goodbye are tales of darkness from sunny Down Under. Strapping Lass and The Club are for those who prefer, shall we say, a little meat to the story...

JUST GO TO CELINA'S WEBSITE to sign up. It's quick, easy and free. Be the first to be informed of promotions, giveaways, new releases and subscriber-only benefits by subscribing to her (occasional) newsletter.

Aspiring or new authors might like to check out Celina's other site http://www.indieauthorschool.com for motivation, inspiration and advice on writing and publishing a book, or even starting a whole new career as an indie author. Get a free eBook, a mini e-course, cheat sheets and other helpful downloads when you sign up for the newsletter.

http://www.celinagrace.com
http://www.indieauthorschool.com
Twitter: @celina__grace
Facebook: http://www.facebook.com/authorcelinagrace

More Books By Celina Grace...

Hushabye (A Kate Redman Mystery: Book 1)

ON THE FIRST DAY OF her new job in the West Country, Detective Sergeant Kate Redman finds herself investigating the kidnapping of Charlie Fullman, the newborn son of a wealthy entrepreneur and his trophy wife. It seems a straightforward case... but as Kate and her fellow officer Mark Olbeck delve deeper, they uncover murky secrets and multiple motives for the crime.

Kate finds the case bringing up painful memories of her own past secrets. As she confronts the truth about herself, her increasing emotional instability threatens both her hard-won career success and the possibility that they will ever find Charlie Fullman alive...

Hushabye is the book that introduces Detective Sergeant Kate Redman.

Available Now

Imago (A Kate Redman Mystery: Book 3)

"THEY DON'T FEAR ME, QUITE the opposite. It makes it twice as fun... I know the next time will be soon, I've learnt to recognise the signs. I think I even know who it will be. She's oblivious of course, just as she should be. All the time, I watch and wait and she has no idea, none at all. And why would she? I'm disguised as myself, the very best disguise there is."

A known prostitute is found stabbed to death in a shabby corner of Abbeyford. Detective Sergeant Kate Redman and her partner Detective Sergeant Olbeck take on the case, expecting to have it wrapped up in a matter of days. Kate finds herself distracted by her growing attraction to her boss, Detective Chief Inspector Anderton – until another woman's body is found, with the same knife wounds. And then another one after that, in a matter of days.

Forced to confront the horrifying realisation that a serial killer may be preying on the vulnerable women of Abbeyford, Kate, Olbeck and the team find themselves in a race against time to unmask a terrifying murderer, who just might be hiding in plain sight...

Available now.

Snarl (A Kate Redman Mystery: Book 4)

A RESEARCH LABORATORY OPENS ON the outskirts of Abbeyford, bringing with it new people, jobs, prosperity and publicity to the area – as well as a mob of protesters and animal rights activists. The team at Abbeyford police station take this new level of civil disorder in their stride – until a fatal car bombing of one of the laboratory's head scientists means more drastic measures must be taken...

Detective Sergeant Kate Redman is struggling to come to terms with being back at work after long period of absence on sick leave; not to mention the fact that her erstwhile partner Olbeck has now been promoted above her. The stakes get even higher as a multiple murder scene is uncovered and a violent activist is implicated in the crime. Kate and the team must put their lives on the line to expose the murderer and untangle the snarl of accusations, suspicions and motives.

Available now.

Chimera (A Kate Redman Mystery: Book 5)

THE WEST COUNTRY TOWN OF Abbeyford is celebrating its annual pagan festival, when the festivities are interrupted by the discovery of a very decomposed body. Soon, several other bodies are discovered but is it a question of foul play or are these deaths from natural causes?

It's a puzzle that Detective Sergeant Kate Redman and the team could do without, caught up as they are in investigating an unusual series of robberies. Newly single again, Kate also has to cope with her upcoming Inspector exams and a startling announcement from her friend and colleague DI Mark Olbeck...

When a robbery goes horribly wrong, Kate begins to realise that the two cases might be linked. She must use all her experience and intelligence to solve a serious of truly baffling crimes which bring her up against an old adversary from her past...

Available now.

Echo (A Kate Redman Mystery: Book 6)

THE WEST COUNTRY TOWN OF Abbeyford is suffering its worst floods in living memory when a landslide reveals the skeletal remains of a young woman. Detective Sergeant Kate Redman is assigned to the case but finds herself up against a baffling lack of evidence, missing files and the suspicion that someone on high is blocking her investigation…

Matters are complicated by her estranged mother making contact after years of silence. As age-old secrets are uncovered and powerful people are implicated, Kate and the team are determined to see justice done. But at what price?

Available now.

Creed (A Kate Redman Mystery: Book 7)

JOSHUA WIDCOMBE AND KAYA TRENT were the golden couple of Abbeyford's School of Art and Drama; good-looking, popular and from loving, stable families. So why did they kill themselves on the grassy stage of the college's outdoor theatre?

Detective Chief Inspector Anderton thinks there might be something more to the case than a straightforward teenage suicide pact. Detective Sergeant Kate Redman agrees with him, but nothing is certain until another teenager at the college kills herself, quickly followed by yet another death. Why are the privileged teens of this exclusive college killing themselves? Is this a suicide cluster?

As Kate and the team delve deeper into the case, secrets and lies rear their ugly heads and Abbeyford CID are about to find out that sometimes, the most vulnerable people can be the most deadly...

Available now.

Sanctuary (A Kate Redman Mystery: Book 8)

Dawn breaks at Muddiford Beach and the body of a young African man is discovered lying on the sand. Was he a desperate asylum seeker, drowned in his attempt to reach the safe shores of Britain? Or is there a more sinister explanation for his death?

Irritated to discover that the investigation will be a joint one with the neighbouring police force at Salterton CID, Detective Sergeant Kate Redman is further annoyed by her Salterton counterpart, one of the rudest young women Kate has ever encountered.

Tensions rise as the two teams investigate the case and when a second body is discovered, Kate and her colleagues are to about realise just how far people will go in the cause of doing good...

Available now.

Interested in historical mysteries?

The Asharton Manor Mysteries

Some old houses have more history than others...

The Asharton Manor Mysteries Boxed Set is a four part series of novellas spanning the twentieth century. Each standalone story (about 20,000 words) uses Asharton Manor as the backdrop to a devious and twisting crime mystery. The boxed set includes the following stories:

Death at the Manor

It is 1929. Asharton Manor stands alone in the middle of a pine forest, once the place where ancient pagan ceremonies were undertaken in honour of the goddess Astarte. The Manor is one of the most beautiful stately homes in the West Country and seems like a palace to Joan Hart, newly arrived from London to take up a servant's position as the head kitchen maid. Getting to grips with her new role and with her fellow workers, Joan is kept busy, but not too busy to notice that the glittering surface of life at the Manor might be hiding some dark secrets. The beautiful and wealthy mistress of the house, Delphine Denford, keeps falling ill but why? Confiding her thoughts to her friend and fellow housemaid Verity Hunter, Joan is unsure of what exactly is making her uneasy, but then Delphine Denford dies... Armed only with their own good sense and quick thinking, Joan and Verity must pit their wits against a cunning murderer in order to bring them to justice.

A Prescription for Death

It is 1947. Asharton Manor, once one of the most beautiful stately homes in the West Country, is now a convalescent home for former soldiers. Escaping the devastation of post-war London is Vivian Holt, who moves to the nearby village and begins to volunteer as a nurse's aide at the manor. Mourning the death of her soldier husband, Vivian finds solace in her new friendship with one of the older patients, Norman Winter, someone who has served his country in both world wars. Slowly, Vivian's heart begins to heal, only to be torn apart when she arrives for work one day to be told that Norman is dead. It seems a straightforward death, but is it? Why did a particular photograph disappear from Norman's possessions after his death? Who is the sinister figure who keeps following Vivian? Suspicion and doubts begin to grow and when another death occurs, Vivian begins to realise that the war may be over but the real battle is just beginning...

The Rhythm of Murder

It is 1973. Eve and Janey, two young university students, are en route to a Bristol commune when they take an unexpected detour to the little village of Midford. Seduced by the roguish charms of a young man who picks them up in the village pub, they are astonished to find themselves at Asharton Manor, now the residence of the very wealthy, very famous, very degenerate Blue Turner, lead singer of rock band Dirty Rumours. The golden summer rolls on, full of sex, drugs and rock and roll, but Eve begins to sense that there may be a sinister side to all the hedonism. And then one day, Janey disappears, seemingly run away... but as Eve begins to question what happened to her friend, she realises that she herself might be in terrible danger...

Number Thirteen, Manor Close

It is 2014. Beatrice and Mike Dunhill are finally moving into a house of their own, Number Thirteen, Manor Close. Part of the brand new Asharton Estate, Number Thirteen is built on the remains of the original Asharton Manor which was destroyed in a fire in 1973. Still struggling a little from the recent death of her mother, Beatrice is happy to finally have a home of her own – until she begins to experience some strange happenings that, try as she might, she can't explain away. Her husband Mike seems unconvinced and only her next door neighbour Mia seems to understand Beatrice's growing fear of her home. Uncertain of her own judgement, Beatrice must confront what lies beneath the beautiful surface of the Asharton Estate. But can she do so without losing her mind – or her life?

Celina Grace's psychological thriller, **Lost Girls** is also available now:

Twenty-three years ago, Maudie Sampson's childhood friend Jessica disappeared on a family holiday in Cornwall. She was never seen again.

In the present day, Maudie is struggling to come to terms with the death of her wealthy father, her increasingly fragile mental health and a marriage that's under strain. Slowly, she becomes aware that there is someone following her: a blonde woman in a long black coat with an intense gaze. As the woman begins to infiltrate her life, Maudie realises no one else appears to be able to see her.

Is Maudie losing her mind? Is the woman a figment of her imagination or does she actually exist? Have the sins of the past caught up with Maudie's present...or is there something even more sinister going on?

Lost Girls is a novel from the author of **The House on Fever Street**: a dark and convoluted tale which proves that nothing can be taken for granted and no-one is as they seem.

Available now

The House on Fever Street
is the first psychological thriller by **Celina Grace**.

Thrown together in the aftermath of the London bombings of 2005, Jake and Bella embark on a passionate and intense romance. Soon Bella is living with Jake in his house on Fever Street, along with his sardonic brother Carl and Carl's girlfriend, the beautiful but chilly Veronica.

As Bella tries to come to terms with her traumatic experience, her relationship with Jake also becomes a source of unease. Why do the housemates never go into the garden? Why does Jake have such bad dreams and such explosive outbursts of temper?

Bella is determined to understand the man she loves but as she uncovers long-buried secrets, is she putting herself back into mortal danger?

The House on Fever Street is the first psychological thriller from writer Celina Grace - a chilling study of the violent impulses that lurk beneath the surfaces of everyday life.

Shortlisted for the 2006 Crime Writers' Association Debut Dagger Award.

Available now

Want some more of Kate Redman and the Abbeyford team? The new full-length novel in the series, Scimitar, will be published late in 2019. You can read the opening chapter below – sign up to Celina's mailing list for details of publication and other news at www.celinagrace.com.

Scimitar

A Kate Redman Mystery: Book 12
Celina Grace
Copyright@Celina Grace 2019

Prologue

SUNLIGHT GLITTERED OFF THE WATERS of the Thames; waves lapped and sparkled as boats and ferries cut through the river. The bright, clear blue sky wisped here and there with faint cotton-puffs of white cloud. Chloe Wapping leant against the parapet of Waterloo Bridge, waving as a boatload of tourists passed underneath her, smiling slightly self-consciously. She brought her sunglasses down from where they had been pushed into her hair and slipped them up her nose before turning to her companion.

"*What* a day."

"Gorgeous," Roman Whitely agreed. "We're set for an Indian summer, I heard."

"Huh." Chloe leant in for a kiss. "I remember they said that last year. 'Stock up on the charcoal' and what did we get? Three weeks of rain."

"Well, let's enjoy it for now." Roman slid his arm around her waist. "Shall we go and get some lunch?"

Chloe concurred with his agreeable suggestion. They wandered across the bridge, up Villiers Street and onto the Charing Cross Road, holding hands. It was their first weekend away together, although they'd been dating for several months. Chloe, a detective sergeant in Abbeyford, a West Country town, was perennially busy with work, and Roman, who worked as a chef, was equally wedded to his job. Chloe looked over at him, as they walked through the busy sunlit streets, and smiled.

Roman caught the smile. "What?"

Chloe squeezed his hand. "Just appreciating the moment. It's been a long time coming."

"Hasn't it just?" Roman squeezed back. They meandered past Charing Cross Station, heading for Covent Garden. "We might have a drink in that pub in the market first, what do you reckon?"

Privately, Chloe thought that was just something that overseas tourists would do, but she was happy and relaxed enough not to point that out. I'm learning, she thought. She'd been single for so long that she'd been worried about how she would cope in a relationship. With Roman, though, it was easy; such a contrast to the drama-fuelled couplings she'd had in the past, not to mention her short-lived marriage. Roman was calm, confident and laid-back, so much so that sometimes Chloe wondered if it was a trait that might come to annoy her, later on. For now, though, it worked perfectly.

Filled with a rush of affection for him, waiting to cross Charing Cross Road, she pulled him closer and raised herself on tiptoes to kiss him. For a moment, there was nobody else in the world; no honking taxis, noisy buses, crowded pavements. There was nobody else in the world apart from the two of them, lip-locked and lost in each other.

Chloe drew back, a little breathless but smiling. "Where—"

She began the sentence but was cut off before she could end it. She saw Roman's eyes widen, his face contorting. Then he pushed her, hard—so hard she flew backwards onto the pavement, hitting it with such force that for a moment she thought she'd broken her back. Her elbow scraped the concrete, a bolt of pain shooting up her arm. Tumbling, her other hand hit the concrete, her fingers hitting the ground so hard they were forced back. Chloe screamed, rolling, until she managed to get a grip of herself and the pavement.

"What the *hell*—"

She was breathless with shock, the words falling from her mouth shakily and indistinctly. Chloe staggered to her feet, adrenaline spiking within her. She looked for Roman, to scream at him, to accuse him, to ask why he had done such a thing. Chloe didn't know. She turned and beheld such a scene of horror so that for a moment she believed she was hallucinating, that she'd hit her head when she fell.

Bodies littered the pavement like broken dolls. So many broken dolls. Blood spattered over the concrete; Chloe could see it steaming. Gasping, she looked wildly about her, looking for Roman, unable to see him, finding only a trail of destruction and carnage. Towards Trafalgar Square, she could see the back of a white van as it ploughed through people on the pavement, bodies tossed aside like confetti. Screams and moans filled her ears as the injured and those bearing witness to the atrocity began to comprehend the situation. Blinking, trying to take it in, Chloe watched as the white van disappeared from view. Her breath hitching with sobs, she began to limp forward, frantically scanning the people lying injured or dead on the ground, searching for Roman, holding her arms across her stomach as if to physically hold herself together.

I should stop, I should help. She told herself that, even as she sped up, whipping her head from side to side. The pavements blurred before her eyes in a surreal tableau. *I should stop, I should help.* But she couldn't; she couldn't make herself stop to help the middle-aged man with the catastrophic head injuries who lay half on the pavement and half on the road. She couldn't stop to help the crying girl who clutched her screaming toddler to herself, one little leg sheeting blood over the girl's pink sun-dress. She couldn't stop because she needed to find Roman. Chloe slowed and the pavement loomed close again as she bent double, stomach cramping, and vomited onto the dusty, blood-spattered pavement.

Gasping and shaking, she straightened up and staggered on, and on, and on.

Distantly, from the direction of the square, came the sound of gunshots.

Scimitar
(A Kate Redman Mystery: Book 12)
Coming Soon

Acknowledgements

Many thanks to all the following splendid souls:

Chris Howard for the brilliant cover designs; Andrea Harding for editing and proofreading; Glendon Haddix and the Streetlight Graphics guys for formatting; lifelong friends and Schlockers David Hall, Ben Robinson and Alberto Lopez; Ross McConnell for advice on police procedurals and for also being a great brother; Kathleen and Pat McConnell, Anthony Alcock, Naomi White, Mo Argyle, Lee Benjamin, Bonnie Wede, Sherry and Amali Stoute, Cheryl Beckles, Georgia Lucas-Going, Steven Lucas, Loletha Stoute, Helen Parfect, Helen Watson, Emily Way, Sandy Hall, Kristýna Vosecká, Jen Moss, Izzy Siu, Chris Lucas, Mabel Lucas and of course, my lovely Jethro and Isaiah.

Printed in Great Britain
by Amazon